DREAMS TO SELL

DREAMS TO SELL

Anne Douglas

This first world edition published 2013
in Great Britain and 2014 in the USA by
SEVERN HOUSE PUBLISHERS LTD of
19 Cedar Road, Sutton, Surrey, England, SM2 5DA.

British Library Cataloguing in Publication Data

Douglas, Anne, 1930
  Dreams to sell.
  1. Edinburgh (Scotland)–Fiction. 2. Great Britain–
  History–George VI, 1936-1952–Fiction. 3. Love stories.
  I. Title
  823.9'14-dc23

ISBN-13: 978-0-7278-8330-8 (cased)

All Severn House titles are printed on acid-free paper.

Severn House Publishers support the Forest Stewardship Council™ [FSC™],
the leading international forest certification organisation. All our titles that
are printed on FSC certified paper carry the FSC logo.

Typeset by Palimpsest Book Production Ltd.,
Falkirk, Stirlingshire, Scotland.
Printed and bound in Great Britain by
TJ International, Padstow, Cornwall.

One

Cold as Christmas, or so it seemed in the Rainey girls' room, yet here it was, March. March, when it shouldn't be still winter, when there was supposed to be a hint of spring. Not so's you'd notice when you'd to face getting out of bed.

Still, Roz didn't mind the cold too much. Always first up, she moved fast, jumping from her bed, pulling on the dressing gown she'd made herself and sprinting down to the bathroom the Raineys shared with two other families. In fact, it was to reach the bathroom, on the half-landing below, before Todd Atkinson came up complaining from the ground floor, which made Roz hurry now, while her sister, Chrissie, in her narrow bed, peacefully slept on. The last thing Roz wanted when she was washing was Todd shouting through the door, as he liked to do, 'If that's one o' you Rainey lassies in there, come on oot, time's up, I've to get to work!' As though they didn't all have to get to work!

Luckily, the tiny bathroom was still vacant when Roz reached it and she was able to wash and do her teeth in peace, only having to face the glowering Todd when she came out, tall and slim in her dressing gown, her dark red hair damp, her cheeks rosy with cold water and her grey eyes bright.

'All ready for you, Mr Atkinson!'

'And aboot time too!' he bellowed, pushing past her, a big man in his vest and corduroy trousers. 'I was just going to rattle the door, I'm telling you.'

Oh, the joy of sharing with neighbours! Roz, running back to her mother's flat, vowed again – yes, again, that one day she'd have a beautiful detached house of her own, with a splendid heated bathroom where she could take a bath every day, not just a freezing cold wash, and lie in the bath as long as she liked with no one shouting through the door!

Maybe she shouldn't complain. If she lived in a tenement there'd very likely be no bathroom at all, so life in an Edinburgh terraced house, now converted into three small flats, could be a lot worse. It was only that working in a lawyer's property office brought her into contact with houses that were so much better. Couldn't blame her for dreaming!

Back in the little room she shared with her sister, she dressed quickly in the clothes she'd laid out the night before – white blouse, dark wool jacket and calf-length black skirt, which still followed in 1949 the New Look fashion Dior had introduced in 1947. Then it was time to run a comb through her hair before starting the breakfast she'd have to make once she'd turfed her brother, Dougal, out of his cupboard bed and knocked on Ma's door. Oh, yes, and pulled the covers off Chrissie.

'No!' squealed Chrissie.

'Yes,' cried Roz, laughing. 'Come on, now, you know you've to get to the café on time.'

'It's all right for you,' Chrissie murmured, sitting on the edge of her bed. At twenty, she was three years younger than her sister, shorter and not so slim – something she minded – but more conventionally pretty, some thought, with a cloud of soft fair hair and clear blue eyes. There were photographs of Flo, their mother, showing her to have looked very much the same as Chrissie in her youth, but life had changed for Flo and so had she.

'All right for me, you say?' Roz asked. 'I'd to get up too.'

'Aye, but you like going to work,' sighed Chrissie. 'I'd just as soon not.'

'Like a lot of folk.' Roz shrugged. 'Suppose I am lucky, to like my work.'

'Of course you're lucky! You're the bright one.'

The bright one? Roz shrugged again. Well, folk said so. She'd done well at school, it was true, and had been lucky enough to win a small cash prize that had meant she could take a typing course, which had led to a job in a city office before she'd got what she really wanted – the post of assistant in a lawyer's property department.

All her life, she'd been interested in houses. Even as a child she'd daydreamed about owning a beautiful house of her own, and if the dreams were a long way from reality, when she'd left school she'd been sure that working with houses would be the next best thing. And so it proved. She was doing well in her job, not just typing particulars but accompanying her boss, seeing houses and gaining experience all the time. Now all she had to do was climb the ladder for promotion and maybe one day she'd be in charge of a property department herself. What an achievement that would be! Except that it was going to be a lot harder than she'd ever imagined, if not impossible.

Leaving Chrissie to roll slowly out of bed, Roz moved away to do her morning chores.

Two

First, with her usual apprehension, she knocked on the door of the room that had once been shared by her parents but now was her mother's alone. How would Ma be? You never knew, you see, from one day to the next.

'All right?' Roz called at last. 'All right, Ma?'

'All right, pet,' came Flo Rainey's faint reply and, with a sigh of relief, Roz hurried on to check on poor old Dougal, her brother, who had to sleep in a cupboard.

Well, not exactly a cupboard, but not much more, it being a tiny room off what had been the principal bedroom of the house in Edwardian days and was now the Raineys' living-room-cum-kitchen. Dougal, now twenty-two and a tall, blond, strapping fellow, had to manage as best he could with a small bed and little space, the only place to put his things being a share of his mother's chest of drawers, making him sometimes complain that if he'd been a lassie, he'd have had a proper bedroom, eh?

'And then there'd have been three of us in a room instead of two,' Roz would remind him. 'And you know how much space we've got.'

That morning, she was relieved to see that he was already up and dressed in a shirt and trousers, a towel round his neck, shaving gear in his hand and his bed clothes in a pile, which was his idea of making his bed. Draped over a chair were the overalls he'd be wearing for his work in a machine tools firm, a job he'd taken on following his national service after the war, and which he never said much about. Roz always supposed he enjoyed it. Or, rather, hoped he did.

'Better get in the queue for the bathroom,' she told him, tying on a large blue pinafore. 'Time's getting on and you don't want those MacGarry boys from up the stair cutting in.'

Evan and Bob MacGarry were brothers in their twenties who shared the top flat and were both in good jobs – draughtsmen, no less – but how did they manage in the flat? Roz often wondered, for they'd lost both their parents and looked after themselves. Still, they were good young neighbours – a great improvement on Todd Atkinson, that was for sure!

'I'm going to make the porridge now,' Roz told Dougal, 'and, no, there's no bacon – we've had our ration, and we don't get eggs till the weekend.'

'Damned rationing,' Dougal muttered. 'Four years after the war and we're no better off. Worse, in fact. Stuff's rationed now that wasn't even rationed in the war, how about that?'

'They say food's so short, we have to help other countries who are worse off than we are,' Roz told him, taking out the porridge pan. 'At least clothes are off the ration; suppose we should be grateful for that.'

'Who cares about clothes? Food's all that matters.'

'Bathroom's free!' cried Chrissie from the doorway. 'Better be quick, though, Dougal. The MacGarry lads will be down any minute.'

'As long as I don't have to see old Atkinson,' said Dougal, disappearing, as Chrissie ran to get dressed and Roz rushed about, preparing porridge and boiling the kettle for tea.

It was pleasant enough in the kitchen end of the main room, she reflected, with the warmth of the little range beginning to give out heat, the kettle singing, the porridge bubbling. If only the living area weren't so cluttered, stuffed as it was with pieces of second-hand furniture, including a heavy sideboard where Flo had placed a photograph of her husband and her children's father, Arthur Rainey, in his soldier's uniform.

Roz never liked to look at that. Too sad. Too much of a reminder that life had never been the same since he'd been killed at El Alamein during the Second World War. Her mother liked to look at it, though, in spite of taking Arthur's death so hard. Always had, even though being so depressed it was the family who'd had to take over for her until she'd felt up to taking a job again. Now she was working behind the cash desk in the same café where Chrissie was a waitress. She was certainly better than she'd been, even if they did still have to tread carefully around her, taking each day as it came.

Doesn't seem too bad today, Roz thought, feeling relieved again as her mother appeared, looking bright enough, a cigarette at her lips and a shawl over her nightdress.

'Is the tea ready?' she asked hoarsely. 'I'll get dressed later.'

'Everything's ready, Ma. And here come the others.'

'Morning, Ma!' called Dougal.

'Morning, Ma,' murmured Chrissie, giving her mother a hug.

And as they all sat down to their breakfast, the family exchanging glances that said all was well, Flo stubbed out her cigarette in the ashtray Roz had placed ready.

'Awful cold this morning, eh?' she asked, sipping her tea. 'When'll spring be coming, then?'

'Och, I reckon it's on its way,' Dougal told her. 'But then, I'm an optimist.'

Three

By the time the kitchen clock showed half past eight, they were all scattered: Flo and Chrissie to the Café Sunshine off St Andrew Square, Dougal to his firm in Fountainbridge, Roz to the offices of Tarrel and Thom's in the New Town. Unfortunately, she couldn't go all the way by tram, which meant she had to finish the journey that morning running through a biting wind, worrying that she would be late. In fact, when she reached Tarrel's offices in elegant Queen Street, she was exactly on time, but it had been a near thing.

Mr MacKenna, in charge of the property department, was nice and easy-going. He was a big, broad man in his forties who couldn't be a better boss, but Mr Banks, the head of the firm, was a stickler for punctuality, correct dress and professional manners. It wouldn't do to be caught by him coming in late, especially with wind-blown hair and a look of anxiety.

Luckily, he wasn't about when Roz arrived, and nor, of course, was anyone called either Tarrel or Thom, both founders of the law firm being long dead, although Mr Banks was a great nephew of the Henry Tarrel who'd first opened his doors as a lawyer back in the 1850s. No property department then, of course, but Mr Banks, being a shrewd businessman, was as keen to move with the times as any other competitor and always backed new ideas, if sound, and if the firm's high standards were observed.

Which, of course, they were, not only by Mr MacKenna in his department and in his general legal duties, but also by his colleagues, Mr Newman and Mr Wray, who were both partners in the firm.

There were no women lawyers, Roz had noticed when she was first appointed. Apart from herself, the only women employed were Miss Calder, secretary to Mr Banks and unofficial clerk to the practice as she knew everything anyone wanted to know, and Norma Ward, office typist – the only person Roz called by her first name. Strictly formal, you could say, was Tarrel and Thom's. But in that respect it wasn't much different from most professional work places in 1949.

Roz loved it, anyway, in spite of not finding herself on the ladder to promotion. She loved the wide entrance hall, where there were always flowers arranged by Miss Calder, and the large rooms lined with books. The solid mahogany desks, the leather chairs, the parquet floors, the smell of polish. All the building spelled quality and quality was what Roz appreciated.

Maybe because her own home, the flat at 35 Deller Street in the St Leonard's area of the city, though immensely better than some of the tenements she knew, was so lacking in the kind of quality she admired at Tarrel's, she felt in spite of herself rather dissatisfied.

She'd no right to complain. In fact, she was grateful that her parents had done so well to get to Deller Street, her dad not earning much, working at the electricity station and always finding the rent a struggle. No, no, she wouldn't complain. Just couldn't help dreaming of one day having some place of quality herself. Why not? Everyone was entitled to dream. Hoping she looked tidier than she felt, she picked up the post that had already been left for her by Miss Calder and hurried into the property department.

Once a fine reception room in the original house, this was still spacious and elegant, though now divided to make a good-sized office for Mr MacKenna and a smaller one for his assistant, Roz. Hers had room only for a typing table and filing cabinets, whilst the lawyer's held his great mahogany desk, his fine bookcases containing law manuals and reference books, and two leather chairs for clients. Prominent on one wall was a large street map, while another showed a collection of black and white photographs of properties for sale, the exterior views having been taken by a professional photographer, the interiors by Mr MacKenna or Roz herself.

She had been pleased to learn how to use a camera and had

become quite proficient at snapping sitting rooms and hallways, afterwards updating the collection regularly at the office as sales could move fast in Edinburgh. Like the rest of Scotland, there was no chain to hold up sales, offers being legally binding, having usually been made as sealed bids to lawyers' private auctions – changes of mind, therefore, being costly and rare.

'All very different from the English practice,' Mr MacKenna had explained to Roz on her first day, 'and better, we believe, as the buyer has no risk of losing the property when someone else tops his offer. On the other hand, he might have paid too much, for no one has any idea what others might bid. Of course, his lawyer will have advised him on the best price.' Here, Mr MacKenna had shrugged and smiled. 'As best he can. We have access to previous sale figures for the area, but we still have no crystal ball.'

'Must be really worrying, then, finding the right price,' Roz had commented.

'All part of the fun of being in the property business, Miss Rainey.' Mr MacKenna's eyes had twinkled mischievously. 'And I'll bet you didn't think there was any fun in that at all, did you?'

'Oh, no, I didn't think that, Mr MacKenna,' she'd answered, wondering if he was being serious about finding his work 'fun', and feeling cheered to think he might be. 'I never thought that.'

'Good for you,' he'd answered, and she'd had the comforting feeling that they were going to 'get on'.

So it had turned out, and it was another reason why she didn't mind coming into work. Getting on with your boss – that was important, eh?

'Morning, Mr MacKenna!' she cried on that wild March day as she took off her coat and Mr MacKenna, looking up from his desk, gave her his usual friendly smile.

'Morning, Miss Rainey. Got blown in by the wind?'

'Oh, heavens, I hoped you wouldn't notice!' She put her hands to her hair. 'I should have gone to tidy up, but I didn't want to be late.'

'Not to worry, you look fine. And you're never late.'

'There's always a first time. The tram seemed slower than ever this morning – honestly, I felt I could have got here as quickly on foot.'

'Cheer up; we'll be taking the car this afternoon, anyway. Got a couple of places to see, haven't we?'

'The flat you valued in the Old Town and the house in the Grange. Are we all right for petrol?'

As petrol was still rationed, trips to properties by car were rationed too.

'Sure, we're fine. Personally, I don't think it'll be long before petrol comes off the ration, anyway. That might be the time for you to think of learning to drive, Miss Rainey. Ever considered it? Very useful in our line of work.'

'Me?' She'd never thought of such a thing.

Dougal could drive, though it was a friend who had taught him, and of course he'd no car of his own, but it would be too expensive for Roz to take professional lessons. Still, the idea of driving appealed. She could just picture herself driving around as though she were Mr MacKenna. Just another dream, of course.

'I wouldn't mind,' she said thoughtfully. 'If it was possible.'

'Everything is possible,' he told her as she went to hang up her coat, sort out the post and collect the office diary in which she kept appointments.

'Ten o'clock,' she read out. 'Mr and Mrs Henryson are meeting you here, Mr MacKenna.'

'And then I'm taking them to the south side. They're wanting something bigger – children growing up like mine.' Mr MacKenna sighed. 'Well, let's hope they go for what I've found. There's one in Winter Place I'd really like them to take off our hands – hasn't had a thing done to it since nineteen thirty-five.'

'I know the one,' Roz said, laughing. 'You take somebody to see it pretty much every week.'

The lawyer laughed too, but then became serious. 'Still, it's encouraging, you know, that so many properties of whatever condition are coming our way. Everybody thought there'd be nothing available for years after the war, but the market's not too bad at all. Nothing new, of course, except prefabs, and they're not coming up for sale.'

Not that Tarrel's would have been selling them if they had, Roz thought, their business being concerned only with traditional housing, but it was good to know that some ordinary folk were getting roofs over their heads. Pity there couldn't be more of them, to ease the terrible overcrowding in some parts of the Old Town, but it would take more than a few prefabs to achieve that.

'Anything else in the diary?' Mr MacKenna was asking. 'I probably won't be back until lunchtime, anyway.'

When she told him that, apart from their visits that afternoon, he just had a call to make to a lawyer wanting to arrange a sealed bids auction, he said he would make the call straight away. Meanwhile, she could get on with preparing their spread for the property page of *The Scotsman* – she hadn't forgotten the deadline, had she?

'Oh, no, Mr MacKenna,' she said swiftly. 'I hadn't forgotten.'

'What am I saying?' he cried, his eyes twinkling again. 'As though you'd ever forget anything, Miss Rainey!'

Oh, yes, I'm very efficient, she thought, returning to her own little office. But when does it all begin paying off? She'd never mentioned her ambitions to Mr MacKenna, though she was sure he was aware of them. Maybe, today, she might?

Four

'Oh, you're so lucky, Roz!' sighed Norma Ward as she and Roz ate their lunchtime sandwiches in the little back room set aside as a staffroom. Bread and the same old cheddar cheese – oh, how boring! But even eating in a café, which they rarely did, the menu wouldn't have been much more exciting. To get back to pre-war standards was taking longer than anyone had ever expected.

'Lucky?' asked Roz, wondering why this seemed to be the day when everyone was envying her for no good reason. 'How d'you mean?'

'Well, getting out of the office the way you do,' Norma answered, gazing at Roz with large brown eyes.

She was a short girl, rather plump, with curly red hair that annoyed her, and a mass of freckles across her turned-up nose. At only nineteen and so very lively, Roz sometimes wondered if she might have been happier in a big jolly office instead of solemn old Tarrel's, which suited Roz herself but not everyone. Norma, however, seemed content enough to stay, which pleased Roz anyway. They got on well.

'I mean, driving about,' Norma added now. 'And with lovely Ronnie, and all.'

'Lovely Ronnie!' Roz burst into laughter. 'Hey, you'll get shot if Miss Calder hears you calling Mr MacKenna that!'

'Well, he is a lovely man, Roz, you have to admit. Always smiling, always so friendly. Not like Mr Wray, eh? He's thin as a skeleton and always frowning. Or Mr Newman – he never even knows who you are!'

'Yes, well, Mr MacKenna is nice to work with, I agree. I'm certainly lucky there.'

'Aye, and his wife's lucky, too, being married to him. She might have been worried about him working with someone like you, but he's no' the sort to try anything on, I'm sure. Anyway, he's more like a father, eh?'

'Of course he doesn't try anything on!' cried Roz, glancing round to see if anyone might be able to overhear, but the lawyers were all out at lunch. Only Miss Calder, who usually took a late lunch hour, would still be around, ready to answer the telephone or the doorbell if anyone called. 'And yes, he's like a father. Been as kind as any dad, I can tell you!'

She jumped up to put the kettle on. 'Honestly, Norma, the things you say! I can tell you this – never in this world would Mr MacKenna try anything on, as you call it, and I don't believe anyone who works here would!'

'I know, and you're right. Mr MacKenna wouldn't even think of it, anyway. He's just devoted to his wife and bairns, and that's the sort of guy I'd like to have. If I ever meet one at all.' Norma sighed and took out a paper bag. 'Like an oatcake, Roz? Ma managed to make some the other day. I've scraped some butter on.'

'Oh, nice! I'll have one with the tea. Then I'll have to be away. Mr MacKenna will be waiting for me.'

'Wouldn't you really like to marry someone like him?' Norma pressed, but Roz shook her head.

'I've got better things to do than think about getting married. My sister, Chrissie, thinks of it all the time, but I've got different ideas. I want to have a career first.'

'Fancy,' commented Norma, crunching her oatcake. 'I don't care about that at all. I'd really rather just get wed. And I should've thought there'd be plenty after you, Roz, you being so attractive.'

'Oh, come on!' Roz, embarrassed, was shaking her head when Mr MacKenna put his head round the door.

'Ready, Miss Rainey? I think we might make a start.'

'Coming, Mr MacKenna!' With one last frown at Norma, Roz hurried to join him in the hall where Miss Calder was just setting down the telephone.

'Valuing?' she asked, giving a brief smile.

In her forties, tall, slim, with thin dark hair drawn back from a high brow, she had worked at Tarrel's since leaving school, first as a typist, then as Mr Banks's secretary – her knowledge of the firm, it was said, being now even greater than his. To begin with, Roz had found her cold – certainly her manner could be that – but after Miss Calder had found her hardworking and willing to learn, they had become friendly enough. And of course it was always good to know that if you needed help on anything to do with Tarrel's, there she would be, Miss Calder, the expert.

'No, just preparing details for particulars,' Mr MacKenna told her now. 'Valuations have already been agreed for these properties.'

'Just what we like to hear,' commented Miss Calder. 'Well, I mustn't keep you, must I?'

'We're on our way,' he said cheerfully, and as they moved into the street, he exchanged a grin with Roz.

'Don't tell anyone I said so but it always makes me feel like I'm back at school when I talk to Miss Calder. Though in fact I'm a bit older than she is.'

'It's just her way,' said Roz, taking her seat in the old Hillman that was the company car parked at the kerb. 'Though I think she probably would have made a good teacher.'

'And all her pupils would have got top marks for their knowledge of Tarrel and Thom's, eh? Well, let's get going.'

Five

Though the Hillman was considered difficult to drive by Mr Newman and Mr Wray, it was Mr MacKenna's view that all she needed was a little coaxing, a little respect, and for him it was true the old lady put on her best behaviour and they'd never broken down in her yet. Not that she started first time, even for him, but at last they were away, threading through the traffic into Princes Street, making for the Mound and the Old Town.

How much busier it was now! During the war, there wouldn't have been a car in sight, unless it belonged to a doctor on a visit, but with the coming of peace, more and more cars were appearing;

some resurrected from owners' garages where they'd been up on blocks and some being new, though these were still scarce and much sought after.

The Old Town flat, the upper floor of a Victorian terraced house close to the Royal Infirmary, was quite different from the overcrowded tenements in other parts of the city and would, Mr MacKenna remarked, be no trouble to sell. When he had made his notes for the particulars and Roz had completed her room measurements, they made their farewells to the owners who were making a move to Glasgow, promising to be in touch with all necessary details of the sale, and returned to their car.

'As I say, we'll have no trouble with that one,' Mr MacKenna commented as they drove away. 'It's just the sort of flat to attract a lot of good bids from middle income families.' He gave a quick smile. 'Though not your sort of place, I suppose, Miss Rainey?'

'Why'd you say that? I thought it was very nice.'

'Ah, but I haven't worked with you for some time without knowing what attracts you. Big, detached, or at least a semi, stone built, or old brick, large rooms, long windows, some garden space or ground at the back and, above all, a feeling of quality. Isn't that right?'

For some moments she sat in silence, her face colouring up to her brow, then she tried to laugh.

'You seem to know me very well, Mr MacKenna. I don't remember telling you all that, but yes, it's true. Houses like that, they're my dream. Just silly, maybe—'

'Not at all. Everyone should have dreams. And people buying houses certainly do. Rarely realize them, of course. Begin with high hopes, then gradually settle for what's available or what they can afford. But it's our job to try to get as close as we can to their dreams, even if we know they're pretty impossible.'

'Your job,' Roz said quietly. 'Not mine. I wish it was, because I know I could do it. Only I'll never be allowed to, will I?'

'Don't say that,' he said uneasily as they turned into a wide road of stone-built houses well fitting his description of Roz's favourites. 'You know you're a massive help to me, Miss Rainey. You're my assistant, after all.'

'But one day I'd like to be more than that.' She took a breath. 'I'd like to be in charge. Don't laugh, but I would. If I were a lawyer, it could happen, eh? But it won't because I'm not.' She sat back in her seat, gazing out at the street of gracious houses in the area known as the Grange, not daring to look at Mr MacKenna.

'Why, Miss Rainey, I never knew you felt like that!' His eyes on her face were large and wondering, his tone kind. 'I think it's good that you have ambition. I fully believe women should, and there are plenty of women lawyers now, you know.'

'But I couldn't have been one. I never went on to further education – it wasn't possible. I had to go to work soon as I'd got my Leaving Certificate. But I believe I could do the job I want even without being a lawyer. I know you have other legal duties at Tarrel's, but if I was an estate agent, like in England, I needn't be a lawyer, need I?'

'You needn't here, if you wanted to open up an office just as an estate agent. There's nothing to prevent you.'

She smiled wearily. 'I don't see me being able to do that, Mr MacKenna. And there aren't many others trying it, either, are there?'

'Well . . .' He glanced at his watch. 'We'd better get on, see Mr and Mrs Boath. Owners of just your sort of dream house, Miss Rainey.'

'Maybe I have too many dreams,' she muttered, following him up to the handsome front door of the house they were to sell. 'Maybe I'd be happier with less.'

She knew it wasn't true – she couldn't imagine life without something to hope for. In any case, the lawyer had no time to reply, as the door was already opening and the lady of the house was welcoming them in.

Six

Just as Roz remembered from the valuation visit, the house was perfect. Admittedly, semi-detached, but so beautifully built and showing quality at every turn, that this seemed to be only a minor point, and did not stop her from dwelling with pleasure on the solid doors and brass fittings, the plaster ceilings, elegant mantels, the long windows with heavy curtains, the fine furniture that so suited its surroundings.

As Roz and Mr MacKenna stood together, breathing in the smell of polish and the scent from bowls of spring flowers, Mrs Boath and her husband, both middle-aged – she very elegant, he quite casual – asked where they'd like to start.

'From the top and work down, I expect,' Mr Boath suggested, 'this being the day you write us up, eh? And then there'll be measuring, I believe you said? Might take some time.'

'No need to worry about that,' Mr MacKenna told him. 'Miss Rainey here is very quick. We hope not to keep you too long.'

'Oh, we've got all the time in the world, now that my husband is retired!' cried Mrs Boath. 'That's why we want to sell, as I think we told you. Our life has shrunk and this place is too big, especially as you can't get the staff any more.' She shook her head with its well-coiffed grey hair, as though confronting tragedy. 'All I have now are dailies and, believe me, they are not the same. Not the same at all.'

'Never mind that now, Anthea,' her husband said shortly. 'Let these people get on. Want me to show the way, Mr MacKenna?'

'No need, thanks. I remember the layout of the house from my valuation. We'll try not to take too long.'

In fact, the work did take time, which was really only to be expected, as everything had to be done meticulously, mistakes in the particulars being considered misleading and causing trouble. Not that Mr MacKenna was likely to make a mistake and Roz could not remember ever getting her measurements wrong, but she always took extra care anyway. The bonus was that she so much enjoyed working in this splendid house, drinking in the atmosphere and admiring everything – though she couldn't help noting that the upper rooms where the maids had once slept were of a different quality to the rest.

Poor things, she thought, how awful to live in this house and just be here to work! How lucky women were to be able to do something else now, and how lucky she herself had been, never to have had to work in domestic service.

'All right?' asked Mr MacKenna when they'd finished and were returning downstairs.

'Fine, no problems.'

'Good, we'll get back then.'

All that remained to do then was for Roz to take a couple of quick photographs of the reception rooms, after which Mrs Boath offered them a cup of tea. Although she declared it 'would be no trouble at all, my help in the kitchen will have it ready in no time', they politely declined, saying they had to get back to the office. As soon as possible, they would be sending copies of the particulars and organizing an advert for the present house in the local paper, while at the same time working on the purchase of the Colinton flat Mr and Mrs Boath had decided on.

'As I don't see any problems with the two negotiations, I think we should be looking at closing dates very soon,' Mr MacKenna told them. 'Just wish all our transactions were so straightforward.'

As he said to Roz in the car driving back to the office, there'd be people queuing up to buy the Grange house, and the Boaths were putting in such a whacking great offer for the flat they wanted, they'd be sure to get it. They were a lucky pair, eh?

Except that the Boaths were now pretty old, Roz was thinking, and their best years must surely be over. Why else would they want to swap the Grange house for a flat, however smart?

'Good work, anyway,' Mr MacKenna was continuing. 'When we get back to the office, we'll deserve a cup of tea there. Except that first I have something I want to say to you.'

'Say to me?' Roz stared at his profile as he drove smoothly back to Queen Street, a cloud of unease suddenly descending over her. Was she at fault, or what? There'd been no hint of anything different in his manner that she could see; no hint that something might be wrong. But now he wanted to speak to her.

'Is it something I've done?' she asked quickly.

'You? No!' He laughed. 'This is nothing to do with you at all, except it concerns you, if that makes sense. The fact is, I'm leaving Tarrel's.'

There was a silence in the car; Roz, stunned, couldn't speak.

Leaving Tarrel's? Mr MacKenna? He couldn't be; she didn't believe it. He'd always been there, a fixture, the only person she'd ever known in the property department. He was her teacher, her mentor – she couldn't imagine the place without him. As she began to try to think of being without him, it suddenly came to her that she wasn't facing only his loss, but the arrival of his replacement. Someone else would be in his job – someone else working with her, telling her what to do, and how that would be of course she'd no idea. All she knew was that her own life was going to change and maybe not for the better.

'It's a bit of a shock for you, I know,' he was saying with a certain awkwardness. 'That's why I've held off mentioning it before – I knew you'd be so surprised.'

'I am,' she managed to say, 'I am surprised. I – well, I don't know what to say. I mean, why, Mr MacKenna? Why d'you want to leave?'

'Let's just stop a moment,' he murmured, drawing up some way from the office. 'Then we can talk in peace.'

Her thoughts flying everywhere as she tried to make sense of the new situation she found herself confronting, she waited for him to speak.

'In a way I don't want to leave,' he said at last. 'I've been very happy here at Tarrel's, very happy. But the time comes to move on and I've had an excellent offer, from my wife's uncle, as it happens. I don't know if you know, Miss Rainey, but my wife is from Aberdeen? She likes Edinburgh, but she'd really love to get back home, so when her uncle, a lawyer, had a vacancy in his firm and offered me the place, I accepted straight away. There'll be a partnership going with it, you understand, so, it makes sense, doesn't it? To take the offer?'

'Oh, yes, I can see that,' Roz agreed, her heart sinking at the finality of his words. No chance, then, that he might change his mind? Of course he wouldn't. To make a move that would please his wife, to become a partner – what more could he want?

'Does this mean you won't be working with property any more?' she asked slowly.

'I'm afraid it does.' Mr MacKenna's smile was rueful. 'I'm sorry to say, I've never had your dedication there, Miss Rainey. True, I've enjoyed my work here, but I'll be happy to take on something different.' He hesitated. 'And hand over the reins at Tarrel's to someone new.'

At the look on her face, he said gently, 'You know, I wish it could have been possible for you to be considered one day for a job like mine. There's no doubt that in time, you could do it easily—'

'Oh, I wasn't thinking I could do it now,' she said hastily. 'I know I'm too young. I'd still need more experience. I was only meaning that I could do it one day, and I wished I could look forward to it, that was all.'

'I'm sorry, Miss Rainey – Roz. Maybe there'll be a change . . .'

A change? There had come a change already, in his using her first name, something unheard of between lawyers and assistants. Oh, but didn't it signal the end of their working relationship, then?

He'd never have used it, even for what was probably a one-off time, if he wasn't leaving. Probably he was going pretty soon.

'I'm not hopeful,' she said quietly. 'When do you leave, then?'

'Advertisements are going out tomorrow for my replacement, but it will probably be sometime in May before he can start. I've agreed to stay until then, so that I can show him the ropes.'

'And not leave a gap with only me in the property department?'

He gave a quick smile. 'Ah, you're a sharp one. Yes, I suppose that was what Mr Banks was thinking. But let me stress that the new man – or, of course, it could be a woman – is going to find you very useful. I don't mind telling you, I've considered myself fortunate to have you for an assistant.'

'It's nice of you to say so.' She hesitated. 'You don't really think it might be a woman, do you?'

Mr MacKenna shrugged. 'Well, it's possible. But not likely for Tarrel's, I agree. Now, we'd better get back. Hope I haven't worried you too much with my news?'

'I'm just trying to get used to it. The thing is, no one's said a word – was it only Norma and me who didn't know?'

'I'm sorry, I've been wanting to tell you for some time but Mr Banks said he'd rather I waited till the advertisement went out. Of course, my colleagues had to know as they were asked if they wanted my job, and Miss Calder had to do the advert.'

'Doesn't matter,' Roz said stiffly. 'Gave me less time to think about it, eh?'

'Look, I really did want you to know,' he said quickly, driving on to park near the office. 'But I'm very glad you know now and can look forward to meeting the new person soon.'

She only wished that that were true.

Seven

Her mother and Chrissie being on late shift at the café that evening, it was Roz's job to prepare tea for her brother and herself. Full of her own problems as she was, it did seem to her, as she fried the fish they were to have, that Dougal seemed a bit on edge. Walking around, picking up the evening paper, putting it down, not yet washed and changed out of his overalls, which was his usual practice when he came home – what was on his mind, then?

'Nothing!' he fired up when she commented. 'Why'd there be anything on my mind? You're the one looking like a thundercloud, eh?'

'I'm not! What are you talking about? Look, why don't you go and change? This fish'll be ready soon.'

Grumbling over her bossiness, he did as she asked, hurrying along to the bathroom and returning in jumper and flannels – his face scrubbed, his hair damp.

'This do?' he asked shortly.

'Fine. I'm just going to dish up.'

Over the meal they were both silent, but when Roz had cleared away and made some tea she admitted to Dougal that she was feeling a bit low.

'The fact is, my boss is leaving and I'm worried. I mean, I don't know who'll get his job and it might be someone awful.'

'Mr MacKenna is leaving? Och, that's a shame,' said Dougal, stirring his tea. 'You've always said he was a nice guy, eh? Why's he going?'

'Got a partnership in Aberdeen, where his wife is from and wants to go back to.' Roz shrugged. 'So, that leaves me waiting to see what sort of chap I'll have to work with, and that's pretty important to me.'

'Should think you'd be better off just getting wed. Then you needn't worry about working. That's where you lassies score over us poor men.'

'Honestly, what a thing to say!' Roz cried hotly. 'Get wed? Who to? But is that all you think matters to women? We've as much right to work as men and we want to, that's the point. Look at how women worked so well during the war—'

'Oh, spare us the lecture,' Dougal groaned. He finished his tea and stood up. 'Look, I'm off out till Ma comes in – just for a pint at the pub, OK?'

'Leaving me with the washing up, of course. I've been working all day as well, you know.'

Roz faced her brother with flashing eyes, but as he shrugged himself into his jacket without speaking, she took a step towards him.

'Listen, there is something up with you, I can tell. And I wish you'd tell me what it is. Maybe I can help?'

He shook his head. 'There's nothing wrong. It's just − well, I'll be able to tell you later. When Ma comes in.'

'You're not going to upset her?' Roz asked anxiously.

'No, well, I don't see why I should. See you later, eh?'

Washing up and tidying the living room, Roz, left alone, felt doubly depressed. It had been bad enough just having Mr MacKenna's departure to worry about, without having to worry about Dougal as well. And it was true, she was worried about him. Though he could often irritate her, airing his opinions, she was fond of him and didn't like to think of his having something on his mind, especially as he was one who always seemed as though he hadn't a care in the world.

There was the added fear that if he was planning to speak to Ma, what he said might not suit, and it was always so necessary to try to make sure that that didn't happen. Even carefree Dougal knew that, but Roz had the feeling now that whatever he wanted to say, he was going to say it anyway.

Not that she could do much about the situation. Better just have a fun evening at home until her family returned, listening to the wireless, tackling that great pile of stockings she'd saved up for mending . . . By which time, Dougal's pint at the pub might have changed his mind about what he wanted to do. She could but hope.

Eight

They all came in together: Flo, looking tired, Chrissie, flushed and seeming excited, and Dougal expressionless, keeping in the background.

'Oh, dear Lord, it there any tea going?' asked Flo, throwing her coat aside and sinking into a chair. 'I'm worn out, so I am.'

'Ma, I've told you there's no need for you to do those late shifts,' Roz told her as she lit the gas under the kettle. 'You should just be going part time − the manageress said you could, didn't she?'

'I need the money,' Flo said flatly. 'And I'm all right − just want a cup o' tea and a ciggy.' Scrabbling in her bag, she found her cigarettes and lit one immediately, before lying back with her eyes closed. 'Och, that's good, eh? That'll do the trick, you'll see.'

'Ma, never mind about your ciggies – what about my news?' asked Chrissie. 'Listen, Roz, I've had such a piece o' luck! This guy I've had my eye on for a week or two has asked me out, and he's a dream boat, I'm telling you! So handsome, isn't he, Ma? And striking. She's seen him, thinks he's grand. A perfect gentleman.'

'A perfect gentleman,' Flo agreed, sitting up and opening her eyes as the smoke of her cigarette rose past her head. 'Works in a bank, very smart, very polite. I could see he was taken with Chrissie, but he's maybe shy – he's only just got round to speaking to her, but now she's meeting him on Friday night. That right, Chrissie?'

'My night off,' Chrissie answered dreamily. 'He's going to meet me from work and we're going to the pictures.'

'What's on?' asked Dougal, taking a chair and flinging out his long legs, as Roz made the tea and set out some dreary-looking cake and biscuits.

'No idea,' Chrissie answered. 'Richard said he'd see what there was and we could choose when we met. I don't care – he's all I want to see, anyway.'

'Richard?' Roz raised her eyebrows. 'Not Dick? What's his other name?'

'Vincent. And he likes his full name.' Chrissie took a piece of the cake. 'Ugh, bet this tastes of sawdust, eh? Ma and me had eggs on toast at the café, but I'm still hungry and this doesn't look up to much.'

'I'll stick with the biscuits,' said Dougal, taking a couple and keeping his eyes on his mother, who said she didn't want anything to eat, just the tea and then she'd be away to her bed.

'Tea's coming up,' said Roz, watching Dougal as she passed round cups, willing him not to speak. This wasn't the time, Ma was weary, couldn't he leave it till morning? But . . .

'Ma, I'd like a word,' he was already saying, as she sipped her tea. 'Won't take a minute.'

'A word?' She gazed at him over her cup. 'What's up, then?'

'Nothing's up. It's just – well, it's about my future.'

His future? Flo and his sisters stared. His future was all arranged, wasn't it? He had his job with the machine tools firm, so where was the problem? They had already sensed that there was a problem. It hung in the air all around, it caused Chrissie's eyes to widen, Roz's gaze to fall and Flo's to narrow as she drew on the last of her cigarette.

'What about your future?' she asked at last. 'I thought we'd got it all settled. You'd be qualified when you'd finished your training and have a good job for life. Seems like a fine future to me.'

'Thing is,' Dougal answered eagerly, 'I don't want it. That good job – no thanks! I mean, think about it – stuck in the same place, doing the same work, day after day, never seeing anything new . . . I couldn't stand it, and that's the truth.'

'Dougal, Dougal, what sort o' folk do you think we are?' Flo cried. 'We have to take what we can get and settle for it. There's no question of having the luxury of going around, seeing different things, whatever takes your fancy. If you've got a regular wage to look forward to, you thank your lucky stars and get on with the job and stop complaining!'

'Ma, why'd we have to take what we can get?' Roz asked. 'I don't agree at all. Everyone's a right to do the best they can for themselves. We've only got one life, remember.'

'No, Roz, Ma's right,' Chrissie countered. 'Dougal's lucky to have the chance of a good steady job and he should stick with it. Think what Ma told us about the thirties – folk'd have given anything for work then!'

'Well, it's not the thirties now and I'm damned if I'm going to settle for something I don't want!' Dougal retorted. 'And the point is, I don't have to. I've got another job lined up and it's ideal. Just what I've been looking for, so don't tell me what I have to do when you know nothing about it!'

'What job are you talking about?' demanded Flo. 'What's this ideal thing you've got lined up, then?'

At that, Dougal drew back in his chair, his eyes losing their fire, his look subdued.

'I'd like to go back in the army,' he said in a low voice. 'Not the Engineers where I did my national service, I want to join the Lowland and Borders Regiment, same as Dad. It's all fixed. They want me and I want them. Don't say anything.'

A silence fell when he'd finished, apart from a shuddering sigh from Roz and a gasp from Chrissie. For a long, long moment, Flo made no move at all, then she stubbed out her cigarette and leaned forward to look at her son.

'Don't say anything?' she repeated. 'Don't say anything, Dougal? You want to do the one thing that'll be sure to upset me and I'm not supposed to say anything?'

'Ma, why the fuss?' he asked, almost squirming in his chair. 'You never complained when I did my national service – what's different?'

'What's different? You know what's different! When you did your service I knew it wasn't your choice and it wouldn't last that long. But to be a regular, that's different, all right. It's the last thing I'd ever want for you, to be a soldier like your dad, in the same regiment, running the same risks. How can you do that to me, Dougal?'

Flo's voice was thickening; there were tears in her eyes as she kept her gaze on her son, but when he attempted to speak again, she waved her hands to quieten him and he fell silent.

'You know what your dad's death did to me,' she said brokenly, 'but away you go without a word and offer yourself to the same regiment as your dad, when you know how I'm going to feel, how we'll all feel, and you don't care, eh? You just want what you want and the rest of us can go hang, is that it?'

'Ma, Dad was a soldier in the war!' Dougal cried desperately. 'Of course he was at risk – everyone was, and some got killed, as did he. But I'll be going into a peacetime army, there'll be no risk and we'll be doing different things, not fighting battles. I'd never have asked you to worry about me like that, honest, I wouldn't!'

'No risk?' Flo repeated with a hoarse laugh. 'In the army and not at risk? You're asking me to believe that? It's a piece o' nonsense and you know it.' She put her hand to her eyes and began to cry in earnest with deep, painful sobs. 'Oh, how could you do this to me, Dougal, how could you?'

'Aye, how could you?' cried Chrissie, rising to put her arms around her mother. 'It's too cruel, so it is!'

'No, it's not cruel, it's not fair to say that. I've explained to Ma how it is, how I'm just joining a peacetime army that'll be nothing like Dad's. She's no need to take it like she has. You see that, Roz, eh? You understand?'

But Roz's eyes were on her mother, who was now sitting back in her chair, her face quite white as her sobs shook her slight frame and, after a moment, Roz shook her head.

'Dougal, what you've said should make sense, but you knew how Ma would see it and you didn't even discuss it with her or any of us, just sprang it on her out of the blue. That was unfeeling, whatever you say.'

'It was just because I knew how she'd be. I knew she'd be so upset that I'd never get away.' Dougal ran his hand over his face.

'We're people too, Roz. We're entitled to lead our own lives, and I'm going to lead mine.'

'It's no good saying anything to him,' Flo murmured, struggling to her feet. 'He's made up his mind, girls – there's nothing we can do.' Leaning on Chrissie's arm, she left her chair and began to move away. 'I'll – I'll have to go to my bed now. I . . . don't feel . . . so well. Roz, will you get me my pills? Chrissie, help me, will you?'

For some time after his mother had gone to bed accompanied by his sisters, Dougal sat on by the range, smoking a cigarette and staring into space, his handsome face blank, smoothed free of all emotion. When Roz and Chrissie finally reappeared, saying they thought their mother would soon be sleeping, thanks to her pills, he ground out his cigarette and stared at them without speaking.

'Well, what are you going to do?' asked Roz, pulling up a chair, as Chrissie said she was going to put on the kettle and make sandwiches.

'I'm starving, eh? Worn out with all this trouble.'

'There shouldn't have been any trouble,' Dougal stated. 'Ma talks about me getting my own way, but she's the one who wants hers, and usually gets it, too. Not this time, though.'

'I asked you what you were going to do,' said Roz.

'I've told you. Get my own way on this. I'm not giving in. Ever since Dad died we've fallen over backwards to look after Ma, and I'm not saying we shouldn't take care of her, just that we have lives too and should be allowed to live 'em.'

'You know she'll be depressed again!' cried Chrissie from the table where she was slicing bread. 'And if you're away, it'll be Roz and me that have to look after her. It's not fair of you to put it all on us, is it, Roz?'

'I think he has a point,' Roz said slowly. 'We should be able to lead our own lives – I mean, that would be the ideal. But we don't live in an ideal world, eh? And families count.'

'What d'you mean, then? You think Dougal should go and we should take care of Ma?'

'Well, Ma's here and she does need taking care of. What else can we do?'

'You happy about that, Dougal?' Chrissie asked roughly. 'You get your own way and we look after Ma?'

'I don't like asking you to, but to be fair neither of you are planning to leave, eh? So, if I am, I hope you won't mind if I do. And maybe Ma will rally anyway. I don't see why not. She's been doing well at the café lately. Folk do get better, you know.'

Roz and Chrissie exchanged glances, then looked at Dougal.

'Want anything to eat?' asked Roz, rising wearily.

'Wouldn't mind.'

'Make the tea, then,' ordered Chrissie, setting down a plate of sandwiches on the living-room table. 'I found a bit o' ham in the larder cupboard – you're in luck, Dougal.'

'Listen,' he said earnestly, 'you don't think too badly of me, eh? Joining the army, it's something I have to do.'

'We're family,' said Roz. 'Just let's leave it at that.'

While their mother slept on, deeply and without dreaming, the three siblings sat together, drinking tea, eating ham sandwiches and still feeling like a family – of sorts.

At least, thought Roz, I've had something else to think about apart from who's going to take over Tarrel's property department.

Nine

Having taken to her bed, Flo refused to speak to Dougal, just turning her face to the wall whenever he came in to see her, and telling the girls she felt too ill to forgive him.

'Oh, Ma, that's silly talk,' Roz sighed. 'You can't go on like that. He's been thoughtless but if he really wants to be a soldier you'll just have to let him go.'

'He knew how I'd feel about it and he just didn't care, that's what hurts. Now he's put me right back to where I was before and it's so unfair!'

'He does care, Ma, but he thinks he has a right to make his own career, and he has a point, eh? Why not just accept what he's done and see how things go? It's true, he'll be in the peacetime army – it'll be less of a worry than if there was a war.'

But Flo refused to be comforted and the doctor, prescribing more bromide to calm her down, said they'd just have to be patient. In his view, she wasn't as bad as she'd been, and if she took her medication and thought about things for a bit, all might be well.

'Aye, and in the meantime we're rushed off our feet at Café Sunshine, with one of us having to take a turn with Mrs Abbot doing the cash desk,' Chrissie complained to Roz. 'And Mrs Abbot is none too pleased about it, as you might guess.'

'Cheer up, you've got your young man, and you have a good time when you go out with him, don't you?'

'Oh, I do, Roz!' The worried lines disappeared from Chrissie's youthful brow and her blue eyes sparkled. 'He's wonderful, he really is! Next thing he wants to do is take me out for a meal, instead of going to the pictures. Somewhere different from the Café Sunshine, too.'

'Well, I'm glad one of us is happy,' Roz murmured. 'Meanwhile, I'm in suspense, waiting to see what happens at work. Everything depends on what sort of chap they take on for Mr MacKenna's job.'

'Might be a woman?' suggested Chrissie, but Roz shook her head.

'No, it wouldn't be and it isn't. I've just heard that three men have been shortlisted. There'll be interviews in a couple of weeks.'

'Could be someone nice.'

Roz's face remained glum. She couldn't see anyone as nice as Mr MacKenna being appointed again. Folk weren't usually lucky twice.

Aware of how much it mattered to her who got his job, Mr MacKenna told Roz, after reviewing the shortlisted candidates' applications, that she really needn't worry.

'I'm confident you'll get on with whichever one is successful. The fact is, they're all pretty much the same. Younger than me – one's twenty-nine, two are just over thirty – all are fully qualified and ready to move on from where they are, and all are keen as mustard about running a property department.'

'Have they had experience?' Roz asked doubtfully.

'One has – that's the twenty-nine-year-old. He's from a firm in the Borders that sells property in a small way, and obviously fancies running something bigger. The two thirty-year-olds are from very small Glasgow firms without much in the way of property interest as yet, but say they're very keen. Shouldn't be ruled out, in my view.'

'But if they haven't had experience of running a department, how will they manage?'

'They'll learn on the job, as I did. I was young like them when I was first appointed here and hadn't actually worked in property. But when Mr Banks asked me to take over, I jumped at the chance and have enjoyed what I've done. Our successful candidate will probably be the same.'

'I suppose so. He'll be lucky, anyway.'

'Yes, well, I'll do what I can to give him a good start and leave plenty of information in my files. And he'll have you, of course – that'll be all he needs.'

'Oh, yes,' Roz agreed coldly. 'I'll be useful, then.'

'I know you'll do your best,' Mr MacKenna said quietly.

She knew she would, too, and said no more.

Ten

That evening, when she returned home after work, she found a pleasant surprise – her mother up and dressed and with a shepherd's pie she'd made herself all ready for tea.

'Why, Ma, you're feeling better!' Roz cried. 'Oh, that's wonderful!'

'I'm better than I was,' Flo admitted grudgingly. 'But I'll have to take care.'

'Oh, yes, but just to see you up – it's so nice!'

Throwing her arms round her mother, Roz was thinking that this was the best piece of news she'd had for quite some time, and if it meant that there might be a softening of Flo's attitude towards Dougal, that would be a tremendous bonus. For surely she couldn't keep up her treatment of him while he ate her shepherd's pie and she sat watching him, knowing he wouldn't be at home for much longer? But Roz knew only too well that nothing could be expected of her mother. Always, you had to take things as they came.

There was the sound of the flat door opening, and Dougal's voice calling. 'Hallo, Roz! I'm back!'

Roz and her mother exchanged glances. The vegetables were ready, the pie in the oven was well browned – all they had to do was serve up. But here was Dougal in the doorway, his eyes widening as he saw his mother up and dressed.

'Ma, you're up. I never thought . . . How are you feeling, then?'

She tossed her head a little, then suddenly sat down at the kitchen table, as though her legs were weakening.

'Better,' said Roz, taking out the shepherd's pie, her face flushed from the heat of the oven. 'Ma's feeling better.'

'Getting better,' Flo corrected. 'My first day up, and I don't feel that grand.'

'It's grand to see you up, though,' Dougal said earnestly. 'You don't know how good that is.'

Flo slowly turned her head to look at him. 'You'd better go and get yourself washed,' she told him tremulously, and as Dougal smiled and Roz smiled with him, they knew the storm was over, that their mother had come back. She had been away, but she was back, at least for the time being. It looked like she'd finally accepted what was to happen and that being so, maybe all would be well. Maybe.

In fact, when Flo had later returned to bed and Roz and Dougal were looking in on her, it was Flo herself who asked how long they'd got before Dougal must leave.

'I put in my notice some time ago,' he said after a pause. 'And I've passed my army medical.'

'Had your medical! You never said.'

'We weren't talking, Ma.'

'Oh, well, never mind – just tell me when you have to leave.'

'End of April, I'll be reporting to the regiment near Lauder.'

'End of April? Oh, that's no time at all – that's too soon!'

'Nearly three weeks, Ma. That's not so bad.'

'So you say!' She put a handkerchief to her eyes. 'I just hope you're right, that's all: that this is peacetime and you won't have to fight.'

'Ma, I'll be training and all that sort o' thing before I even get posted. You've no need to worry.'

'No need at all,' chimed Roz, then leaped to her feet. 'There's the door – it's Chrissie. Oh, Ma, I wish she'd seen you up and dressed!'

'Heavens, what a fuss!' cried Flo, but when Chrissie came in, it was enough for her to see Dougal smiling beside Flo's bed to know that Ma was better and had come back to them once again.

'Oh, Ma!' she cried, running to hug her mother as she lay back against her pillows. 'Oh, Ma, I'm that glad, eh?'

'I'm sure I don't know what about. Your brother's still going to join the army, you know.'

'Ma, he'll be all right, and you'll be all right. That's what's grand, eh?'

'I hope so,' sighed Flo. 'Look, is no one going to make us a cup of tea?'

Eleven

On the twenty-first of April, three young lawyers, formally dressed in dark suits, arrived at Tarrel and Thom's at precisely two o'clock, to be shown by Miss Calder to the clients' waiting room.

'If you'll wait here, gentlemen? Mr Banks will be along shortly to welcome you. In the meantime, may I get you some coffee?'

The three lawyers – Mr Appin, Mr Franklin, and Mr Shield – thanked her and declined, each sitting down, trying to look at ease. When Miss Calder had withdrawn to inform Mr Banks of the candidates' arrival, Norma, who had been hovering in the background, ran along to the property centre, agog with her news.

'They're here!' she told Roz, who was at her desk, trying like the candidates to appear at ease. 'The interview men are here! Miss Calder's put 'em in the waiting room. But where's Mr MacKenna?'

'He's already with Mr Banks.' Roz jumped up, abandoning any attempt to look calm. 'What do they look like, then? Are they nice? Did you like them?'

'Honestly, I only saw 'em for a couple of minutes.' Norma's round brown eyes were shining. 'But I thought they looked OK. Well, one's a bit overweight, but there's one who's really friendly. I mean, he was smiling a lot, but it might have been nerves, eh?'

'I just wish it was all over,' Roz muttered, turning away. 'It's too nerve-racking.'

'Anybody'd think you were being interviewed yourself, Roz,' Norma said, laughing. 'Why are you getting so worried?'

'Well, it makes all the difference to your job how you get on with your boss, eh? It's very important, I'd say.'

'You've been spoiled, having Mr MacKenna, that's your trouble. How about me? My boss is Miss Calder!'

'At least you know where you are with her. These fellows are completely unknown.'

Roz moved around the main office, tidying papers that didn't need tidying, straightening Mr MacKenna's pens and adjusting photos on the property wall.

'I'm going to meet them, you know. Mr MacKenna is going to show them round the department before they have their interviews. We've cancelled all appointments for today.'

'Oh, the fellows might be along soon, then!' Norma cried. 'I'd better get back to the front desk – Miss Calder wants me to look after it this afternoon.'

As soon as Norma had left, Roz took her compact from her handbag and studied her face. Must look my best, she thought, but, oh, Lord, see those violet shadows underneath my eyes! Looked as though she hadn't slept for a week, and it was true that last night, at least, she had lain awake for far too long.

That was partly because she had been worrying over Dougal's leaving and how Ma would take it when it actually happened, for though she was now well enough to return to work – just in time before Mrs Abbot sacked her – there was no guarantee that she would stay well when the goodbyes came. It was partly, also, of course, to do with what was happening today. Her own D-Day, as they'd called that day of invasion in the war – her own crucial day of reckoning, for this would be the time when her life at work would be decided just as surely as the successful candidate's.

Norma had asked why she was so worried, and Roz had tried to explain the importance of getting on with your boss. But it was more than that, really. More that she'd become so used to Mr MacKenna's easy ways, so cushioned against difficulties, that she wasn't sure how she'd cope with someone who might be different. Almost certainly would be different – that was the point.

Oh, grow up! she told herself. You can do your job well, whatever happens. Just don't worry about how the new man does his and how that might affect you. Powder your nose, put some more lipstick on, and look your best. The candidates could walk in any minute now.

Sure enough, almost as soon as she'd put her compact away, they did walk in, shepherded by Mr MacKenna, all three looking around with interest at the department. And her.

'Gentlemen, this is Miss Rainey, my assistant,' Mr MacKenna told them. 'My prop and stay ever since she joined the department. Someone I really couldn't do without, and who will be as helpful, I know, to my successor.'

As a quick blush rose to Roz's brow, the young men nodded and smiled. Mr Appin, the plump one, soon looked away, as did Mr Franklin, who was wearing tortoiseshell glasses and was almost as thin as Mr Wray, while only tall Mr Shield's gaze rested on her a little longer. And it was a friendly gaze, quite intent, from fine hazel eyes beneath well-marked dark brows, darker than his thick, light brown hair, and Roz rather enjoyed returning it. Only for a moment, though, as Mr MacKenna was beginning to outline some of the routine work of the department, moving the candidates on to study the property photographs before showing them Roz's own little office and asking her to explain her duties.

She managed that quite well, surprising herself with the ease with which she went through her work, before leaving it to Mr MacKenna to add a last word or two.

'As you know from the job description,' he began, 'the duties here include a certain amount of general legal work apart from managing this department – you'll have to be prepared for whatever comes along, but in any event, Miss Rainey here will hold the fort. She will also assist on visits to properties in taking particulars.'

Glancing at Roz, as he spoke, he added: 'I believe she considers it one of the perks of this job that she gets to see the houses. Isn't that right, Miss Rainey?'

'Oh, yes, Mr MacKenna,' she agreed eagerly. 'Houses are my real interest.'

'Yours, too, of course?' Mr MacKenna asked the candidates, at which there was a chorus of agreement and a smile from him.

'They have to be, it goes without saying, if you look after a property department. Buying a house is the biggest investment most people have to make, and we're here to help them to get it right. Wanting to do that is what's drawn you to this particular post, I suppose I can say?'

'Oh, certainly,' plump Mr Appin said at once. 'That's certainly true for me.'

'And me,' chimed Mr Franklin, while Mr Shield nodded without speaking.

'Fine.' Mr MacKenna looked at his watch. 'Well, we'd better return now to Mr Banks, I think. Follow me, gentlemen. Thank you, Miss Rainey.'

'Thank you,' the young men echoed with enthusiasm, giving her farewell smiles as they left, Mr Shield's being as friendly as the look in his hazel eyes.

Feeling completely unsettled as she sat down at her typewriter, Roz's head was in a whirl. She'd seen the three candidates, who would now be taking it in turn to suffer an ordeal by interview, and it had all been pretty painless for her, hadn't it? The chaps had been very nice and polite. One in particular had been very friendly, she had to admit, and that was Mr Shield.

Mr Shield – he had a really pleasant manner, hadn't he? One that he could probably turn on for anyone, but that didn't make it any less attractive. Could she see herself working with him?

Roz stared at the paper in her typewriter.

She could, she decided, she'd like to, but what she'd like and what Mr Banks wanted could be two different things. Slowly, she began to type in the details of a bungalow that had recently come on to the market, wondering when the interviews would be over and Mr MacKenna would return. And would she get to know who the lucky winner was?

Sometime after four o'clock, she helped Norma to carry a tray of tea into the waiting room where Mr Appin and Mr Franklin were sitting in silence.

'No Mr Shield?' asked Norma brightly. 'Is he still having his interview?'

'He's been in there ages,' Mr Appin muttered, accepting his tea and drinking it fast.

'Longer than either of us,' said Mr Franklin, shovelling sugar into his cup, as though he felt he needed it.

The girls, returning to the staffroom, exchanged glances as they drank their own tea.

'Oh, d'you think that Mr Shield's going to get it?' Norma whispered. 'What a nice fellow, eh? You must be keeping your fingers crossed, Roz.'

'Oh, I don't know – you can't really tell what someone will be like from first meeting, can you? We'll just have to wait and see.'

Wait, Roz did, of course – for Mr MacKenna's return, anyway. He looked weary, she thought, when he finally appeared sometime after five o'clock, but pleased. Things must have gone his way, then?

'Well?' she asked anxiously. 'Who got it?'

'There's been nothing official said to the candidates – we're going to write to them.'

'They've gone?'

'Oh, yes, to catch their trains.'

'Nothing official. What's unofficial, then?'

Mr MacKenna smiled broadly. 'Mr Banks and I have both agreed – it's to be Mr Shield.'

Mr Shield. As she took in the news, her face told her thoughts and Mr MacKenna laughed.

'You're pleased, aren't you, Roz? It wasn't just that he'd had some experience, he was the best all round and we think he'll be an asset to the firm. But why do I have the feeling that you're not going to miss me at all?'

Twelve

It wasn't the case, of course, that Roz wouldn't be missing Mr MacKenna, her mentor, her father figure, when he departed. Having always worked with him at Tarrel's and finding it so pleasant, it would take more than a new fellow to replace him, however good he was at smiling. True, she was pleased Mr Shield had got the job and she felt more at ease about the future but, come the day when she arrived at the property department and Mr MacKenna wasn't there, she was still going to feel a huge gap that would take time to fill.

For now, though, everything was nicely routine at work and all she had to worry about was Dougal's departure, which was so soon approaching. Flo was, for the time being, bearing up well, which was so surprising. No one could quite believe it, but it was Dougal himself who appeared on edge. Perhaps he was worrying about whether he'd done the right thing? After all, it had all been his idea; he'd not asked for advice, seemed so sure he knew what he was doing, but as the time grew closer for his departure maybe he was beginning to have second thoughts?

'I bet he is,' Chrissie declared. 'I mean, who'd want to be a soldier? Always being ordered about, told what to wear, made to clean your stuff or be in trouble – I mean, your life's not your own, eh?'

'Fellows seem to enjoy the life, they say,' Roz replied. 'And they get to go places, see the world, do different things. That's what appealed to Dougal.'

'Aye, but look at him now – face like a wet weekend! I think he's got cold feet.' Chrissie sighed. 'Why is there always something to worry about in this family? The one thing that cheers me up is seeing Richard.' She gave a dreamy smile. 'He takes me right out of this world, Roz. Makes me forget all my troubles.'

'That's grand, Chrissie.' Roz hesitated. 'But you will be careful, eh?'

'What do you mean? I know how to take care of myself, eh? I'm not going to end up in the family way, if that's what you're hinting!'

'No, it's not. All I'm saying, is, don't get too involved, in case – you know – it doesn't last.'

'Thanks for that!' Chrissie cried. 'Thanks for thinking Richard is going to get tired o' me, before we've known each other five minutes!'

'Look, I didn't mean that. It's just – well, you know what I mean, Chrissie. I'm only thinking of you.'

'You needn't, then! You're not exactly the one who should be handing out advice when you haven't even got a fellow of your own!'

'OK, OK,' Roz said impatiently. 'I'll say no more. Look, we're all on edge, eh? With Dougal due to go so soon? Let's not fall out.'

'Just as long as you go easy on telling me what to do,' Chrissie said sulkily. 'I've enough to think about, worrying about Ma. If she takes to her bed again after Dougal goes, Mrs Abbot will give her the push, no question.'

'Worrying about Ma?' Roz's grey eyes darkened. 'We're all in the same boat there.'

On Dougal's last evening before he left for his regiment, Flo and Chrissie came home early from the café so that all the family could be together for tea. Not that anyone expected it to be a cheerful meal, but it seemed the right thing to do, and though Flo constantly kept her eyes on her son and there was little conversation, all went off better than hoped. Afterwards, however, when Roz and Chrissie had cleared away and washed up, Flo's face began to take on the blankness the family dreaded and their hearts began to sink.

'I'd . . . better pack my bag,' Dougal said, clearing his throat. 'Though I'm not taking much. I'll be kitted out there.'

'Kitted out?' Flo asked, her gaze on him now expressionless as she drew on a cigarette. 'You mean you'll be in the same uniform as your father?'

'Aye, I will. What else?'

'Doesn't it make you feel bad, to think o' him?'

'No, I feel proud. I felt proud when I told 'em about him at my first interview and they were impressed.' Dougal's voice was strong, his manner definite. If he'd had misgivings of sorts, he'd lost them now. 'And when I get to wear the same uniform as he did, I'll feel good, Ma, so you've no need to worry about it.'

Flo was silent, finally looking away, and Roz said hastily, 'Dougal's right, Ma – you've no need to worry about how he feels.'

'Maybe I'm worrying about how *I* feel, Roz. You all know what I think about Dougal leaving us for the army.'

'But we thought you'd got used to the idea!' cried Chrissie. 'You've not said a word lately!'

'Doesn't mean I've not been thinking about it.'

'Ma, have a heart!' Dougal said roughly. 'It's all fixed – I leave tomorrow. Don't make it hard for me!'

'Hard for you?' Flo tossed her head. 'What about me? Yes, you leave tomorrow, so when do we see you again, I'd like to know? This is your thanks to me for bringing you up, worrying about you—'

'Ma, I'll be back on a weekend pass before you know I'm gone!' he cried. 'They've told me that new recruits soon get a trip home, so you can see how I'll be and you needn't upset yourself or us any more.'

He leaped to his feet. 'Now, I'm going to pack my bag in your room and then I'm going down to say goodbye to the lads at the Crown. If you're in bed when I come back I'll come in to say goodnight and I'll expect you to wish me luck. But don't you or anybody else see me off tomorrow because I'm leaving early like I told you, for the first train out.'

Red in the face, Dougal fixed his mother with a last fierce glare, then stalked away and the three women in his family, sitting speechless in their chairs, heard the crash of Flo's bedroom door behind him.

Thirteen

Oh, my, thought Roz, oh, Lord! That's torn it! Dougal was so pleased Ma had seemed to have got used to him going, he'd not been able to take it now she was playing up again. But what would happen now? Ma would never accept it, her son speaking to her like that – she'd be away to her bed, eh?

But Flo made no move. She seemed turned to stone, sitting in her chair, cigarette in hand, her eyes cast down while Roz and Chrissie waited fearfully for some sort of reaction. Only when the cigarette began to burn her fingers did Flo give a start, put out the stub and turn her eyes on her daughters.

'Did you hear what he said?' she asked huskily. 'Just then – what Dougal said to me? "You needn't upset yourself or us any more" . . . that's what he said. "Needn't upset yourself or us any more". . . Have I upset you girls? Have I upset him? Is he blaming me?'

Chrissie, shaking her head, looked at Roz as though she couldn't find the words to say all that she wanted to, and it was Roz who had to find an answer.

'Ma, of course we're upset if you're upset. That's always been the way, eh? We can't be happy if you're not happy, can we?'

'I've made you all unhappy? Because I'm ill?' Flo's face was twisting with pain. 'I've never meant to, never! I've always done my best – but you don't know what it's like, when the darkness comes down. It's like night to me, black, black night, and I try to struggle up, out of it, but there's nothing I can do, nothing, till it goes . . .'

She began to cry, putting her hand to her eyes like a child, until Roz ran to her and put an arm around her.

'Ma, don't cry, you'll soon feel better again. The night does go, eh? You've been so much better lately.'

'Aye, till Dougal had to go, till there's no way out. He's away tomorrow, and then there'll be the worry – the fear. I had to take the telegram, you know, when your dad went. I can remember it now – just how it was, all those years ago.'

'Ma, there won't be any telegram about Dougal!' Chrissie cried. 'He's not going to war, he's told you. It'll all be different for him!'

'He's in the army. He's at risk, he'll always be at risk, and how do we live through it? Tell me that.'

'Would you like a hot drink, Ma?' asked Roz desperately. 'Some cocoa, maybe?'

'That'd be good,' Chrissie hurried to agree. 'I'll make it. I'll put some milk on now. Then you could go to bed, Ma, and Dougal will come in to see you, like he said.'

'If he wants to,' sighed Flo.

'Of course he wants to!' cried Roz. 'You know he does!'

'Aye, well, I think I will away to my bed, then. But in the

morning, I'm going to be up to see him off. Whatever he said, that'd be only right, eh?'

'We'll all be up,' Roz told her, glancing round to see Dougal in the doorway, his small case in his hand.

'All done!' he cried cheerfully, going to his mother. He drew her to her feet, kissed her on her cheek and held her close.

'Shan't be long, Ma. I'll just say cheerio to the lads, and then I'll be back. But you go to bed if you want to and I'll come in to say goodnight.'

'All right, son,' she murmured. 'That'll be grand. I won't be asleep, that's for sure.'

Will any of us sleep tonight? Roz asked herself.

And it did seem as though there was hardly any night at all before they heard Dougal getting up, and then they were up and kissing him goodbye and watching him stride away into the morning, his hand giving a last wave as he went for an early tram.

'How d'you feel, Ma?' Roz asked softly. 'You going back to bed?'

'No, might as well stay up now.' Flo's voice was weak, her face a mask, but it seemed as though she had made up her mind to go to work.

'It'd be good if you could go to work, Ma, if you feel up to it.'

'I'll feel no better if I stay at home, that's the truth of it.'

Roz and Chrissie exchanged glances.

'Mrs Abbot'll be pleased, anyway,' Chrissie remarked, trying to sound cheerful.

Flo's only reply was, 'Oh, well, nice to know I can please somebody, then.'

And as the sisters looked at each other again, they knew that whatever they did, however things worked out for them or Dougal, the way ahead would have its problems.

Fourteen

The days lengthened, grew truly spring-like, as hopes strengthened that this post-war time would lead to lasting peace. Even the long-standing civil war in far-away China looked like coming to an end, with the Communists poised to defeat the Nationalists and create a

republic, while southern Ireland had already quietly declared itself
a republic with the name of Eire. All very interesting, if you liked
to read the newspapers, but all that mattered to the Raineys left at
home was that nowhere did it seem likely that a Scottish regiment
might be called upon to fight somewhere foreign – which was
exactly what Dougal had said.

'You see, Ma, it's true,' Roz told Flo. 'He's in a peacetime army;
he won't be going to war, and look at the postcards he's sent – he's
enjoying himself, eh?'

'I'm sure,' muttered Flo. 'We're out o' sight, out o' mind, seemingly. Are we enjoying ourselves, then?'

'I am!' cried Chrissie. 'I've got Richard.'

At that, Flo's expression softened and she even smiled. 'Well, that's
true, Chrissie. And he does seem a nice lad.'

'A perfect gentleman?' asked Roz, also smiling to see her mother
for once forgetting Dougal. 'When am I going to meet him, then?'

'Oh, not just yet,' Chrissie answered. 'But you will meet him, Roz,
I promise, and then you'll understand why I think he's so nice.
Meantime, what's happening with you? When's your new boss starting?'

'Next week,' Roz said swiftly. 'I'm already collecting for Mr
MacKenna's leaving present. We're going to get him a new briefcase.'

'And then he'll be away?' asked Flo. 'Shame, eh? When you got
on so well?'

'He'll have a day to show Mr Shield the routine and then he'll
be off to Aberdeen.' Roz sighed. 'Sold his own house here, you
know, in no time at all. Some friend wanted it and Mr MacKenna
let him have it without it going to sealed bids, which is just the
sort of thing he would do.'

'You'll just have to hope that this new chap is as nice,' Chrissie
told her comfortingly. 'He's younger, anyway.'

'As though that matters,' said Flo, looking into space. 'I wonder
when Dougal's coming home for that weekend he mentioned? I
hope he won't be wearing his uniform.'

Oh, dear, thought Roz, catching Chrissie's eye. There they were
– back to Dougal again. She supposed it was only to be expected.

The big day came at last – Mr Shield's first and Mr MacKenna's last.
Roz, who had spent half the previous night worrying what to wear,
eventually wore what she usually wore to work – white blouse, dark
jacket, dark skirt – and arrived at the office hoping to be first there.

Mr MacKenna, however, was already at his desk, with Mr Shield in his formal suit with hair well flattened sitting next to him, surrounded by files and papers.

'Ah, here's Miss Rainey,' Mr MacKenna said cheerfully, as both men rose to their feet. 'She'll soon sort us out.'

'I'm not late, am I?' she asked, as Mr Shield favoured her with his smile. Mr MacKenna smiled too.

'Haven't we had this conversation before? No, it's just that we came in early, to get on with the handover.'

'Is there anything I can do?' asked Roz.

'I don't think so, thanks. I'm just going through my notes and the legal stuff with Mr Shield here.'

Roz hesitated, her thoughts concerned with the presentation of the briefcase that was to take place in the afternoon.

'Will you be going out to lunch at the usual time, Mr MacKenna?'

'Oh, yes, Mr Banks is taking us both out, with the partners.' Mr MacKenna looked apologetic. 'Sorry we couldn't all have gone.'

'That's quite all right.'

She smiled, aware of a sympathetic look in the new lawyer's eyes. As though she'd expect to go out to lunch with Mr Banks and the partners! From the door, she asked if they would excuse her as she must just check something with Miss Ward, and as they returned to their files she sped along the hall to Norma at Reception.

'The briefcase,' she said to Norma urgently. 'It's still there under the counter, eh?'

'Sure it is. Why wouldn't it be?'

'I don't know, I'm just worried because I had to collect the money and help Mr Newman choose it, then wrap it up and all that. If anything happens to it, I'm responsible.'

'Honestly, anybody'd think it was the royal regalia!' Norma cried, laughing. 'Look, here it is, and our farewell card as well, with all our signatures.'

'Oh, thanks, that's grand.' Roz studied the large parcel wrapped in red paper and tied with a bow. 'Just as long as we know where it is when it's time for the presentation.'

'That's not till this afternoon.'

'I know.' Roz laughed. 'Should be back from their lunch by then, I suppose.'

'Oh, yes, they're all going out to lunch, eh?' Norma's brow had darkened. 'No question of anybody inviting us, you'll notice.'

'Did you think they would?'

'Well, you should've been asked, Roz. You've worked with Mr MacKenna for a long time.'

'I think he would have liked to invite me, but he's the one being taken, you see. It wasn't his place to tag me along.'

'Well, maybe the new chap will have different ideas.' Norma's eyes gleamed. 'If you ask me, I think he'll be different altogether from the guys we've got now.'

As Miss Calder came tapping along the hall, Roz shook her head warningly, and Norma, colouring up, rapidly began to sort a sheaf of papers on the reception desk.

'Everything ready for the presentation, Miss Rainey?' Miss Calder asked. 'Mustn't mislay the briefcase, must we?'

'No, Miss Calder. It's safe here in Reception.'

'That's good. Now, when Mr Banks and the lawyers have gone to lunch, I'd like you both to help me put out some glasses in Mr Banks's room. There's going to be wine and sherry provided, so that we can all drink Mr MacKenna's health and wish him luck.'

'Ooh, nice!' cried Norma.

'What a lovely idea,' said Roz.

'Yes, Mr Banks is always thoughtful like that, of course. Don't forget to put out a glass for Mrs MacKenna. She's coming in to say goodbye, too.' Miss Calder gave a brief smile. 'We didn't see her often, but she was always very pleasant when she looked in.'

'Very pleasant,' agreed Roz, who'd always found her so on the rare occasions when they'd met.

'Now, our new Mr Shield isn't married,' Miss Calder went on, rather unusually staying a moment to chat. 'But then he is very young.'

Catching Norma's look, she laughed a little. 'Perhaps you don't think so, Miss Ward, but to me he seems that. Not of course that I mean he is too youthful,' she added hastily, yet giving the distinct impression she did mean exactly that. 'Well, I must go – I have things to do. You too, girls. Don't forget to put out the glasses and some small plates for potato crisps. I'll leave out some packets.'

As she tapped away, Roz said yes, she must get back to the property department, but the irrepressible Norma couldn't resist a last word or two.

'Fancy her going on about Mr Shield's age,' she whispered. 'Bet I know what's bothering her.'

'What?' asked Roz, mystified.

'Well, what she probably thinks is that he's too young to be working with you. Now don't look like that – you know what I mean.'

'I do not!' cried Roz. 'What's it matter how old we are?'

'Well, Mr MacKenna was old enough to be your father, eh? And Mr Shield isn't. So, if the two of you are always together . . .'

'Oh, Norma, you're hopeless! Mr Shield's only just started and you're talking like that? He's here to do a job, and so am I, and that's all there is to it!'

'OK, OK, I'm just joking. No offence, Roz.'

'All right, but let's just cut out all that stuff, eh?'

'Sure.' Norma drew her finger across her throat and laughed. 'I promise never to say another word!'

'That'll be the day,' said Roz, hurrying back to the property department and, without meeting the eyes of either Mr MacKenna or Mr Shield, made for her own office and closed the door.

Fifteen

In fact, the lawyers were not late back from their lunch, Mr MacKenna having said that he needed to be back in good time to complete his handover to Mr Shield before the end of the day. Even so, the men were all looking remarkably cheerful when they came into the office, with even the usually gloomy Mr Wray seeming animated and Mr Newman, not one who normally troubled to pay compliments, actually telling Mr MacKenna he would be much missed.

'Yes, indeed, Ronnie,' he said solemnly, 'Aberdeen's gain is definitely our loss, as you might say.'

'I certainly do say,' chimed Mr Banks, the senior partner, now in his fifties and a little overweight, his once-dark hair grey and receding, but his formidable manner unchanged, even though his smile was affable. 'You've been a tower of strength to Tarrel and Thom's.'

'Please,' groaned Mr MacKenna, bowing his head, 'I've had enough kind words for today. Don't forget you have Mr Shield here and he'll do a splendid job – as long as we finish our handover!'

'Too right,' agreed the newcomer, who had been standing modestly by. 'I still have plenty to learn.'

'Well, you have until four o'clock to learn it,' Mr Banks told him. 'Then, I'd like us all to meet in my office.'

'Very nice,' said Mr MacKenna, very deadpan. 'We'll look forward to it.'

Back in the property department, while the two lawyers continued with their work, all there was for Roz to do was to wait on edge in her own office until it was time to join Norma and Miss Calder in Reception, where they were already greeting Mrs MacKenna, who'd just walked in through the door.

So like her husband, Roz thought, smiling and shaking her hand. So easy-going, so pleasant – what lucky lives their children must lead! No anxiety, no stress. Did they know how well they'd done in life's lottery? Today, Mrs MacKenna, who was not normally interested in clothes, had made a special effort to look smart in a neat blue suit and matching hat, with a touch of make-up on her broad, good-natured face.

'All set?' she whispered at the reception desk. 'Ronnie doesn't know a thing about this, you know.'

'I'm sure he'll have an idea,' said Miss Calder. 'We don't usually have a cup of tea in Mr Banks's office.' She leaned forward. 'Actually, we're not even having tea. Mr Banks is providing wine or sherry – must have managed to find some somewhere. It's a little early, but why not?'

'Why not indeed?' cried Mrs MacKenna. 'Oh, we're going to miss you all so much! What are we doing, going up to Aberdeen?'

'Come along to see Mr Banks,' Miss Calder told her. 'Girls, you too – to help with the drinks.'

'As long as we get a drink ourselves,' Norma muttered to Roz, who knocked her in the ribs, for the lawyers were joining them and their little celebration was about to begin.

First, Mr Banks with great panache opened his wines, which were then served by Roz and Norma to everyone except Miss Calder, who chose sherry. Crisps were handed, more wine was accepted, and as the noise level rose, it seemed amazing that such a small crowd could appear to be so many.

'I feel I'm at a proper party, don't you?' Norma whispered to Roz. 'Who'd have thought old Banks could put on such a do, then?'

'One of these days someone's going to hear you, Norma, and

then there'll be trouble,' Roz whispered back, but she was feeling wonderfully mellow after the one glass of wine she'd allowed herself, not being used to it and not wanting to feel tipsy when it came to saying goodbye to Mr MacKenna. Or even to look flushed in the face, as Joan MacKenna was looking now, or strangely bright-eyed like Miss Calder after her small sherry.

'Who cares what I say?' asked Norma, who was looking rather bright-eyed herself. 'Listen, I'm going to have another glass of wine. Are you?'

'No, because Mr Banks looks as though he's going to speak. There – he's banging a spoon on his glass. Be quiet, Norma!'

'Ladies and gentlemen,' Mr Banks was beginning, 'it now gives me great pleasure to say a few words about Ronnie MacKenna, who is sadly leaving us for foreign climes – well, Aberdeen . . .' Pause for laughter. 'No one could have worked harder for, or done more for, Tarrel and Thom's, not only in his general work for clients, but also – and more particularly, perhaps – for the property department, which, I think it is fair to say, he has really created to make it what it is today, a most valuable asset, admired by all . . .'

There was a good deal more on similar lines, all the sort of things that a boss might say on the departure of a good member of the team, but sounding quite genuine on Mr Banks's part. Well punctuated, too, by cries of 'Hear, Hear!' from Ronnie's colleagues, before ending with an invitation to everyone to raise their glass in a toast to Ronnie and Joan.

'To Ronnie and Joan!' went the cry. 'Good luck in Aberdeen!' Followed by calls for 'Speech, Ronnie, speech!'

And with good grace, Mr MacKenna spoke easily and naturally of his time with the firm, of how much he'd enjoyed it, especially working with such fine colleagues – and here he felt he must mention the special contribution of Miss Roz Rainey to the success of the property department, at which there were murmurs of approval – and of how he was confident that success would continue under the leadership of Mr Jamie Shield. Not just continue, but flourish, as Tarrel's itself would flourish, and would not be forgotten by the MacKennas, who were both so sorry to be saying goodbye.

'Any time you're in Aberdeen,' everyone was told, 'you'll have our address – look us up, you'll be very welcome!'

During the applause that followed, Miss Calder slipped out of the room, to return with a bouquet of flowers which she presented to Joan. This was the signal for Mr Banks to produce the brightly wrapped parcel that he would be presenting to her husband. But to Roz's astonishment, it was into her hands he placed it and told her with a smile, 'Now, Miss Rainey, you know what to do with this, eh?'

'You want me to—?'

'Yes, yes, come along now, Mr MacKenna is waiting.'

Swallowing hard, Roz took the parcel and under the kindly look of her ex-boss, put it into his hands. 'This is from all of us,' she murmured. 'We hope you'll like it.'

'Why, it's a briefcase!' he cried, stripping off the wrapping paper. 'So, you've all seen my old one, eh? I never did think it would make Aberdeen, but this is wonderful. I love it. Thank you. Thank you all very much! I couldn't be more pleased!'

'Well done,' a voice said quietly in Roz's ear as people gathered round Mr MacKenna to look at the briefcase, and she turned to find Mr Shield at her side, his look still seeming sympathetic. 'You were taken by surprise but did that so nicely.'

'It was a surprise – I never thought Mr Banks would ask me to do it,' she told him, but his gaze had moved to Mr MacKenna.

'A hard act to follow,' he murmured. 'I can tell you had quite a rapport there.' His eyes swung back to her. 'But I want you to know I'm really looking forward to working with you, and I think we'll do well too.'

'Thank you; it's nice of you to say so.'

'You'll see – we'll make a good team,' he was continuing, but she had already taken a step away. With his wife beside him, Mr MacKenna was coming over to her, his hand outstretched, his face serious, his eyes as kind as always.

'Miss Rainey – Roz – we're away. Just came to say goodbye.'

'But we don't want to!' cried Joan. 'Oh, it's too sad.'

'My thoughts exactly,' Mr MacKenna said gently. 'Ah, how hard it is to find the words, eh? But you know already what I want to say, don't you? Now I'll wish you all the best for the future, and I'm certain it'll be a good one. You'll do well, Roz, never fear, and remember, I meant what I said about Aberdeen.'

'Look us up, any time!' cried Joan.

They shook hands, all three, and there was even an embrace from Joan, but Roz, not trusting herself to speak, could only smile and watch as others gathered round for the last goodbyes and waves at Tarrel's fine old door where Joan had parked the family car.

'No more dear old Hillman!' cried Mr MacKenna, taking the driving seat. 'Best of luck with that, Mr Shield – treat her well and you'll have no trouble.'

'Come on, dear,' ordered Joan. 'Don't keep everyone waiting.'

And as they all waved again, the MacKennas' car moved slowly away down Queen Street, then put on a little speed, turned a corner and was gone.

'What a shame, eh?' said Norma as people moved back into the building. 'And it was all so nice and friendly at the drinks, eh? Did you ever hear so many first names, then? Now, I suppose it'll be "Miss Ward, will you clear away the glasses?"'

Roz made no reply, but feeling a touch on her arm, heard someone say, 'See you tomorrow, Miss Rainey.'

'Oh, yes, Mr Shield,' she answered. 'Tomorrow.'

Sixteen

For the first day of the property department's new regime with Mr Shield in charge, Roz decided to wear something different. The weather was warm; she no longer needed her jacket, and for that first morning substituted it with a deep blue cardigan, a blue blouse that matched and a pretty, patterned scarf, borrowed from her mother.

'Not bad,' she decided, studying herself in the bedroom mirror, but as she left for work on Day One, her main interest was not how she looked, but whether or not she would arrive at the property department before Mr Shield. It would give her confidence to arrive before him, that was the thing – it would underline that she came to work on time and was there when he arrived, ready to assist and show him what she knew. Also, it would give her the chance to get used to seeing the office without Mr MacKenna.

Too late. Mr Shield was already in the office when she arrived, sitting, working, at Mr MacKenna's desk. Oh, wouldn't he be? The advantage she'd thought to gain by being there before him was not going to happen, and all she could do was return his smile and echo his 'Good morning' as she put the post on his desk, just as she'd done for Mr MacKenna.

'Miss Rainey!' He rose to shake her hand, his eyes lighting up as they rested on her. 'Nice to see you. I'm just frantically reading the notes Mr MacKenna kindly left me – with any luck, I won't have to ring him up for an hour or two!'

He laughed and seemed at ease, wearing this first morning a casual tweed suit, though she couldn't help noticing that the collar of his shirt was not very well ironed and that his thick hair was looking just a little unruly. He was not as well-turned-out as she'd seen him before. Was he not, after all, quite so much at ease as he was trying to appear? Was he even . . . rather nervous?

Immediately – and she felt a little ashamed about it – she warmed to him, feeling that he was just like other people – well, her, anyway – and not the wonderfully efficient new broom he might want folk to think him. This really was someone she could help.

'Mr Shield, I'll just sort the post for you, shall I? I usually did that for Mr MacKenna. And then if there's anything particular I can do for you, please say.'

'Oh, Miss Rainey, I'm not sure where to start!' He ran a hand through his hair, then hastily tried to flatten it. 'But, yes, I'd be very glad of your help, as I was told I would be. To begin with, I'd like to see the file on house prices here, they being very different from Border prices, you understand. Obviously, I'm going to have to bone up on those before I do my valuations.'

'Certainly, I can help you there. Just out of interest, what part of the Borders are you from, Mr Shield?'

'Kelder – that's a small market town some miles from Berwick. I don't know if you know it?'

'Not really. I've only been to Berwick once, on a school trip.'

'Beautiful country, Miss Rainey. I've always lived there.'

Roz smiled. 'Hope you're not going to be too homesick, then, living in a city?'

'Oh, no, I want to be here. I'm very glad they gave me the job.' He shrugged. 'Bet they wouldn't have done if an Edinburgh man had applied. Guess I was lucky they didn't.'

She hesitated, wondering if she should say she was sure it wasn't just luck that he got the job, but decided against it – might sound patronizing, eh?

'I'll get you the recent prices file,' she told him.

She was turning away when he said lightly, 'Just one more thing, Miss Rainey—'

'Yes, Mr Shield?'

'Well, it's what I called you just now – Miss Rainey. All a bit formal when there are just the two of us in the office, don't you think? May I not call you Roz?'

Her eyes widening, she could only stare. Was he serious? Did he not know what Mr Banks would say to that idea?

'My name's Jamie,' Mr Shield added cheerfully, seeming unaware of her reaction. 'I was christened James, of course, but I've never been known as James.'

'Mr Shield,' she said slowly. 'We don't use first names here. Norma Ward – she's the typist – is the only person to call me Roz, and she's the only one I call by her first name.'

'Oh, come on, last night at Mr MacKenna's farewell, first names were being bandied about all the time! Why, I heard him being called Ronnie and you being called Roz. How about that, then?'

'That was just for a special occasion. Normally, Mr Banks likes things to be formal. It is usual in most offices, from what I've heard.'

'Not at Hanna and Hanna's, where I worked,' Mr Shield said firmly. 'We were all first names there. Not in front of the clients, of course, just between ourselves, which is what I was suggesting to you. But if you're not happy about it, please forget I asked. The last thing I want is to upset you, and on our first day at that!'

His expression was so rueful, she found herself shaking her head and laughing.

'I'm not upset at all. I think it was very nice of you to suggest it and I wish I could've agreed, but, you know, I think . . .'

'It might not go down well with Mr Banks? I understand. Our Mr Hanna was a bit younger, you see, rather a different guy altogether.' Mr Shield sighed and returned to his desk. 'Let's stick to the status quo, then, all right?'

'Right, Mr Shield. I'll get you your file.'

'And maybe a cup of coffee?'

'And coffee too.'

First names or no first names, thought Roz, I'm still the one to get the coffee, eh?

At the end of the day, though, she felt much more cheered than she'd feared she might have done. True, she missed Mr MacKenna and the familiar routine with him, but Mr Shield had turned out to be just as pleasant as when she'd first met him, and she was sure now that they would have a good working relationship. Though he might have seemed nervous to begin with, from the way he tackled his work on that first day, it was clear to her that he was going to have no problems with it. He might even have ideas for improvements, being keen, she guessed, on stamping his own identity on the job.

Of course, one of his suggested changes would not have gone down well if Mr Banks had got to hear of it. First names in the office? It was just what Roz would have wanted if it was possible, but at Tarrel and Thom's, clearly it was not, and had better not be mentioned again. Just as Mr Shield's other idea – of going out to lunch with her, his assistant – would be thought quite out of the question.

As she made her way home, reviewing the day, Roz allowed herself a smile as she recalled the way he'd seemed to take it for granted that they'd go out to lunch, with or without his colleagues, this again being the practice in his previous job, where everybody went out together.

'You mean, you didn't go out to lunch with Mr MacKenna?' he had asked, when she'd explained to him that she usually had a sandwich at twelve o'clock with Norma in the staffroom. 'So what did he do, then?'

'Why, he went to lunch with Mr Newman and Mr Wray. Not Mr Banks – he lives quite close in Queen Street and always goes home to lunch with his wife.'

'I see.' Mr Shield studied her for a moment, then snapped his fingers. 'I get it, Miss Rainey. You had to go separately from Mr MacKenna? So that you could be here to look after the department?'

'Not really. We're often away together when we go to see houses, and telephone calls are switched through to Reception.' Roz gave a patient smile. 'The lawyers go to a pub they know, and like to be together, I think. I expect they'll be calling for you, Mr Shield.'

'Maybe. I believe I'm to spend time with them this afternoon, and also with Miss Calder, who knows everything there is to know about this place, I've been told.'

'Quite true,' said Roz, as she was proved right and Mr Wray put his thin face round the door and asked the new man if he'd like to join him and Mr Newman for lunch round the corner. The food wasn't marvellous, he was quick to say, but as good as you could expect in today's straitened times.

'Sounds fine.' Mr Shield took his raincoat from its peg. 'See you later, then, Miss Rainey.'

Being free to go to lunch herself, Roz had joined Norma in the staffroom where, over their cheese sandwiches, she'd resigned herself to giving a blow-by-blow account of her morning's work with the new head of department.

'And did you get on with him?' asked Norma. 'Is he as nice as we thought?'

'Just as nice, I'd say. I think things will work out well.'

'There you are, then.' Norma gave a long sigh. 'You've turned out lucky again, Roz. Working with a dishy man like Mr Shield, while who do I get – Miss Calder!'

Poor old Norma, thought Roz, arriving at home. Wish she could find something to take her mind off my good luck she's always talking about. But, oh dear, now I'll have to go through my day all over again for Ma and Chrissie – it's their early evening home.

In fact, hers was not the only exciting news that evening. First, there'd been another postcard from Dougal to say he'd be coming home in two weeks' time with a weekend pass.

'Isn't that grand?' cried Flo, for once looking really relaxed and pleased.

'And I've got news too, or at least an idea,' said Chrissie. 'It's for you, Roz.'

'Me? What sort of idea?'

'Well, Ma knows Richard, but you don't. You said you'd like to meet him but when I asked him if he'd like to come home sometime he said it'd be too much for Ma. As she'd not been well, you know.'

'Well, that's a relief!' cried Flo. 'I get all flustered with strangers coming here.'

'Oh, Ma, Richard's not a stranger! You know him from the café! Anyway, Roz, what I thought was you could come to the Sunshine one evening and meet him there.'

Chrissie's eyes on her sister were very bright; she seemed as excited as though she was arranging something very important. And so it must be, for her, thought Roz, seeing as it concerned Richard, and he was now the centre of her universe.

'You and Richard could both have something to eat and a nice chat together, eh?' she asked quickly. 'What do you think?'

'If it's what you want, of course I'll come,' said Roz. 'But what about Dougal? He'll have to meet Richard too.'

'Oh, yes, he'll be next, when he's got some leave. But you first, after I've fixed it up with Richard. And, Roz, you will wear something smart? Richard takes a lot o' notice of how folk look.'

Seventeen

'I think things will work out well,' Roz had told Norma of her future in the property department, and in the days that followed it seemed she was proved right. Not only did Mr Shield's grasp of his new duties smooth away any anxieties she might have had, but the way he dealt so easily and charmingly with clients quite charmed her too. Though it would not be true to say that he was any better at his job than Mr MacKenna, he certainly brought his own gifts to it, she had to admit, and would be, as she'd heard someone say, an asset to the firm.

Another bonus for working with him was the definite pleasure she took in their driving out together to visit properties. Apart from his saying at times that he felt like cursing the 'dear old Hillman' and that he was already planning to ask Mr Banks for a new car – or, at least, a better second hand one, which was all they could hope for, she knew that he enjoyed these trips as much as she did. This was his chance to learn from her which were the pricey areas of the city and which were not, and being as quick as he was it didn't take him long to absorb all she told him. Later, in the office, where he'd marked up which areas were which on the street map on the wall, remembering accurately all she'd said, he told her how helpful she'd been, his gaze so sincere, so intent, she'd felt particularly pleased.

Perhaps the best thing of all about the drives was that when they took particulars of houses she specially liked it was to find that he liked them too; that he was, in fact, as fascinated by property as she was.

'I don't know why it is,' he told her, driving back to the office one afternoon, 'but ever since I was a boy I've been interested in houses. Just to admire them, you know, and imagine how it would be to own one of them myself. Of course, I never had the faintest hope then of that happening.'

'Snap!' cried Roz. 'It was the same for me. I used to cut pictures out of Ma's magazines, and then I'd do drawings on bits of cardboard of all the rooms and stairs and bathrooms and such, and Ma would say, "Couldn't you draw something else? Why always houses?" I knew I'd never have a lovely one myself, at least, I couldn't see how, but I suppose I liked to dream. Still do.'

'Well, that's what our clients do, isn't it? They're looking for a dream and we have to find it for them.' Mr Shield laughed. 'And sell it. You might say that's what our business is – selling dreams.'

'Which aren't always the right ones.'

'No, but buyers have to settle for what they can get and can afford.' He sighed. 'I always knew as a family we couldn't afford anything much. Dad did his best – he had a wee tobacconist's shop and we lived over it. He always wanted me to have a profession and I'm glad I managed to qualify as a lawyer just before he died.'

'That must have meant so much to you,' Roz said quietly. 'I'm so sorry you lost him.'

'Yes, he's still a huge miss to my mother and me. In fact, I feel a bit guilty, coming away to work and leaving her, though she does understand I need to move on. At present, she's in a small rented house, but I'm planning to buy her a cottage one of these days – something of her own. How about you, Miss Rainey? You live with your family?'

'With my mother. My dad worked for the electricity station at Portobello, but he was killed in the war. At El Alamein.'

'I'm sorry to hear that.'

'Yes, it was a terrible blow. But I have a sister, Chrissie, and my brother's just joined the army as a regular. We live in a flat in St Leonard's.' She shrugged. 'It's all right, but no dream. We have the use of a bathroom, though.'

'And so do I – in my flat in Marchmont. No dream, either, but I share it with a guy I knew at university, so it's not expensive. Gives me a chance, I hope, to save up for Mother's cottage.'

Interesting, Roz thought, to learn about her new boss, and to feel so much at ease with him. Seemed Norma was right to say she'd been lucky. So far, at least.

Arriving back outside the office in Queen Street, she had begun to gather up her papers ready to leave her seat when Mr Shield slightly touched her arm to detain her.

'You know we were talking of using first names the other day?' he asked lightly, fixing her with a steady gaze.

'Yes?' she answered cautiously.

'Well, I want to ask – would you really mind if I called you Roz just when we were alone together? I know it wouldn't be the right thing in front of clients, or even colleagues – knowing Mr Banks's views – but if we're just in the car or the office on our own, it seems so formal, you know, to call you Miss Rainey.'

'I suppose it does. It's just what I'm used to.'

'I know, but I do want us to be friends. So much pleasanter if you're working together, don't you agree?'

'Oh, yes, I do. I want to be friends, too.'

'Well, then.' He gave one of his smiles. 'How about calling me Jamie?'

'Jamie,' she repeated softly, as though trying the name for size. 'It seems strange.'

'No, just friendly.'

'Only in the car, then,' she said after a pause.

'Or in the office, if we're on our own.'

'I'm not sure about the office. People are always coming and going.'

'We're not exactly committing any crime, Roz.'

At his saying of her name, she felt a strange little thrill and lowered her eyes, which was foolish, eh? Surely her eyes couldn't give her away?

'Just before we go in,' he went on, 'may I ask, is Roz short for something?'

'Rosalind.'

'Shakespeare's Rosalind? *As You Like It*?'

'No.' Roz smiled. 'Ma doesn't go in for Shakespeare. It was a name in a show she saw once, something by the man who wrote the waltzes – Johann Strauss, I think – and she liked it so much she gave it to me. Only it was, in fact, Rosalinda, and she thought Rosalind was more suitable.'

'But you became Roz, anyway. I think it suits you.' Jamie reached over to take his briefcase from the back seat. 'Ah, well – back to the grindstone, eh?'

Feeling as though something had very slightly changed since they'd

been away from the office, Roz went to make a cup of tea, first
studying herself in the mirror in the staffroom. She looked . . . how
did she look? Self-conscious, maybe? Surprised? Or, no different?

He's just being friendly, she thought. It's his way. They were all
first names where he worked before, he said so – it doesn't mean a
thing that he wants to use first names here. All the same, he was
Jamie now, and she was Roz. Without a doubt, something had
changed.

Eighteen

Going into work the following morning, Roz's feelings were
confused. On the one hand, she found herself believing that Jamie
Shield was, as she'd earlier decided, just being friendly with all that
first name stuff. On the other hand, though, there was the way he
looked at her, which was – well, different from the way Mr MacKenna
had looked at her, or any of the lawyers at Tarrel's.

She'd had some experience in the past of young men who'd been
attracted to her – without any encouragement from her – and it
seemed to her that their way of looking at her had been rather like
Jamie's. But then she could be wrong – she could be imagining
things, seeing something that wasn't there, and would feel a fool, all
right, if that proved to be true. In fact, she felt rather foolish already,
and was certainly not looking forward to meeting Jamie's eyes,
whichever way they were looking at her.

The first thing she saw, however, when she went into the property
department for their short morning – on Saturdays they finished at
noon – was a leather holdall by Jamie's desk. Was he going away?
If so, he hadn't told her.

As she was slowly preparing for work, he came in from the hall,
papers in his hand, his eyes once again appearing to light up when
he saw her.

'Roz, there you are! I've just been checking some conveyancing
work I had to do for Mr Wray while waiting for you.'

'I'm not late,' she said quickly and he laughed.

'Always so touchy about that! Of course you're not late. I just
wanted to tell you I'll be leaving early today – I'm catching the

lunchtime train to Berwick. I've squared it with Mr Banks that I can make the time up later.'

'You're going down to see your mother? I saw your bag when I came in and wondered if you were going away.'

'Sorry, I forgot to mention it. I'll probably be going down to the Borders once a month. Keep everybody happy.'

'Your mother will be thrilled, I bet. We're expecting my brother next weekend – it'll be his first time home since he joined up and Ma's so happy.'

Which was true and a wonderful thing to be able to say, Roz thought, wondering if she should cross her fingers. Oh, long may it last, anyway, that Ma was happy and willing to keep on forgiving Dougal for his enlistment.

'He's liking it in the Lowland and Borders?' asked Jamie. 'I was in the King's Own Scottish Borderers myself, during the war. Came out to finish my studies at St Andrew's.'

'Every day you tell me something interesting,' she remarked, smiling, as she moved towards her own office. 'I didn't know you went to St Andrew's.'

'A very pleasant place to be after war service. But I can't believe you find me interesting. I'm a lawyer, for heaven's sake!'

'A property lawyer – there's the difference.'

He was studying her again, his eyes searching her face. 'You're the one that's interesting, all the same,' he said quietly. 'I'd like you to tell me more about yourself. Perhaps we could . . .'

He stopped, shrugged a little, said no more.

'Could what?' she asked, after she'd waited.

'Nothing. I was just thinking aloud.' He turned aside, looked at his desk.

'That the post?' she asked.

'Yes, I haven't opened it yet, but don't worry, I'll sort through it. You carry on with what you want to do.'

'Coffee at ten o'clock?'

'Yes, please!'

By eleven o'clock he was gone, trilby hat pressed over his thick hair, raincoat over his arm, holdall in one hand, hurrying for the station, while Roz was left to make a few delegated phone calls to clients, finish off some typing and tidy up. The weekend stretched ahead, a long, long desert with no oasis of work. Or seeing Jamie.

At the thought that came unbidden to her mind, she caught her breath. What had that meant, then, that thought? Since when had she looked forward to seeing him? Since yesterday and that business of calling each other by their first names. Since she'd begun to wonder about the way he looked at her, and compared it with other looks from young men who'd made their feelings known, to her impatience and lack of response.

But there was no way Jamie was going to make his feelings known, because he probably hadn't got any in the way she was imagining again. 'Perhaps we could . . .' he'd begun, but had not finished whatever he was going to say. Had it meant anything? 'Nothing', he himself had said. He'd just been 'thinking aloud'. Not with much purpose, then.

Twelve o'clock struck on the grandfather clock in Tarrel's hall and, with her face showing all the questions in her mind, she put on her outdoor jacket, combed her hair and closed the door of the property department behind her. All she had before her was an empty flat and a lonely lunch, with both her mother and Chrissie at work but, leaving the office, she heard Norma calling to her and waited.

'Roz – your sister's on the phone. Glad I've caught you!'

'Chrissie? She never rings me.' Roz, turning pale, was instantly thinking the worst. Something had happened to Ma. She'd collapsed at the cash desk – been taken to hospital – 'Quick,' she told Norma, 'give me the phone.' Then, 'Chrissie, what's wrong? Is it Ma?'

'What do you mean? Nothing's wrong with Ma. Richard said he could come to the café this evening and I'm wondering if you could, too? If you're not doing anything else?'

'This evening?' Roz was breathing evenly again, her colour returning. 'Bit short notice.'

'It'd be nice, though. Shall I tell him yes? Look, Roz I've got to hurry – I'm not supposed to use this phone.'

'All right, I'll come. What time?'

'Seven o'clock? Oh, that'd be grand, Roz. Ma's got an early night, so she won't be there, but I'll look after you. 'Bye, Roz, and thanks!'

'Everything all right?' asked Norma with interest.

'Fine. Chrissie just wants me to have a meal at the Sunshine.'

'Oh, nice! A free meal, eh? And I was wondering if you'd have liked to go to the pictures with me. There's a good film on – *Kind Hearts and Coronets*. They say it's a scream. One fellow plays all the parts. Thought it might have cheered us up.'

'Who says we need cheering up?'

'Well, you're looking a wee bit down. And where was Mr Shield going in such a hurry? I saw him scooting out of here a full hour before the rest of us.'

'He's going back home to the Borders for the weekend. To see his mother.'

'Doesn't seem like a mother's boy,' commented Norma.

'No, I wouldn't call him that. His dad's dead, and he's been living at his mother's place to keep her company. I think it shows he's a caring sort of fellow.'

'Oh, I'm sure.' Norma shrugged. 'Well, looks like we'll have to make the flicks some other time. Have a good time at the café, Roz – hope you enjoy your free meal!'

'If I get a discount, I'll be lucky,' Roz answered, turning away, half glad to be going somewhere for the evening, half apprehensive that the somewhere would include meeting Chrissie's young man. You never knew, he might be all she claimed him to be. On the other hand, he might not. She would soon find out, either way.

Nineteen

As soon as she entered the Café Sunshine, Roz recognized Richard. 'Handsome', had been Chrissie's oft-repeated description, coupled with 'striking' – and there was only one man in the café who fitted that bill.

Oh, yes, he was handsome all right, and striking, Chrissie'd got it right there. Black hair, combed to fall in a wave over a high forehead. Straight nose, level dark brows, fine eyes so dark they seemed to be without expression. He had been sitting alone at the side of the warm, crowded café where, at that moment, there seemed to be no sign of Chrissie, but suddenly rose as though making a decision, and smiled.

'Is it Roz?' he asked, his Scottish voice low and pleasant, as she came towards his table. 'Richard Vincent.'

'How did you know me?' she asked as they shook hands.

'Chrissie's description was very accurate.'

'Of you, too.'

They both laughed.

'Chrissie's given us this table,' Richard went on, pulling out a chair for Roz with a display of the good manners Flo so much admired. 'Though I can't see her at the moment.'

'Gone to fetch orders, I expect.' Roz's gaze was going over the people at the tables, talking, chattering, all at ease, as she was not. Of course, she knew the café well enough. Knew it was popular with city workers during the day and those who liked an inexpensive meal out in the evening, and pleasant enough for both Chrissie and Flo to want to keep on working there, in spite of the brooding presence of Mrs Abbot, the stately, hawk-nosed manageress, who was patrolling the tables now, smiling at the customers but keeping a sharp watch on the progress of their meals.

Ah, here at last came Chrissie, flushed with the heat as she walked through the swing doors at the back of the café, carrying a loaded tray to another table, her eyes lighting up when she saw Roz sitting with Richard.

'Oh, Roz, grand you could come!' she cried as soon as she was free to reach their table. 'And you've met Richard?'

'Yes, Chrissie, we've met,' he said easily. 'Now we want our menus. Don't look so scared – we're customers. You've a right to take our orders.'

'Oh, I know, but here's Mrs Abbot—'

'Good evening, Mr Vincent, good evening, Miss Rainey. Nice to see you both here,' said the manageress. 'And you have the menus? That's excellent. We have some specials tonight – we've been so lucky with our deliveries. I can really recommend the steak pie.'

'Aye, it's good,' Chrissie chimed, taking out her notebook. 'Shall I say two?'

'It's so warm tonight, I'd just like the egg mayonnaise salad,' said Roz, reading the menu for herself, but Richard said he'd try the pie, he not being a salad man.

'Very good.' Mrs Abbot, collecting their menus, gave a small, pinched smile. 'Now, I'll leave Chrissie to see to your orders. Enjoy your meal.'

'Egg mayonnaise salad,' Richard said softly when they were alone. 'More like egg salad cream, but I daresay it'll be all right.'

'You're eating here, anyway,' remarked Roz.

'Chrissie's idea. I normally just come for lunch, but she was keen for us to meet and thought you'd find it easier in the evening.' His gaze was steady on her face. 'What do you think of it, then?'

'Café Sunshine?'

'No, her idea for us to meet like this.'

'She'd have liked you to come to the flat.' Roz's gaze was as direct as his. 'But you didn't agree.'

'I was thinking of your mother. She works hard enough here as it is.'

'Well, now that we've met anyway I'd like to say that I'm very glad to meet you, Richard. I've heard a lot about you.'

'And I, you. The bright one of the family, I'm told. You work in Tarrel's law firm. They've a very good reputation.'

'I'm not a lawyer; I work in the property department.'

'Oh, I know. Mad on houses, Chrissie says. Unfortunately, I'm not ready to buy yet, though my father – he's an accountant – says you can't go wrong with bricks and mortar, and my sisters both have properties.'

'Oh, you have sisters?'

'Two, both married; one in Peebles, one in London.'

'But your father's in Edinburgh?'

'Oh, yes, both parents have lived here for years. They have a house in the Grange.'

'I see,' said Roz, who knew the price of houses in the Grange. 'Are you renting something, then?'

'No, I'm living at home at present.' He gave a slightly mocking smile. 'Anything else you'd like to know, Roz?'

She flushed, looking down at her knife and fork, and let a silence fall which was eventually broken by Richard.

'Sorry,' he said quietly. 'I don't mind talking about myself, anyway.'

She looked up to meet those dark eyes of his which still told her nothing, in spite of his apologetic words. Impenetrable – that was the only way to describe them. Were they his screen against the world? Would you ever know a man like this? With a sudden inner rush she was reminded of Jamie's candid gaze, so open, so friendly, and knew that her view of Richard was made by contrast transparently clear. She didn't like him. He was hiding something. Was it to do with his intentions – or lack of them – towards her sister?

'I didn't mean to seem to be interrogating you,' she said after a pause.

'I've said I don't mind.' He leaned back in his chair, raising his hands, and looked at her as if he could read her thoughts. 'I've nothing to hide.'

'And I am Chrissie's sister.'

'Of course. I take your point.' He straightened up. 'But talking of Chrissie – here come our orders. Poor girl, how hard she works!'

'I wish she had another job,' Roz said quickly. 'She needn't be a waitress, but she never looks for anything else.'

Of course, the truth was Chrissie was only waiting to get married, but that was not something to be said to her young man.

'One steak pie!' Chrissie cried, her eyes radiant. 'One egg mayonnaise!'

'Here, let me help you,' said Richard, leaping to his feet and unloading her tray. 'There we are, all shipshape, except that you should be eating with us, Chrissie.'

'I never eat with you here,' she said fondly. 'And I want you and Roz to have a nice chat, just the two of you.'

'Why, I think we've had that,' said Roz. 'I won't stay late – Ma could do with company, I expect.'

'Oh, you'll have a sweet, Roz!'

'I think I'll just have coffee after this.'

'I was expecting to take you home with Chrissie,' Richard remarked, beginning to eat. 'Sure you won't have a pud? They're not bad here.'

Roz shook her head, saying she'd be quite happy with just her salad, and longed now to be away, finished with this sparring match she saw herself having with Richard. Somehow, he'd guessed that she was trying to decide whether she could trust him with her younger sister, and had decided not to make it easy for her, though she couldn't really point to anything he'd said that should make her think that. All the same, she did think it, and now just wanted to go home. Where of course she would have to face Ma – just wait for the interrogation there!

'I'd better go,' Chrissie murmured, 'Mrs Abbot's got her eye on me. Roz, I'll see you at home. Glad you've met Richard, though. That was what I wanted.'

'I'm glad, too,' said Roz, her eyes meeting his, expecting no message and receiving none. Yet, later, as they both stood up and shook hands in farewell, she was as certain as before that he knew just what was in her mind. Opening her bag, she took out her purse.

'Please put that away, this is on me,' he said at once, and laughed. 'I think I can run to an egg mayonnaise for you, Roz.'

'And don't forget, I can get a discount for my family,' put in Chrissie.

'Better and better! Seriously, Roz, I'm very pleased to have met you. Sorry you can't stay.'

There was a slightly awkward pause as Roz looked from one to the other of the two faces before her, knowing that they were thinking this had been no ordinary meeting but some sort of test for Richard. Had he passed? would be their question. But how much did Richard care?

Finally, Roz made her goodbyes again and got herself out of the Café Sunshine to make her way home, where she must decide what to say to Flo.

'Roz, you're back!' cried Flo. 'How did it go, then? How did you like Richard? So handsome, eh?'

'Very handsome,' Roz replied, taking a chair and pulling off her smart shoes to rest her feet. 'Oh, yes, he's just what Chrissie said.'

What else could she say to her mother? Richard was handsome, a perfect gentleman, and so on, but she, Roz, didn't like him. Why didn't she like him? Because she felt he wasn't right for Chrissie. Because – oh, God, she didn't trust him. How could she say all that to her mother without upsetting her? Without risking – well, Roz knew what she'd be risking. Yet she couldn't say she was happy about him, could she? 'Like a cup of tea?' she asked brightly.

'Yes, in a minute. Tell me about Richard first. Did you really like him?'

'Well . . .' Roz cleared her throat. 'He's very nice, very well-mannered, but I'm not sure he's right for Chrissie.'

Flo's eyes widened. 'Whatever do you mean? He's perfect for Chrissie. Why, he's a catch, Roz, you canna deny it. He comes from a nice family, he's a professional man and could give her a wonderful life! Why would he not be right for Chrissie?'

'Because she wants to get married and he might not.' Seeing the look on her mother's face, Roz said hurriedly, 'Of course, I could be wrong.'

'You could,' Flo said coldly. 'Are you sure you're not a wee bit envious, Roz? That Chrissie's found someone like Richard and you've not?'

'Ma, what a thing to say!' Roz cried, leaping up. 'I'd never be envious of Chrissie, only happy for her if she found the right man.

And maybe she has – maybe I just don't know him well enough. Look, I'll put the kettle on.'

All she wanted now, as she made the tea, was to back pedal on what she'd said and take the anxious look from her mother's face before there was real trouble. Heavens, she'd been a fool, eh? Opening her big mouth like that.

'It's all right, Ma,' she said comfortingly as she brought over the tea. 'I've probably got it all wrong and Richard is the one for Chrissie. Men can be difficult to read, eh? Don't worry, anyway. Chrissie knows what she's doing.'

'That's right,' Flo agreed, sipping her tea. 'We can leave it to Chrissie, eh? And I'm sorry I said – you know – about you being envious. I know you've got your own ambitions. You're not worried about not having a young man.'

'That's right, Ma,' said Roz, relieved. 'I'm not worried at all.'

Twenty

When Jamie arrived back at the property department on Monday morning, he brought Roz a present.

'For you,' he said, bowing low and putting into her hands a large paper bag containing something that felt soft – even crumbly. She was very intrigued.

'Why, Jamie, whatever is it?' Roz was blushing deeply as she continued to hold the bag.

'Come on, it's just something to eat. Why don't you have a look at it?'

Rather gingerly, she drew the soft lump out of the bag and unwrapped it, then raised her wide eyes to Jamie's. 'It's a cheese?'

'Yes, a cheese. It's called Kelder White.' He laughed at her look. 'Why so astonished? Cheeses are still made locally today and some of 'em are a damn sight better than that dreary stuff you told me you had at lunchtime. So, I thought you'd like to try one from my home town.'

'Why, Jamie, I don't know what to say! It's such a kind thought, to bring me this, and it really is just what I wanted!' Her blush fading, her grey eyes were sparkling as she looked up at him. 'Thank you very much. I'll put it in the staffroom, eh? There's a little larder cupboard there.'

'Fine. And let me know what you think of it this afternoon.'

As she moved to the door, holding the cheese, she looked back, aware that he was still watching. 'But how was your weekend? I never asked.'

'Very pleasant. I really enjoyed being home, but now I'm glad to be back here.'

'And your mother was well?'

'Very well. Cooking as though there was an army in the house, instead of just me. She always thinks men need hot food on the hour, or they'll collapse!'

'My mother's a bit the same.'

They stood for a moment or two, exchanging glances, then Roz hurried away to the staffroom and Jamie, sighing deeply, sat down at his desk and looked at the letters she'd opened for him.

Their work that day was confined to the department, with Jamie busy meeting more clients than usual, most encouraged by the summer weather to rush into moving, one way or another, while Roz had an extra load of particulars to type and post out, as well as continually answering the phone. Even so, lunchtimes were still lunchtimes and when Jamie came back from his, Roz was able to tell him how much she and Norma had enjoyed his Kelder White cheese.

'Oh, such a treat!' she told him. 'To have something different and with such a lovely taste! Can't thank you enough.'

'What's a piece of cheese?' he asked, smiling. 'Not exactly a luxury item.'

'Why that's just what it is! It's real luxury, to have something nice to eat.'

She didn't add that she'd had to put up with a lot of conjecture from Norma on why Mr Shield had brought Roz a cheese from the Borders, which she'd managed to dampen down by being non-commital until Norma's questions had dried up. Pity she'd had to eat the cheese at lunchtime, but if she hadn't, the whole point of the gift would have been lost, and she didn't want that – not when she'd been so touched by Jamie's thought.

It seemed he'd had another, though whether it was anything to do with Roz or not she didn't know, for after he'd begun with the words, 'I was thinking,' the telephone rang, and he stopped.

Someone wanted to make an appointment for a valuation, Roz

told him, before moving to her own office where she thought he'd follow. When he didn't, she shrugged as she rolled paper into her machine. What had he been thinking, then? She would never know at this rate, would she? It couldn't have been important, anyway. When she popped her head round his door there was no sign of him, and she guessed he'd gone to continue his other work. Returning to her desk, she felt ill at ease, still being unsure of whether he had special feelings for her or not, or indeed whether she had any real reason for wondering if he had. And what about her own feelings? She answered that question by typing as fast as possible until it was time to get to the post.

It was almost five o'clock before she saw Jamie again when he came back to the department, saying he'd been with Miss Calder who had been showing him the firm's legal archives – very know-ledgeable lady, eh?

'You didn't come for any tea and I didn't know where you were,' Roz remarked.

'Sorry about that. I had a cup with Miss Calder.'

'Oh, well—'

Roz was turning to leave as he stood watching.

'I'll just say goodnight.'

'Goodnight? The sun's cracking the flags still.'

'Goodbye, then.'

'That's even worse.' Jamie laughed. 'Listen, Roz, I was wondering . . . It's such a nice evening . . . Couldn't we have a drink together?'

She stopped in the act of picking up her bag and stared, her lips parted, her expression stunned. 'A drink?' Even to her own ears, she sounded incredulous.

'Yes, a drink.' Jamie was shaking his head. 'You might be looking at me as though I've suggested an orgy, but that's all I'm offering – a drink at the Adelphi in George Street. Don't know if you know it, but it's very pleasant.'

'It's kind of you to ask me, Jamie.'

Roz was hesitant – one part of her thrilled, the other wondering what those at Tarrel's would say if she and Jamie were seen going out together. 'The only thing is, I'm not sure if it'd be a good idea.'

'Not a good idea? Why not? It's just two colleagues having a drink after work.'

'Mr Banks might not approve.'

'Mr Banks?' Jamie groaned. 'In other words, God? I tell you, Roz, I sometimes wonder if I'll ever get used to working in this place. No first names, no drinks with female staff – what does he expect to happen if we're a bit more friendly?'

'It's just the way things are, Jamie.'

'Well, my offer still holds. I like you, Roz. I want to be able to talk to you outside a work situation. Be honest – what's wrong with that?'

'Nothing, really. Well, there wouldn't be, if things were different.'

'But you like me, don't you? You wouldn't mind spending time with me?'

'I do like you, Jamie. I wish I could spend time with you.'

'Look—' He glanced at his watch. 'We're wasting time. You probably don't want to be late home, so let's away.'

'You mean, still go to the hotel?'

'Sure I do. Let's take the risk, eh? Hell, live dangerously. Why not, for once?'

She laughed. 'Why not?'

They moved together to the door, where Jamie suddenly stopped.

'We can go separately, if you like? I don't want you to be worrying, Roz.' His face was rueful. 'So much for living dangerously!'

'Might be better,' she agreed. 'Norma's probably still around – if she sees us together she'll never let me forget it.'

'OK. What's that other saying? Discretion is the better part of valour? You leave first and we'll meet in the hotel entrance.'

But they *were* living dangerously – Roz, feeling like an excited conspirator and not looking back as she walked ahead to Tarrel's front door, called cheerfully to Norma at Reception, 'Goodnight, Norma, I've got to run!'

'Goodnight, Roz!' cried Norma. 'See you tomorrow!'

And away went Roz, walking fast, to George Street and the Adelphi Hotel.

Twenty-One

The Adelphi Hotel was not only pleasant, it was smart; a frequently written-up venue in the glossy magazines for dinners, receptions or cocktails for the well-to-do. Certainly not a place Roz had ever been to, but was fascinated to see, while at the same time worrying that she wasn't wearing the right clothes.

'Wear something smart,' Chrissie had ordered for the meeting with Richard, and Roz couldn't help wishing that she'd had the same advice before coming to the Adelphi. Why on earth had Jamie chosen it?

As they took seats in the cocktail bar, she glanced round at the clientele and, at the sight of the women's outfits, looked so glum that Jamie at once asked her what was wrong. Didn't she like the Adelphi?

'It's too grand, Jamie. I'm not wearing the right clothes.'

'You look perfect. Always do.'

'But why did you choose it?'

'Simple. It's not the sort of place we're likely to meet anyone from Tarrel's.'

She raised her eyebrows. 'You were already thinking we shouldn't be seen together?'

'No, I just want privacy. To be with you.' He touched her hand. 'But let's forget Tarrel's. What would you like to drink?'

'I don't know – I don't drink much.'

'How about a gin with tonic you can add yourself? Then you can put in as much tonic as you like? I'll have the same.'

When their drinks came they each sipped a little, then nibbled the salted nuts provided, and were silent.

'Hey, we're supposed to be talking,' Jamie murmured. 'Why are we sitting dumb?'

'I feel sort of shy,' Roz confessed.

'Shy of me? Come on, no one's ever shy with me. If there's one talent I have, it's being able to talk and to get others talking too. So, come on, Roz, tell me about yourself.'

'You know it all already. I've told you about my dad, and my folks. There's not a lot to add.'

'I think there's something.' His look was steady, his hand placed for a moment over hers, dry and firm. 'Something you didn't tell me, isn't there?'

She sighed and sipped her drink. 'I suppose there is. It's about – well – my mother.'

The next moment, she was telling him about Flo: how she'd been hit so hard by Arthur's death that she'd sunk into a depression which was still with her, on and off, and was something her family had to watch out for and try to bring her through. Swiftly, easily, the words flowed, and Roz knew she was talking to him as she'd never really talked to an outsider before, and that she felt the better for it. He'd been quite right about himself, hadn't he? He could get people talking, without a doubt.

'Thank you,' he said softly. 'Thank you for telling me about your life, Roz. I hope it wasn't hard for you?'

'No, it was helpful. I've never talked about poor Ma before – I mean, to someone who wasn't family.'

'It seems to me that you've all been very brave, having to face complex problems, and all so young.'

'I suppose we got used to it. Though you never know when the moods will come – that's the difficult part. Poor Dougal, my brother, caused a lot of trouble when he wanted to join the army, but in the end Ma accepted it, which was a big relief.'

'And you, Roz, you're all right? I mean, you're happy with what you're doing at Tarrel's?'

She topped up her drink with tonic again. 'I'm happy, yes, because I love working with property and I admire Tarrel's, but – well, I'll have to admit, I do feel a bit resentful that it's not likely I'll ever run the department.'

'You easily could.' Jamie drained his glass. 'But you're not a lawyer, is that it?'

'As far as Tarrel's are concerned, yes, that's it. A woman as well!' Roz laughed. 'I'd be the last person Mr Banks would consider.'

'And you're so right for the job! It's a damned shame. Have you considered trying an ordinary estate agent's?'

'You know how many there are here.'

'You could go over the Border. There are plenty in England.'

'As I told Mr MacKenna, I'm not likely to do that.'

'Thank the Lord!' cried Jamie. 'I don't want you going anywhere. Like another drink?'

'No, thanks, I must go.'

They sat for a moment, looking into each other's eyes, before Roz grabbed her bag and stood up.

'It's been lovely, Jamie. Thank you.'

'It was lovely for me too, Roz.'

He paid the bill and they moved out into the evening sunshine still lighting the elegant George Street.

'May I take you home?' Jamie asked as they stood together, but Roz shook her head.

'No need. I'll get a tram.'

'I'll walk with you to the stop, then.' A few minutes later, as her tram came into sight, he asked, 'You don't regret it? Coming out for that drink?'

'I don't regret it at all. It was good; I enjoyed it.'

'Would you come out with me again, then?'

She looked away. Her tram was grinding to a halt and people were getting off while others waited to board. Her eyes moved to his. 'I'd like to . . .'

'But?'

'Well, there is what we talked about.'

'I don't think we need worry. We could have a meal in town, somewhere right away from Tarrel's. No one need see us.'

'Let's decide later, then. I must get this tram.'

'Promise we will?'

She smiled, waved, stepped on to the tram and, with the usual squeaks and clanks was borne away, while Jamie stood watching until the tram was out of sight.

So, now she knew, Roz thought, going home on a high, her head spinning at what she'd discovered. Jamie Shield was attracted to her, had definite feelings for her. She'd not been wrong about those looks of his, after all.

How did such knowledge make her feel? Wonderful, she would have liked to cry from the top deck of the tram. Yes, wonderful, because she couldn't deny that she was attracted to him, probably as much as he was to her, though she hadn't been willing to admit it until now. But of course she couldn't really cry 'wonderful', from the tram or anywhere else, because – well, because there was Mr Banks.

It was all very well for Jamie to say that Mr Banks was old fashioned, out of touch, and that there was no harm in colleagues going out together, even if they were man and woman and worked in the same department. Maybe that was true, but Roz could also see it from Mr Banks's point of view. He was the boss, he had to make his law firm pay and get the most efficiency from his staff – and if his staff became tangled with each other, how efficient would they be? That was the way his mind would work and who could blame him?

On the other hand, even if she and Jamie were attracted to each other, they might never become truly involved. Who was to say that they would go so far? Why, she'd all along said herself that she wasn't keen on commitment and wanted to have a career, and quite likely Jamie would say the same. Heavens, what was she worrying about? They'd had one drink together. Why get all worked up at such an early stage?

As she left the tram, Roz decided she would indeed go for a meal with Jamie, somewhere in town, as he'd suggested, where they wouldn't see folk from Tarrel's. Just for the moment, the future could take care of itself, eh? Decision made.

It was a relief, all the same, to let herself into the empty flat and not have to face questions over where she'd been from Ma or Chrissie, who were still at work. Lovely to sit down, have some tea and something to eat, and go over her time at the Adelphi with Jamie all over again.

Twenty-Two

For the next few days Roz and Jamie conscientiously tackled work, not allowing themselves to show anything new in their manner towards each other. As Roz had reminded herself, they'd only had one drink together. There was no need to behave in any other way than colleagues should. Except – well, they'd had that drink. And there was also that talk of having a meal together, even if it hadn't been arranged. Roz had thought Jamie would ask her as soon as he saw her on Tuesday, but it wasn't until the end of the day on Wednesday when he asked her quietly if she would be free the following evening.

'Thought we might meet – as we said we would?'

'Well, we said we'd discuss it,' she replied.

'Still thinking it's a risk?' His tone was light, as though making clear he didn't really believe in any such thing.

Her grey eyes very direct on him, she knew what she'd decided. Might as well say. 'I'd like to meet, Jamie. If you're happy about it.'

He gave a long sigh. 'Roz, I've only just found the courage to ask you. I thought you might have decided against me.'

She shook her head, smiling, a little relieved. 'Where shall we go, then?'

'I know just the nice little anonymous place we'd like. Off Marchmont Road, a small restaurant near my flat. Alan – my flatmate

– and I have been there a couple of times. The food's what you'd expect, but what they've got they cook quite well. Any good?'

'Sounds perfect. What time shall we meet?'

'Seven o'clock there, if that's all right? The name is Platters.'

'Platters. Fine, I'll see you there.'

'You're sure you can get a tram? I feel I should be taking you myself.'

'Jamie, I've lived in Edinburgh all my life. I think I know how to get around.'

'Of course you do, and I'm the country boy. But I'm learning to get around too in my spare time.'

'Going where?'

'Looking at properties, streets, areas. Figuring out where the building boom will go when it starts, as it will, when things improve. Edinburgh's going to see some changes, you know.'

'Not too many,' she said uneasily.

'Hey, it'll be right for us! More development can only be good news for people in the property business.'

'We've already had changes. All that ribbon development in the thirties – bungalows all over the place.'

'Not knocking bungalows, Roz? They get bought and sold too, remember?'

'But they have no character, Jamie! And you like character, too, eh?'

'Personally, yes, but for my bread and butter, I'm willing to buy and sell what comes my way. But what are we doing, talking like this? Forgetting what's important!'

'And what's that?'

'Our meeting tomorrow. Agreed?'

Their glances meeting, she said softly, 'Agreed.'

There was no way out of telling Flo and Chrissie that she would be having a meal with someone the following evening. Biting on the bullet, she told them as soon as they came home from work on Wednesday.

'You finish early tomorrow night, eh? Thought I'd better say I won't be having tea. I'm going out for a meal.'

'Oh?' Flo's eyes were wide. 'That's something new.'

'Who with?' asked Chrissie, with interest. 'Not one o' the lawyers?'

'He is a lawyer, as a matter of fact. The one I work with.'

Flo and Chrissie looked at each other.

'That fellow who took over from the nice one?' asked Flo.

'Mr Shield, yes. But he's nice too.'

'H'm. Thought you wouldn't be allowed to go out with him.'

'It's just for a meal, Ma.'

'Just the two of you?'

'Well, yes,' Roz said, hesitating slightly and wishing an end to the questions.

'You call him Mr Shield?' asked Chrissie.

'No, I call him Jamie, but only when we're alone.'

'Fancy. Thought those stuffed shirts at your place never used first names, eh?'

'He asked me if we might use first names. Seemingly, where he worked before it was quite the thing.'

'H'm,' said Flo again. 'Well, I hope you know what you're doing. How about putting the kettle on?'

'What are you going to wear?' asked Chrissie. 'Are you going somewhere grand?'

'Exact opposite. Somewhere small and quiet in Marchmont. And I'm not worrying too much about what I wear.'

'Marchmont? Not many cafés there, eh?'

'This one's near his flat.'

As Roz filled the kettle she could almost hear the wheels in her mother's mind moving round and round.

'So he's got a flat? Of his own?'

'No, he shares it with another fellow. Don't worry, Ma, I'm not going there anyway.'

'Not yet,' said Flo.

'Ma!' Roz said warningly, and no more was said until they were drinking tea and eating some tasteless Madeira cake, when Flo seemed to relax a little and reminded Roz and Chrissie that Dougal was due home on Friday.

'D'you think he'll be in his uniform?' she asked anxiously. 'I don't want to see him in that.'

'He'll change for the weekend,' Roz told her quickly. 'Don't worry about it, Ma.'

Might as well save her breath, she thought, sighing. Only Ma would decide what to worry about, or not.

Twenty-Three

Marchmont, home to Jamie and where Roz was to meet him at Platters, was an area of mainly tall stone houses, most given over to flats. Though the architecture had a certain sameness about it, it was a popular neighbourhood, near the Meadows, one of Edinburgh's largest parks, and Bruntsfield Links, a piece of land of great antiquity. Somewhere to walk, then. Somewhere to breathe fresh air and pretend to be in the country. No wonder the flats were sought after and fetched a good price.

Oh, nice, thought Roz, arriving at the outside of Platters at exactly seven o'clock on Thursday evening and admiring its white painted woodwork and hanging baskets of summer flowers. But where was Jamie?

'Roz!' she heard him call as he appeared from the main door and came towards her with outstretched hands. 'Well done, you found it! And dead on time, too!'

'You know I don't like to be late,' she told him, laughing. 'But this place looks so pretty, Jamie – it's very unusual, eh?'

'Different from most Edinburgh restaurants, that's true. But come on, let's go in – I'm starving.'

Inside was just as pleasing, with shaded lights and vases of flowers on the white-clothed tables, most of which seemed to be occupied, making Roz wonder if they were too late to be served. But it was all right – Jamie had booked and a waitress showed them to a table by a window, handing them menus with a friendly smile.

'No' a lot o' choice,' she whispered, 'but the lamb casserole's very nice.'

'Sounds good,' said Jamie. 'What do you think, Roz? Shall I order for us both?'

'Yes, please.'

Roz, who was taking more notice of the well-dressed diners than the menu, was glad she'd put on her best jacket and pretty blouse, for this place was a good deal smarter than she'd imagined. And expensive? Not used to dining out, she was beginning to feel a little uneasy, and when Jamie apologised for the lack of wine, Platters not yet having a licence, she sighed with relief. At least she needn't worry about keeping her head from drinking wine, whatever else might keep her from thinking straight.

When the waitress had taken their order, Roz leaned forward. 'I didn't know we were coming anywhere like this,' she whispered. 'I mean, it's grander than I thought.'

'Only the best for you, Roz,' Jamie said cheerfully.

'But it's expensive, eh?'

'It's not too bad. It's not exactly your Caledonian, or the North British Hotel. As I say, Alan and I come here sometimes when we feel like a change from getting our own meals.' Jamie reached over and touched her hand. 'Don't worry about it, anyway.'

'But we could still see somebody from Tarrel's here, I should think. And you didn't want that.'

'They won't come here – it's not their sort of place. Can't see John Wray or Tony Newman liking hanging baskets, or Mr Banks either, for that matter.'

'I just wish we didn't have to worry.'

'Look, we needn't worry.' His eyes were serious. 'The thing is, we're together, having a lovely meal – or will be when it comes – and what could be better than that? Just relax and enjoy the evening.'

Still troubled, her smile was reluctant, but gradually, as she looked across at Jamie and realized how much she wanted to be with him, she did relax and the smile became genuine, even radiant.

'That's more like it,' Jamie said with relief. 'No more "ifs" and "buts", eh?'

'I'll do my best.'

Their food came and was good, as Jamie had said it would be, and as they ate and talked, Roz's misgivings finally left her and she found herself at ease.

'You know what, Jamie, tonight is the time to talk about you, eh? The other day it was all me, but I want to know about you. So, tell me!'

'As I said, you know all about me already. Where I come from, who my parents were, what I like to do.' He shrugged. 'What else is there to say?'

'Well, I don't really know what you like to do, apart from work. I mean, what is there to do in Kelder?'

'Precious little! You have to go into Berwick for entertainment – and that's a wonderful place, full of history and so on, but not exactly buzzing with night life, you might say. What do I like?' He twirled his glass of soft drink. 'I like to walk, go to the cinema when I can, photography – look, I told you I was a pretty uninteresting fellow. Can we stop this interrogation now?' he added, jokingly.

'Who do you walk with?' she pressed on. 'Have you a lot of friends in Kelder?'

'Sure,' he answered readily. 'Fellows I went to school with, people I worked with . . .'

The waitress appeared to take their plates. 'Like a sweet?' she asked. 'There's castle pudding or apple tart.'

They chose apple tart and, when the waitress had left them, Roz, fiddling with her spoon, asked, 'Jamie, how about girls?'

'Girls? You mean, girls in my life?' He gave a disarming smile. 'The answer's yes. At my age, it'd be unlikely that there wouldn't have been one or two.'

'I see,' she said quietly.

'You're younger than I am, of course, but there must have been some fellows for you, Roz. Am I right?'

'None that meant anything to me.'

'Well, there you are. All in the past. Why don't we talk about the present? Guess what I'm going to do?'

'Two apple tarts,' interrupted the waitress. 'With custard, I'm afraid – there's no cream.'

'What are you going to do, then?' asked Roz, beginning to eat.

'Buy a car,' he told her, taking pleasure in seeing her eyes widen. 'Second hand, of course – there aren't many new ones about as yet and they're hard to get – but it'd make all the difference to me to have my own wheels. Everything'd be so much easier, you see. Why, I might even use it at work, if they'd give me a petrol allowance. That old Hillman's not going to last much longer but I don't see old Banks replacing it in a hurry.'

'You're going to buy a car,' Roz repeated, her eyes alight. 'That would be wonderful, Jamie – if you can afford it.'

'I've enough. And I won't be going for a Jaguar or a Humber, or anything like that. It'll be something small and easy to run. The sort you could learn on, Roz. It's time you learned to drive.'

'That's what Mr MacKenna told me. He said it would be useful. I thought lessons would be too expensive.'

'Driving school lessons? Sure, but you'd have me. I can teach you.'

'Would you?'

'You bet. As soon as I get the car. I'm already looking at adverts – I might even try auctions.' Jamie laughed. 'What I need is a sale from one careful lady owner! And remember to take that description with a large pinch of salt.'

It was still warm and very light when they left the restaurant, the June evening being only a little while after the longest day, and they walked slowly, enjoying the air.

'Isn't this what they call white night time?' Jamie asked, taking Roz's hand. 'You know, in places like Shetland it never gets dark at all at this time of year.'

'I've heard that. Sometimes I wonder if it will ever get dark here.'

'Nice for most people. But perhaps not lovers, who prefer the dark.'

Roz gave Jamie a quick glance. 'I like it like this. We get enough dark nights in winter.'

'True,' he said easily. 'But what are we going to do now? I wish I could have shown you my flat, but Alan will be there, working on some plans. He's an architect.'

'I think I'd better make for my tram anyway,' she said quickly.

'Not by yourself,' he said firmly. 'I'm taking you home tonight. Don't say there's no need. You surely don't want to say goodnight yet, do you?'

Her eyes rested on him again. 'No, I don't, Jamie, it's been so nice. I do appreciate it all, you know that.'

'My pleasure, Roz. Now, which tram do we get?'

'If we walk up to Melville Drive we can get one for St Leonard's.'

'Could always get a taxi?'

'A taxi? Don't be silly. You've spent enough.'

'I quite like trams,' he said thoughtfully when they reached the stop. 'They're a bit of a novelty to me, you see. We don't have them in Kelder.'

'No novelty to me,' Roz laughed. 'I seem to have spent half my life on trams, or else at tram stops.'

'And now you're at another stop. But here comes a tram – will that one do, Roz?'

'That'll do. And look, I've got the coppers for the fare. It would have cost us at least a shilling for a taxi.'

Holding hands, they were quiet on the tram and also when they left it, until they reached Deller Street, where they stood outside Roz's home and she told him that that was where she lived.

'It's very nice, Roz. Not old, but attractive.'

'Has no quality, we'd never claim it had.'

'Never mind, I like it. Listen, you're not going straight in, are you?'

'Ma and my sister will be at home. You could come in, if you like.'

'Well, maybe not tonight.' Jamie looked around. 'Still not even dusk! Oh, Roz, I don't want to leave you – isn't there somewhere we can go?'

'I don't think so, really.'

His gaze on her very intent, he suddenly drew her into his arms. 'There's no one about,' he whispered.

'I know,' she whispered back.

And then their mouths met and the kiss was long until finally they parted.

'Couldn't we meet again soon?' Jamie asked. 'On Saturday, or Sunday?'

'My brother's coming for the weekend. I can't see you then.'

'Oh, yes, you told me. All right, we'll just have to wait. Thank God I'm getting a car soon.'

'I'll see you tomorrow, anyway,' Roz said, drawing away. 'Jamie, thank you again. It was a lovely evening.'

'So polite . . .' He shook his head. 'Till tomorrow, then.'

'Tomorrow.'

He watched her go into the house, turn and then wave before walking slowly away. As for Roz – she was floating. Did folk say on cloud nine? Somewhere wonderful, anyway.

Twenty-Four

In the morning, things were different. Looked different, anyway. When Roz had gone to bed, all was wonderful. The memories of being with Jamie, the talk, the feeling of being special, the startling pleasure of his kiss – she'd scarcely been able to sleep for thinking of them. But with the cold light of day came worry. That same worry she'd had from the beginning, of how the attraction they had for each other could possibly be concealed. And if it weren't concealed, what would happen?

She didn't, of course, want to conceal it. She wanted to shout her feelings for Jamie from the rooftops. At the same time, she didn't want to lose her job, and she knew Jamie didn't. Perhaps there should be no question of it, but of what she knew of Mr Banks, Roz was sure he would not take kindly to the idea of two of his staff being attracted to each other. Going out for drinks, having a meal, kissing . . .

The only way to be safe was to step back, to go no further. Even since she'd thought about it on the tram, the attraction between herself and Jamie had progressed very quickly, like a fire taking hold. Who knew how it would end, if not damped down? To be sure of causing no trouble that was what must happen, but, oh, God, it was the last thing she wanted.

'What's the matter with you?' asked Chrissie, rattling cornflakes out of the box. 'Last night you looked like sunshine – now like you might have had bad news – what's up?'

'Nothing's up!' cried Roz. 'I don't know what you're talking about!'

'Having second thoughts about going out with your boss?' Chrissie smiled. 'Look, if you had a good time with him, don't worry – I mean, whether he's the boss or not. It's time you enjoyed yourself, instead o' just thinking o' that job o' yours.'

Scraping butter on her toast, Roz made no reply.

Flo fluttered in, smiling and clutching her shawl around her shoulders. 'Today's the day!' she cried. 'Dougal's coming home!'

'Not till this evening,' said Roz, rising to make more tea. 'But it'll be grand to see him.'

'I canna wait,' said Flo, taking a chair and pushing aside her cereal bowl. 'Is there no porridge, Roz?'

'Too warm for porridge, Ma. Have some cornflakes.'

'I'm too excited to eat anything. Have you got my tea there?'

'Anybody'd think, the way we're going on, that Dougal had been away for months,' Chrissie murmured. 'Talk about putting the flags out!'

'It's a big thing for him, this going back into the army,' Flo said coldly. 'Not something you've had to do, Chrissie.'

Roz, making the tea for her mother, shook her head at Chrissie, who had just opened her mouth – clearly ready to say Dougal hadn't had to do it, either – but, at Roz's look, shrugged and said nothing.

'We must think o' something special to do tomorrow,' said Flo. 'I've got the day off, anyway. But I'll have to find him something nice to eat, eh? Not going to be easy.'

'I can do some shopping if you like, Ma,' said Roz, at which Flo brightened.

'Would you, pet? That'd be a help. I get so tired.'

'Trust Ma to rope you in,' Chrissie said later. 'Getting her to do anything these days is like pushing a stone up Arthur's Seat.'

'Just be grateful that she's swung right round over Dougal and we're not having to worry about her being depressed.'

'For now,' said Chrissie.

'For now. That goes without saying.'

Last night, thought Roz, hurrying for her tram, she was so thrilled about seeing Jamie again at work that nothing else was in her mind. But now, though she was in fact longing to see him, she couldn't help letting her fears overtake her, so that all she could do was think about telling him – what? They must back pedal? Think of their jobs, instead of their feelings?

It was in distinctly low spirits that she arrived at the property department and with some apprehension looked for him, but for once saw she was there before him. A breathing space, thank God! Quickly, she put down the post and ran into her office, where she took the cover off her typewriter and sat down at her desk. Then leaped up and combed her hair. Sat down again, sorted through papers, tried to stop her fingers trembling.

'Roz!' she heard him say. And there he was in her little office, bending down, his arms around her. 'Oh, Roz, good morning. I was awake all night, thinking about you!'

She couldn't believe that he seemed about to kiss her, and sprang up from his arms.

'Jamie, we're at work! What are you thinking of?'

'Of you, like I said.' He was laughing, stepping away from her. 'Oh, I'm sorry. I'm behaving like a schoolboy, but there's no one here, no one to see. I couldn't resist coming in to find you, then kind of lost my head.'

'It's all right.' Her eyes fastened on his face. She was lost in gladness at seeing him again, and though she knew she must be strong and tell him what they must do, being in his arms again had not helped her resolve.

'But Jamie, we really can't be like this, can we?' she managed to say. 'The fact is, I've been thinking—'

'Thinking?' Suddenly, he was quite serious, his smiles, his banter quite gone. 'I don't like the sound of that. What have you been thinking, then?'

'Well, I was so happy last night, you see, but then it seemed to me this morning that – what you said about risk . . . maybe we shouldn't take it.'

'You're afraid you'll lose your job?'

'Yours as well, Jamie. That'd be more important, because you're a professional. I could get something else, but you'd be throwing a lot away.'

'So, you want to give me up?'

His hazel eyes without their smile seemed strange; she could no longer meet them.

'No!' she cried. 'No, I don't want to, Jamie! I just think . . . maybe we shouldn't go any further. It's too difficult. How can we keep it a secret?'

'Tell me what you mean by "it",' he said quietly. 'Would it be love?'

'Love?'

'Love. Are you saying you love me, Roz?'

As she seemed unable to speak, he took her hands and made her look at him.

'Because I love you, Roz. Yes, it's been quick – love at first sight, in fact. It happens, you know. Happened to me when I saw you in this very department, with those other two guys who were in for the job and your Mr MacKenna. I didn't really believe it at first, but then I began to think you might feel the same. We had that drink, that meal, I kissed you and . . . Look, for God's sake, do you care for me, Roz?'

'I do, Jamie. I do care for you.' There were tears in her eyes. 'I do love you.'

He gave a little sigh and very gently kissed her brow.

'All right, I'll tell you what we'll do. We'll be very careful. There'll be no repeat of me coming in and going on as though we're not at the office. We'll be absolutely without reproach until we meet outside of work. And then, you see, we'll have the car.'

'The car?'

'Yes, I'm going to look at one tonight, and I've two more lined up for tomorrow. By Monday I should have one and then we'll have transport to go out of town, go wherever we like as far as we can from Tarrel's. How does that suit?'

'Oh, Jamie, it suits!'

'Fine.' They exchanged long, rapturous looks but nothing more, until Jamie turned to go back to his own desk. Just once, he looked back at her.

'Better do some work, I suppose?'

'Oh, yes!' she cried. 'To work!'

But it was some time before she could settle.

Twenty-Five

It was in the late evening that Dougal came home, at the same time that Chrissie arrived back from work and the MacGarry boys were about to climb their stairs.

'Hey, who's this Scottish soldier, then?' cried Bob, the younger of the two brothers, both tall and black-haired, their bright eyes slate blue. He slapped Dougal on the shoulder. 'But you're looking well, eh? As though you've been on your holidays.'

'Holidays!' cried Dougal, laughing. 'I wouldn't say that.'

'But you do look well,' said Chrissie, throwing her arms round him. 'I'm sure you've put on weight.'

It was true – in his well-fitting tunic and trews, a forage cap on his fair hair, Dougal did look well, and if he had put on a little weight, it only made him appear stronger and more at ease with himself. There was no doubt that he had not been suffering in his first few weeks of army life.

'Like the uniform,' Evan commented. 'You have to wear it on leave, too?'

'No, I'm going to change soon as I get in the flat. Nice to see you guys – we'll have to have a drink sometime.'

'You bet,' the brothers promised and ran lightly up their stairs, while Dougal followed Chrissie as she opened their front door.

'How's Ma?' he asked in an urgent whisper, putting his hand on her arm.

'She's fine. No problems at all. You're the absolute blue-eyed boy now, I'm telling you.'

'Only while I'm away. I'm back now. How's Roz?'

'Got a young man. Just like I've got my Richard.'

'Dougal, is that you?' came Flo's voice. 'Oh, come away in, then, we've been waiting for you!'

'Oh, Ma!'

She and Roz were standing together, Roz smiling, but Flo, her lower lip trembling, was only just keeping back tears as Dougal, dropping his kitbag, strode towards her and hugged her close.

'It's all right, Ma, I'm back and I'm well.' He laughed uneasily. 'Now, don't I look well? Nearly as well as you!'

'You've filled out!' she exclaimed, holding his arms, her smile wavering. 'And you're in your uniform, eh?'

'I'm just going to change, Ma – I needn't wear it over the weekend.'

'How about a hug for me?' asked Roz, gently moving her mother aside to kiss her brother's cheek. 'Dougal, you look grand!'

'You too,' he said, holding her at arm's length and studying her. 'You look terrific – have you had a new hairdo?'

'No, there's nothing new about me, nothing at all.'

'What a lie!' cried Chrissie, laughing. 'She's got a new young man, and he's her boss!'

'This I'll have to hear about,' said Dougal, 'as soon as I change.'

'Hurry up, then,' said Roz. 'Then we can have something to eat. Your favourite, Dougal – ham and egg pie. Ma's been fussing over it all evening, but don't ask me where she got the eggs.'

'Know something?' asked Dougal. 'I'm very happy in the army, it's just what I expected, but it's nice to be back here, too.' He picked up his kitbag and set off for his mother's room. 'Very nice,' he said firmly. 'These weekend passes are a damned good idea.'

If only it could always be like this, Roz thought, as they later sat round the table and ate the meal Flo had prepared. So relaxed, so much at ease, all of them happy. Of course, she'd no way of knowing how other families were, but she was sure they didn't live as the Raineys usually did, perched on a knife-edge, fearful if things were going well that they might soon experience the opposite. Perhaps this time they wouldn't? Ma did seem well and so happy to have Dougal back – maybe their luck was ready to change?

Roz smiled to herself as her mother passed the last portion of her ham and egg pie to Dougal and beamed around the table – talking of luck, Roz's had changed, hadn't it? Something she'd never expected to happen, and still couldn't believe, had quite suddenly changed her life. Not that she had forgotten her ambition, or her pleasure in her work – they were there still, a part of her she'd never give up, but something very precious had come to her out of the blue and already meant so much, she couldn't imagine being without it.

It was just a wee bit worrying that Dougal had seen a difference in her that she was hoping others wouldn't, and if her happiness was sending out such signals, she must try harder at work not to give anything away. But another factor she might have considered – which was where the new-found love between her and Jamie would end – she purposefully put from her mind. With such an ecstatic beginning, she'd let the future take care of itself.

After their meal, when they'd cleared away, the women of the family listened while Dougal, comfortable in his own clothes, smoked a cigarette and entertained them with tales of the sergeant major, the other 'lads' in the barracks, how tough it was being drilled into being a soldier and yet how enjoyable.

'Fancy!' and 'Imagine that!' cried his family, marvelling at how well Dougal seemed to have settled in, though Flo was worrying about what the recruits had to eat and what the sergeant major was really like. Not too hard on the lads, was he?

'He's got to be hard, Ma,' Dougal explained. 'Got to get us into shape. Of course, I've done it before, in my national service, so it's not been too bad for me, though I'm finding that being a regular is not the same as just being called up. The thing is that you know all the time when you're called up that it's only temporary, that you won't be staying. Being a regular, it's going to be your life, eh? It's different.'

Roz, glancing quickly at her mother, saw that a shadow had crossed her face at Dougal's words, and she hastily tried to talk of something else. Their day tomorrow, for instance. Chrissie had to go to work, but Flo and Roz were free.

'What would you like to do?' Roz asked her brother. 'Anything special?'

'Let's decide tomorrow. I'm easy, anyway.'

'So, how about a nightcap, then?'

'By which you mean tea or cocoa?' Dougal grinned. 'Not something stronger? No, I'm only joking. Cocoa's fine.'

He stretched out his legs and gave a satisfied sigh.

'It's grand to be home, eh?'

'Grand to have you,' Flo said, rising from her chair and putting her hand on his shoulder. 'Even if only for a weekend.'

'It's just begun, Ma! And we've the whole day tomorrow.'

'We'll make the most of it,' said Roz.

Twenty-Six

They had a splendid time on Saturday – Flo, Roz and Dougal – not going anywhere out of the ordinary, just sightseeing, almost like tourists, in the famous parts of Edinburgh they hardly ever visited. The Princes Street Gardens, the castle, the Royal Mile – even Logie's, the rather grand department store, where Dougal treated Flo and Roz to a light lunch surrounded by so many Edinburgh ladies he had to smile.

'Makes a change from the pub, eh? But it's time I gave you two a treat. Just wish Chrissie hadn't had to work today.'

'Aye, but can you afford to treat us?' Flo asked anxiously. 'Army pay for new recruits canna be much.'

'I've saved a bit, Ma, and I wanted to do something for you and Roz. You've been grand to me, and that's a fact.'

'Think so?' Flo lowered her eyes. 'Maybe I took my time understanding what you wanted, but you know how it was?'

'No need to say any more,' he told her earnestly. 'That's all behind us. But listen, what d'you want to do now? I wouldn't mind going back to the castle to look at the National War Museum, but maybe you'd like to go home?'

'I think I will, Dougal. I do feel a bit tired. But you and Roz can go. I'll have a wee rest.'

When they had seen their mother on to her tram, Roz and Dougal made their way back to the castle, which housed the National War Museum of Scotland as well as regimental collections, the famous old Mons Meg gun and various gun batteries – all too much for Flo to spend time on but of interest to Dougal.

'And you know, I feel dead ashamed,' he told Roz as they began to look round at the military exhibits. 'I've lived here all my life, but this is the first time I've looked at this stuff. I'm glad I'm seeing it now.'

'Me too. I suppose it's the same old story – when you live in a place, you're the last to visit the sights.'

Roz dropped into a seat and fanned herself with her handkerchief, for the day was hot and the museum crowded. 'Too many people,' she murmured, 'and when the festival begins it'll be worse than ever.'

'Canna think why we need a festival,' said Dougal, also mopping his brow. 'But I'll not be here to see it, anyway. How about a cup of tea? There's a café somewhere or other.'

'I think we do need a festival,' Roz remarked, reflecting on the annual Edinburgh International Festival begun in 1947 by Rupert Bing, an opera man. 'We're a great city – we should be on the map.'

'With Culture with a capital C, eh?' asked Dougal, laughing and pulling her to her feet. 'Come on, let's get that tea.'

Over the tea, he fixed her with his clear blue eyes and bent towards her. 'How about filling me in on your young man?' he asked lightly. 'Did I hear Chrissie saying he was your boss?'

'I don't think I want to talk about him,' Roz answered, taking a small cake.

'Why not? He's a lawyer, eh? You've done well to land him.'

'Land him?' she cried, her eyes flashing. 'I haven't *landed* him, Dougal. What a thing to say. We've only been out together a couple of times.'

'But you're keen, I can tell, and I bet he is, too. I don't see why you shouldn't talk about him.'

'Because it's not the sort of thing that would be approved of at Tarrel's – I mean, folk who work together getting, well, friendly.'

'You mean more than friendly, eh? Bad for their work?' Dougal shrugged and ate a cake almost in one bite. 'I expect it happens all the time. That's why some men fall for their secretaries.'

'Oh, don't!' Roz exclaimed. 'You make it sound so – underhand. Look, I said I didn't want to talk about it. Maybe we'd better be getting back now.'

'Right you are.' Dougal stood up, ready to pay the bill, but Roz was before him.

'I'll get this – you paid for our lunch.'

Outside, in the warmth of the afternoon, she put her summer hat over her dark red hair and turned to give Dougal a long, serious look. 'Do you think things'll work out, Dougal? Between Chrissie and this Richard?'

'Don't see why not.'

'It's just that she's so sure of him, it worries me. I don't know why, but I have the feeling that he's not as keen as she is.'

'Why, that's a piece o' nonsense, Roz. You can't know that. Have you even seen him?'

'Sure I have. Chrissie fixed up a meeting at Café Sunshine – after he'd made an excuse not to come to our flat.'

'One meeting – you can't know what's in his mind from that. Ma thinks he's ideal.'

'Oh, I know. The perfect gentleman.'

'Well, how's she feel about your lawyer, then?'

'She hasn't met him yet.' Roz's smile was suddenly radiant. 'If she does, I can tell you, she'll be bowled over!'

As they began to walk down the steep road from the castle, Dougal grinned. 'Like someone else I know, not a hundred miles from here.'

At which, Roz knocked his arm and told him to shut up, laughing all the same.

Oh, it was so nice having him back, she thought – if only the weekend weren't so short! But time moved on, however you might want to hold it back, and after a pleasant, leisurely Sunday morning, when Dougal had his wish and had a long lie in, there was just the family dinner to enjoy before he had to be on his way.

'Lovely bit o' beef,' he told Flo, when he came to kiss her goodbye. 'Och, it's been grand, Ma, being back!'

'It was Roz who sweet-hearted the butcher for the beef,' Flo told him, 'and I was lucky to have an egg, eh? For your Yorkshire pudding!'

She's doing well, her girls thought, watching her give Dougal a last hug, not crying yet, though there were tears in her eyes. Just as long as she didn't relapse into depression once he'd gone. At least she'd seen how well he was, and enjoying army life, even if he'd been glad to have his weekend at home. Peacetime was not the same as wartime, you had to agree.

When he'd embraced them all a second time and said he'd be back in no time, they had to watch him leave for the station again on his own, waving to him until he was out of sight, then turning back to what seemed a very quiet flat.

'Don't worry, Ma,' said Chrissie, putting her arm round Flo's shoulders. 'He'll be back soon, and look how well he is!'

'Aye, he's fine – for now.' Flo managed a smile. 'It was good to see him, eh?'

'Very good,' the sisters agreed. 'And you'll be all right, Ma.'

'Maybe I will. Think I'll just have a lie down, though. I feel so tired – don't know why.'

'Thank goodness,' Roz whispered when their mother had left them. 'I think we needn't worry this time. What are you going to do now?'

'I'm meeting Richard. We're going for a walk. What about you?'

'Oh, I'll do my usual – tidying up – ironing – mending . . .'

And think of Jamie, she thought, smiling to herself. Wonder if he's bought that car yet?

Twenty-Seven

Jamie was standing at Tarrel's open door when Roz arrived on Monday morning. He took her hands and held her surprised gaze with laughing eyes. 'Oh, it's good to see you! I've been waiting here for hours – well, five minutes.'

As she opened her mouth to speak he put his fingers over her lips.

'Now don't tell me you're not late – of course you're not. There's no one here yet.'

'Thank goodness for that,' said Roz, looking past him to the reception desk. 'I can just imagine what Norma would say if she could see us now.'

'Never mind about Norma. Come and see what I've bought.'

'Jamie, you haven't!' Roz's eyes were sparkling.

'I have. I've got the car. Bought it at the Saturday auction and it's a little beauty. Quick – come and see it – just at the kerb here.'

He rushed her outside on to the pavement where, parked by the kerb as he'd said, was a dark blue car, very well polished, very neat, very smart, looking exactly like what Jamie'd wanted – something owned and loved by one careful owner.

'Oh, Jamie!' Roz breathed. 'It's lovely! What make is it?'

'Austin Eight Light Saloon. Very reliable, and practically nothing on the clock. Of course, it's been up on blocks for the whole of the war and the lady who had it has now given up driving.'

Jamie was taking out keys and opening the door. 'Like to sit in?' he asked. 'Quick, before people start arriving!'

Roz, glancing round and seeing nobody, quickly seated herself in the passenger seat, smiling delightedly as she looked first through the windscreen, then back at Jamie, who was hovering about like a mother hen with a chick.

'Like it, Roz?' He rubbed at a tiny spot on the side window.

'Oh, I do, Jamie! It's a lovely car. I never thought you'd find one so good.'

'Cost me more than I'd expected, but I've been saving up for years for something like this and it's worth every penny. Better hop out now and I'll lock up.'

Just in time, Roz left her seat, for Mr Newman had appeared round the corner, his eyes showing unusual interest as he saw the blue car at the kerb.

'Well, well, what have we here? Something new for you, Mr Shield?'

'That's right. I was just showing it to Miss Rainey.'

'Looks in good condition.'

'Best I'll get at this time, I think.'

'And it's an Austin Eight? Now, I've got a Wolseley. Does quite well . . .'

Who'd have thought it? Roz was smiling. Mr Newman had an interest outside work?

'I'd better go and collect the post,' she told the two men, now deep in car talk.

Jamie waved his hand. 'Right you are, Miss Rainey.'

'Hey, what's going on?' asked Norma, arriving at the same time as Miss Calder. 'Ooh, is that yours, Mr Shield? What a smart car!'

'Very nice,' said Miss Calder, 'but I think I hear the telephone ringing, Miss Ward.'

'Just going!' cried Norma, flying into the hall, followed by Miss Calder and, more reluctantly, Mr Newman and Jamie. New acquisition or not, work called, and no one wanted to be still outside on the pavement when Mr Banks arrived. Meanwhile, Roz was already in the property department, waiting for Jamie.

As soon as he came he shut the door and came to take her in his arms and quickly kiss her. 'Ah, Roz, did you miss me over the weekend?'

'I did, but I bet you didn't miss me!'

He stepped back, shaking his head. 'I did! All the time I was looking at cars, I was thinking of you and which one you'd like.

When I got the Austin, I was thinking of our first drive together and where we'd go.'

'Oh, Jamie,' she said softly. 'It'll be so lovely!'

But as he made to kiss her again, she firmly pushed him away. 'Didn't you say that in the office we were going to be beyond reproach?'

'Oh, God, did I say that? It's going to be pretty difficult.'

'It's the way it has to be, Jamie. Don't make it even harder.'

He moved to his desk and sat down, sighing. 'Roz, you're wonderful. You hold me to what I promised. So, here goes, let's get to work.'

'Let's,' she agreed. 'So, there's the post on your desk and I can tell you that you have a valuation trip this morning and another one this afternoon. Want the details?'

'Think I know them. But does this mean we've no houses to see together?'

'Not today. I've got plenty to do here, while you're out.'

'How about this evening, then? Can we go out this evening? I'm talking about our first trip in the car.'

'Oh, Jamie, so soon?' Roz's face was alight. 'Where shall we go? And when?'

'How about I pick you up at your home at seven and we'll take it from there. All right?'

'All right!'

He gave another long sigh. 'Now we've fixed that I can really concentrate on work. Beyond reproach, that's me!'

'Me, too,' sang Roz, going into her office and taking the cover off her typewriter. It was true, she had plenty to do and, like Jamie, really felt she could settle down to it, now that she knew she would be seeing Jamie after work. And in the car!

Twenty-Eight

He was prompt, but she was waiting for him when he drove up in the warmth of the summer evening and leaped out to take her hand.

'Roz, you look amazing!' he cried, his eyes going over the new green dress she'd recently bought in the sales, and she laughed.

'Almost as good as your car?'

But she knew she was looking her best, the slim-fitting new dress showing off her slenderness, its colour contrasting with her dark red hair.

'You're both equally perfect,' he told her, opening the passenger door. 'No, I mean it. But hop in, then, and I'll tell you where we might go. It's a lovely evening, just right for our first drive.'

'You've already decided where we're going?'

'If you agree. Thing is, I've bought myself a book on the Forth area and there's a whole load of interesting places to see, but I thought this one for a start.'

Reaching into the glove pocket, Jamie produced a guide book and, flicking over the pages, found what he was looking for.

'See, this is it – Blackness. It's a little village about five miles from South Queensferry, but it has an ancient castle, a fortress that I'd really like to see. Have you been there?'

'No, but I know about it.' Roz studied the picture of the castle, an ancient-looking building perched on a promontory over the sea. 'The castle's the main place of interest there, I think, but you won't be able to go round it now.'

'Oh, I know, but we can look at the outside, walk by the sea, have a drink at the pub. And there is a pub. What do you say?'

'I say yes, please.' Roz sat back in her seat, sighing with pleasure, as Jamie switched on the car's engine. 'It's so nice, I just want to drive out anywhere.'

'With me?'

'With you.'

Dominated by the massive Forth railway bridge, looking splendid in the evening sunshine, South Queensferry was full of visitors strolling round, or sitting on benches outside the pubs and cafés, almost tempting Jamie to stop.

'Looks so inviting, eh? But Blackness it is, and I guess it won't be so crowded.'

'And less likely to have folk from Tarrel's visiting,' Roz remarked. 'Remember, we don't want to see them, do we?'

'You mean we don't want them to see us. But stop worrying about people from work, Roz. We're out together, on our own, we're free! And in our own transport. There's nothing to worry about.'

'Sorry, I won't mention them again.' Roz gave another contented sigh. 'You know, I can't believe I'm really here. Bowling along to Blackness – it's just so different from what I usually do. I feel I must be dreaming.'

'Better get used to driving out with me, Roz, for that's what you'll usually be doing now, in your time off, anyway. Now, let me check the map – with only five miles to go from Queensferry, we'll soon be there.'

Blackness village turned out to be very small – just a few houses, a harbour, a pub, a boat club, and, some way away from the nearest house, the castle. A long, narrow, brooding edifice, described in Jamie's guidebook as a 'ship that never sailed' because of its shape, it was certainly the dominant feature of the village and as dramatic as he had expected.

'Wish we could have got to look round it,' he murmured as they stood as close as they could to its entrance gates. 'It's just how you imagine a castle to be, a proper fortress, eh? And there must be wonderful views of the bay from that promontory.'

'It might have been a fortress, but I seem to remember hearing it was damaged by Oliver Cromwell,' said Roz. 'Seemingly, he damaged an awful lot of places when he invaded Scotland.'

'One of the ruins Cromwell knocked about a bit, eh?' Jamie laughed. 'According to my book, it's been everything – a residence, a prison, an armament store – but it's been repaired and people can look round it now so I'll have to come back for another visit. For now, though, let's walk a bit, shall we?'

It was very pleasant, strolling beside the sea wall, looking out on the wide expanse of the bay where a few sailing boats were moving through the evening calm, and though they were not alone, Roz and Jamie saw no one they knew and walked together naturally, arm in arm.

'Fancy a drink?' asked Jamie as they reached the pub. 'We can sit outside, if you like.'

'I wouldn't mind a lemonade.'

'I'd better have the same, seeing as I'm driving.' Jamie looked back to where he'd parked the car. 'Hope it's all right. I'm already beginning to worry someone might steal it.'

'Why, you locked it!'

'Ah, but you don't know how car thieves operate. They've got all sorts of tricks. Come on, let's have that drink.'

'And get back to the car?' asked Roz, amused.

'Now I didn't say that!' he protested.

All the same, they didn't linger over their drinks and, as no car thief had tried any tricks on the Austin, were soon back in their seats and driving away.

'This countryside's so lovely,' Jamie commented. 'Why don't we just drive round a bit?'

Drive round and stop was what he actually meant, for when he found a little lane leading nowhere, with only a distant view of the Forth Bridge to remind them of where they were, he drew up and turned his eyes on Roz.

'Want a driving lesson?' he asked cheerfully.

A driving lesson? It was the last thing she'd expected.

'Maybe not now,' she answered cautiously. 'It's getting late.'

'Nonsense, it's as light as day!'

'But I'd need a licence, wouldn't I? Some sort of provisional thing?'

'Yes, I suppose you would. All right, another time, then.' He took her hand. 'It wasn't my first reason for stopping the car, anyway – to give you a driving lesson, I mean.'

'No?'

'Come on, you're teasing. You know I want to kiss you again. You want me to, don't you?'

To answer, she leaned forward and pressed her lips to his, at which he dropped her hand and took her into his arms.

'Oh, Roz! You don't know what it's been like, waiting to do this!'

'As a matter of fact, I do,' she whispered. 'I've been waiting too.'

For some time, they held each other, kissing more and more passionately, until both drew back, breathing hard and gazing into each other's eyes.

Then Jamie gently touched Roz's face. 'Suppose I'd better take you back?'

She said nothing, only let him see, from the look in her grey eyes, how little she wanted to go.

'Only bright spot, Roz, is that we see each other tomorrow. That gets me through.'

'I don't know, I find it a bit of a strain – being together yet having to be so careful.'

'That's because you worry too much. I don't worry – I hope for the best.'

'I do worry. It's the way I am.'

'Well, just try to think the way they did in the war.' He kissed her quickly. 'You remember the slogan? "Don't worry, it may never happen"? It's very important to keep that in mind. Now, we'd better be on our way.'

When Jamie parked outside the flat in Deller Street, Roz asked a little hesitantly if he'd like to come in to meet her mother and sister, as they'd be back from the café by now. She'd no idea what he would say, yet was still surprised when he, too, was hesitant.

'I'd like to meet them, of course, but, I wonder . . . would it be better another time?'

'Another time?' She tried not to sound cool. 'All right, if you prefer it. I just wanted them to meet you, to see why I want to be with you.'

'I see. Oh, well, then, tonight's the night. Yes, I'd like to meet them, Roz. Lead on.'

He took her hand, seemingly agreeable, yet it seemed to her he was still unwilling and she couldn't help wondering why. Did he think she was treating him already as a prospective fiancé? That wasn't true. She was sure he and she were the same, overcome by sudden love, not even thinking where it might lead. Just enjoying for the moment what they had.

'This way,' she told him. 'We're on the first floor. And they are home – I can hear their voices.'

Twenty-Nine

Flo and Chrissie, not long back from the café, were sitting in the warmth of the evening, their shoes off, the window open, both pleasantly relaxing, until Roz's call had them looking towards the door.

'Roz! Is that you?' cried Flo.

'It's me, Ma, and I've brought someone to see you, just for a minute.'

'Oh, no, a visitor? Where are my shoes?'

As Flo scrabbled for her shoes and Chrissie slid into hers, Jamie stood in the doorway and Roz took his arm.

'Ma – Chrissie – this is Jamie Shield, from Tarrel's. Jamie, this is my mother and my sister, Chrissie. Ma, you got my note, eh?'

'Note – oh, yes.' Flo, having put on her shoes, was standing up and staring at Jamie, who was smiling endearingly and stretching out his hand.

'I'm very glad to meet you, Mrs Rainey, and Chrissie – if I may call you that?'

'Oh, yes, that's fine,' said Chrissie, her surprised gaze going over his face. 'Very pleased to meet you, Mr Shield – Jamie.'

'Very pleased,' echoed Flo, as she and Chrissie shook Jamie's hand. 'So you've been out this evening? Such good weather, eh?'

'We've been to Blackness, Ma, in Jamie's car. He's just got it and it's lovely.'

'Blackness? Fancy.' Flo put her hand to her hair in a distracted fashion. 'Would you like a cup o' tea, then? Chrissie – the kettle—'

'Thank you very much, Mrs Rainey, but I won't stay,' answered Jamie. 'It seemed a good opportunity to look in, but I won't disturb you. I know you're just back from work. So nice to meet you both, though.'

'And you,' Chrissie said politely. 'Heard such a lot about you.'

'Oh, dear, hope it wasn't too bad?'

'All flattering,' Roz told him with determined cheerfulness. 'I'll just show you out, then? Sorry it was just a flying visit, Ma, but like Jamie said, it just seemed a good opportunity.'

'It was grand to meet you, Jamie,' Flo said, seeming to have recovered some poise. 'Very nice of you to call in. Maybe you'll come again?'

'Thank you, Mrs Rainey, I'd like that. Goodnight, then. And goodnight, Chrissie.' Slightly bowing his head, Jamie gave a final smile and followed Roz from the room, leaving Flo and Chrissie to collapse back into their chairs.

'I'm afraid we caught them on the hop,' Roz murmured as she and Jamie reached the car.

'I rather thought we might, you know.'

Though he'd acquitted himself well meeting her mother and Chrissie, it seemed to Roz, studying him in the light that was just fading, that he was strangely ill at ease. Again, she was puzzled, but there was no way she could question him and, as he moved to kiss her goodnight, she thought perhaps she was just being overly sensitive, imagining something that wasn't there. And when the kiss came she could think of nothing else anyway.

'Another lovely evening,' she whispered, releasing herself from his arms. 'So special to be with you, Jamie.'

'With my special car?'

'With or without your car.'

'Well, this is the bit I don't like, saying goodnight. Who said parting is such sweet sorrow? There's no sweetness in it, as far as I can tell. Goodnight, darling Roz. See you tomorrow.'

'Better not call me darling. It might slip out at work.'

'Worrying again?' He shook his head at her. 'You know I'm a very careful guy.'

He was relaxing, becoming more his usual self, and as he took his seat at the wheel, blew kisses at her until the engine started and he was on his way.

'Goodnight!' she called. Darling Jamie . . . She could be careful, too.

'Well, that was a surprise!' cried Flo, when Roz came into the living room. 'I'd no idea you'd be bringing your young man home with you!'

'I'm not exactly calling him my young man, but I wanted you to meet him. You and Chrissie.' Roz glanced swiftly at her sister. 'What did you think of him, then?'

'Very nice,' Flo answered at once. 'Very open, good-natured face, and a lovely smile. I liked him.'

'I did, too,' said Chrissie. 'I thought he was sweet.' She paused for a moment. 'Reckon you'd be safe with him.'

'Safe?'

'I mean, he'd look after you. I can tell, he's the sort.'

'But I don't need looking after!' Roz was smiling, but her eyes on Chrissie were watchful. 'Is Richard that sort, then?' she asked. 'To look after you?'

'Of course he is!' Flo cut in. 'You can rely on Richard. Isn't that right, Chrissie?'

'Sure it is. You've no need to ask.' Chrissie yawned and stretched. 'Roz, how about you making us two poor tired souls a cuppa, then?'

'That's the ticket,' said Flo, striking a match to light a cigarette. 'But what a shame Jamie couldn't stay, eh? I hope he does come to see us again.'

'See no reason why he shouldn't,' Roz replied, making the familiar trek to the kettle.

Thirty

With August came the festival, and as crowds of visitors, many of them foreign, filled the streets in amazingly good weather, Roz drank in the atmosphere as never before. She felt so full of high spirits it was as though she was part of the programme, though she didn't even have tickets to any operas, concerts, or ballets – and in fact had never taken much interest in the previous two festivals, believing she couldn't afford anything anyway.

So what was different? Jamie, of course! He made the difference. Being in love made the difference. Everything seemed in sharper focus and brighter colours because of him, because of their love, and though she couldn't be with him when she moved through the streets in her lunch hour, or going home after work, the thought of him added to all that she could see and feel. Even if, she had to admit, just lately he could sometimes seem mysteriously to be a little 'down'.

They tried as often as they could to be together, but it wasn't easy. Their evening or Sunday drives always had to be out of Edinburgh to places they thought their colleagues wouldn't go, and though Roz was just glad to be with Jamie at all, she knew he found it irksome. And sometimes, when they were out and she'd been looking away, she would look back to see his eyes fixed on her and find in them something she couldn't quite understand. Regret? Sadness? All she could be sure of was that when her eyes were on him she only ever felt happy.

One morning he came into her office, his more usual cheerful self and, seating himself on her desk, asked her about the festival that she'd been enjoying so much without actually attending.

'Have you really never gone to anything at the festivals, Roz? That's a shame, if they were anything like this one – there's some marvellous stuff on.'

'Well, it's pricey, Jamie. I'm like a lot of Edinburgh folk – I think it's not for me.'

'But if you could afford it, there are things you'd like to see? This year, there's that Scottish thing – *A Satire of the Three Estates* – we ought to see that. And then there's a woman with a beautiful voice – I've got some of her records – Kathleen Ferrier, who's giving a recital.' Jamie waved his hands. 'So, why don't I get us tickets, then? I'll bet they've got some left, though I might have to queue to get them.'

'They say all the best things are sold out. People from abroad will have booked ages ago.'

'I could try, anyway. And if all else fails we can have a drink at the Assembly Rooms bar. That won't break the bank!'

'Haven't you forgotten something?' she asked softly. 'We don't want to be seen together. I'll bet folk from here will be all over the festival.'

'Oh, God!' Jamie abruptly left her desk. 'Why is there always this barrier? Why have we to keep thinking of other people?' He moved to the window and stood with his brow against the pane, staring out at the sunshine. 'All I want is to be with you, and all I find are difficulties.'

'Why, Jamie, we're often together,' she cried, hurrying to him, turning him to face her. 'We go out in your car, we see places, it's wonderful. Absolutely keeps me going, thinking of it, when I'm not with you.'

'Is that right?' he asked tenderly. 'I suppose that's true for me, too, but I do feel so bitter that we happen to have met here and that makes such a hell of a difference. You can understand, Roz? You feel the same?'

'I do, but I just think I'm so lucky, anyway, to have you and be with you when we can. I'm willing to put up with everything else for that.'

'Ah, Roz, that's so like you.' He pressed her hand. 'All the time, you keep me right.'

'Well, if I do, we'd better get back to work.' She laughed a little. 'There's the telephone!'

They were all right again, back on an even keel, until the weekend when Jamie said it was sweet sorrow time again, as he must go home to the Borders. Well, of course, Roz understood, but it did occur to her that it would have been nice if he'd asked her to go with him. Seemingly, their families were not to be involved, for Jamie had never suggested seeing her mother again, and she had the feeling that she shouldn't suggest it either. And now he was to visit his own mother who might or might not know of Roz's existence. He kept saying how important she was to him, how he only wanted to be with her, yet she didn't even know if she played any part in his life away from her.

Where were they going then? Maybe the time had come to think of that? Or maybe not? Roz decided she must just get through the weekend somehow. Perhaps go to one of the 'Fringe' events that were outside the festival proper but becoming quite popular?

'Och, they're just a load of amateurs,' said Norma when Roz asked if she might be interested in going with her, 'but you know they've had some good reviews. How about one of the comedy shows? I could do with a good laugh. You too, eh?'

'Why me?'

'Well, Mr Shield's away this weekend, eh?'

When Roz stood speechless, Norma grinned.

'Come on, Roz, you don't need to pretend with me. I know there's something between you. What of it? It's no crime, is it?'

'Oh, Norma, you won't say anything?' Roz had turned a little pale. 'We work together – you know it'd never be approved of here.'

'Roz, I promise I won't say a word and I've not said anything up till now, have I?'

'Do you think anyone else has noticed us?'

'Not likely! They're all such sticks, they can never see anything that's not a legal document! Now I could tell about you two just by seeing the way you look at each other – even by the way you say each other's names.' Norma smiled triumphantly. 'But I live in the real world, eh?'

'I thought, maybe Miss Calder—'

'Miss Calder? She's just the same as the lawyers. When did she ever see anybody in love? Oh, come on, Roz, stop worrying! Let's fix up to go to a show on Saturday night and forget Tarrel and Thom's!'

'Oh, yes, let's,' agreed Roz with feeling.

They did go to a comedy show – one held by an amateur group in a church hall – and Roz did manage to forget her worries, joining in the laughter with Norma and not mentioning Jamie's name at all. It was only when she was on her way home in the tram that the worries came back, for how sure could she be that Norma was right and others weren't seeing what seemed to be so plain to her? Mr Banks, for instance? He certainly hadn't said anything so far, but then he might just be waiting to see her and Jamie together somewhere before asking them to step into his office and – what? Give them the sack?

Searching for some comfort, Roz decided she was worrying too much. Maybe they wouldn't be in such trouble after all, even if they were found to have fallen in love. As Norma had said, it was no crime. But in her heart, Roz knew that it wouldn't do either of them any good either, especially not Jamie, who was the professional and would be held responsible. And if the truth were told, their relationship was affecting their work, which was just what Mr Banks would fear. Though Jamie had said they would be absolutely above reproach they hadn't been, for often they couldn't resist spending time talking to each other, looking at each other, just being with each other, instead of concentrating on clients.

Taking a hard, objective view of the situation, Roz felt bad and guilty, and longed to be with Jamie, to have him, somehow, make her feel better. But the only solution she was beginning to see was that she should leave Tarrel's. Find another job. It wouldn't be too difficult, except that it might not be with property and there would be the end to her dreams. But if she still had Jamie, wouldn't it be worth it?

Here the tram rattled to her stop and with some relief Roz alighted and made her way home through the still warm, light evening. Not a word of her worries to Ma, she told herself as she let herself in to the flat, and was only to find out when she went into the living room that her worries at that time would be of no interest. How could they be, when Chrissie, her face white, was sobbing quietly into a wet handkerchief, while Flo, looking stricken, was sitting opposite, shaking her head and murmuring words of comfort that were so clearly not being heard?

'What's wrong?' cried Roz. 'For God's sake, what's happened?'

Her mother turned expressionless eyes on her. 'He's given her up, Roz. It's Richard. He's leaving Edinburgh and he doesn't want to marry her.'

Thirty-One

'Oh, Chrissie!' Roz ran to kneel by her sister's side, to put her arms around her, smooth her poor damp face with a clean handkerchief and whisper again, 'Oh, Chrissie!'

'I trusted him, Roz,' Chrissie said hoarsely, her throat swollen with tears. 'I knew from the start he was the one, and he felt the same about me. He did, he did! Ma, you knew that, eh? You saw how he was with me? Unmistakable, you said, how he felt?'

'Aye, he was very keen,' Flo murmured. 'Bit slow at first, but then he was always after you, wherever you were in the café. We all saw that.'

'Yes, and then he asked me out,' Chrissie cried eagerly. 'He was always asking me out. And we got so close, I knew that the next thing would be . . .' Her voice shook and trailed away as she crumpled Roz's handkerchief and wiped her eyes again. '. . . would be getting wed,' she finished. 'It had to be – we were so in love!'

'Did he ever say . . .?' Roz asked hesitantly. 'Did he ever say – I mean – put it into words? That you would be getting wed?'

'No, he didn't need to; it was just so plain, Roz, it was understood. That's when I fixed up for you to meet him, because he already knew Ma, and he admired you, said you were so clever when I told him about your job – I wanted him to know all my family, and Dougal would have been next. Oh, there was no question, no question, I tell you – we were going to be married!'

'So what happened?' Roz asked desperately, glancing at Flo, whose face was so blank with misery, warning bells were already beginning to sound that she would not be able to take this blow. 'Tell me what happened, Chrissie.'

'We went for a meal in a little café near the Meadows,' Chrissie said dully. 'It was packed out with festival folk, and Richard said he wanted to talk, but it was too noisy. So we went to the Meadows and sat down on a bench . . .'

'Yes?' asked Roz. 'He talked? What did he say?'

Chrissie's drenched blue eyes were looking away towards Flo, who was now lighting a cigarette, and Chrissie leaned forward.

'Ma, could you give me a cigarette, please? Pass one over, and the matches.'

'I'll not have you smoking, Chrissie!' cried Flo. 'You gave up and now you want to start again? No, it's bad for you. I should give it up too.'

'I need a cigarette, Ma. I'm not starting again, but I want a smoke now. And don't say I should have tea instead, because I don't want any tea.'

Chrissie, now red in the face, leaned over and snatched Flo's Woodbines and matches. With trembling fingers she lit a cigarette.

'There, that's better!' she cried. 'That helps; it'll get me through.'

She moved her gaze to Roz. 'You were asking what Richard said? He just took my hand and told me he'd been asked to move to England. The bank was opening a new branch in Newcastle and it would mean promotion.'

Chrissie gave a hard little laugh.

'I thought I knew what was coming next. He was going to ask me if I'd go with him. If I'd marry him. And I was just going to say, "Oh, yes. Oh, Richard, yes!" when he looked into my face and said, "I'm afraid this means goodbye, Chrissie." So, Roz, that's what he said.' She laughed again. '"Goodbye."'

As Flo gave a groan, Roz took Chrissie's hand and squeezed it. 'I can't believe it,' she said quietly. 'That he could be so cruel.'

But she did believe it. Thinking back to her meeting with Richard, she knew she'd sensed in him a disregard for others that had explained her distrust, and that had made her afraid for Chrissie. Yet now she'd been proved right it still seemed hard to take in that he could have been quite so callous. What had he thought? That Chrissie was just a waitress, of no account, enough to please him for a time before being put aside when he was tired? He must have known that she believed him to be serious. Couldn't he have let her down lightly, made it clear from the start there would be no future for them?

Roz felt her colour rise as anger swept through her and she longed to have Richard in front of her so she could tell him what she thought of him. As if he'd care! People like him were invincible; there was no way of touching him, because he didn't care.

'You're well shot of him,' Flo declared, putting out her cigarette and rising. 'He's a rotter, and that's all I can say. It's a good job he's not left you with a bairn on the way, eh?'

'Ma! As if there was any question o' that!' Chrissie cried. 'I'm not that sort o' fool!'

'Like I say, just as well. Look, if no one else wants a drink, I do. I'll make some cocoa.'

'Are you all right, Ma?' Roz whispered as she went to help, taking out cups and a pan for the milk.

'All right? When Chrissie's like she is?'

'You know what I mean, Ma.'

'I'm not going to be ill, Roz. Chrissie needs me and I'll be here for her. No need to worry about me.'

Thank God, thought Roz.

They all had cocoa – Chrissie too, and then she said she'd go to bed.

'And you needn't go to work on Monday,' Flo told her. 'Mrs Abbot will understand.'

'I'm not going back to the café, Ma.' Chrissie, standing with her hand on the doorknob ready to go to her bed, was looking so small, so much a shadow of her usual self that the hearts of Flo and Roz went out to her. But what could they do? Only time would help.

'I can't face it,' she added wearily. 'Working where he came . . . All the girls laughing behind my back because I thought I was so grand, eh? Catching someone like Richard.'

'They won't be laughing,' said Roz quickly. 'They'll feel sad for you, because they'll know you loved him. You weren't trying to be grand.'

'Aye, they're nice lassies,' put in Flo. 'They'll understand.'

'I still don't want to work where he used to come,' Chrissie declared. 'You can tell Mrs Abbot, Ma, that I'm not coming back.'

'See how you feel, pet. You might feel more like going back after a break.'

But Chrissie only shook her head and went to get ready for bed, while Roz and her mother looked at each other.

'This has been a bad day, eh?' asked Flo. 'And one I never thought I'd see. He always seemed the perfect gentleman.'

'He was no gentleman, Ma.'

'No, well, I'm thankful you're all right, eh? With your nice Jamie?'

'I hope so.' Roz collected the cocoa cups for washing as Flo stared. 'Why, you've no worries, have you?'

'Oh, no.' Roz's face relaxed. 'I can't wait to see him again when he comes back on Monday.'

Thirty-Two

As soon as Jamie came into the department on Monday morning he made straight for Roz's office, where he found her already waiting. They embraced and exchanged kisses, guilty though Roz felt about it, and soon freed herself from his arms and said she had something to tell him.

'Not bad news, I hope?' he asked lightly, though not smiling.

'Not good. First, I have to tell you that Norma knows about us.'

'Oh, Lord, that's all we need. How? How does she know about us?'

'Just by looking at us, seemingly. She told me on Saturday night before we went to a Fringe show.' Roz took Jamie's hands. 'But it's all right, she won't say anything – she's promised. We can trust her, Jamie. She wouldn't let us down.'

'Maybe not, but it's the first crack, isn't it? I mean, does she think anyone else suspects?'

'She's sure they don't. They're not likely to notice what she notices, she says.' Roz's grey eyes were searching Jamie's face. 'Anyway, you've always said not to worry, eh? That we'd be all right, and Mr Banks probably wouldn't throw us out?'

'I don't believe he would, but something like this – I have to admit – it wouldn't do me any good.' Jamie laughed without mirth. 'Five minutes into the job and I've fallen in love with my assistant?'

'Well, there's nothing we can do, unless . . .'

'Unless what?'

'I find another job.'

'Another job? Oh, God, no – that would mean I wouldn't see you.'

'Yes, you would. We'd meet like we do now, after work. It's what most folk do, Jamie.'

'You wouldn't want to go, though, would you? It wouldn't be fair. Look, let's leave it for now. See what happens. What's the other bad news, then? You said Norma was the first bit.'

'Oh, Jamie!' Roz heaved a deep sigh. 'It's my sister, Chrissie.'

Briefly, she told him what had happened, how Chrissie was devastated and unable to go to work, and he listened carefully and with sympathy, gently stroking her hands.

'What a cad!' he cried when she'd finished. 'You always did say you couldn't trust him. Why, I'd like to look him up and give him a punch he might remember! Smooth guy, wasn't he? I'd roughen him up a bit.'

'Not you,' she said, smiling weakly. 'No, he's the type to get away with whatever he does. All I want now is for him to go to Newcastle as soon as possible, and for Chrissie to get over him.' She moved abruptly to her desk and picked up the post. 'Listen, we'd better get on with some work. Every day I feel more and more guilty.'

'We're selling just as many houses as before, and organizing sales better than ever. You've no need to feel guilty, Roz.'

'How do we fit it in between kisses?' she asked, trying to sound amused. 'I think I might be better off in that new job I mentioned, after all.'

But Jamie only shook his head as he left her for his own office, his shoulders drooping, and it came to her that he was in one of his 'down' moods again. How different he'd been when he returned from the Borders last time, bouncing in with a cheese for her, wanting to take her out for a drink! This time there'd been nothing like that, and if he'd been more worried than she'd thought by her news about Norma, that in itself was a sign he wasn't his usual cheerful self. She could imagine a time when if she'd told him that he'd have laughed it off and said they'd nothing to worry about. Not now.

Had something happened on his weekend? Or was his mood just part of the frustration he'd expressed before when they'd discussed their situation? She resolved to speak to him and discover what was in his mind.

'How was your weekend?' she asked at their coffee break. 'You didn't say.'

He drank some coffee. 'Fine. I always like to see the Borders.'

'And your mother? Was she well?'

'Just the same. Baking, cooking.'

'Missing you, I expect.'

'Can't be helped, I'm afraid.'

'I was just thinking you seem a bit down again. Did anything happen? I mean, to upset you?'

He put his cup aside and stood up. 'No, why should it? Look, what is all this? Why do you think I seem down?'

'You're usually so cheerful, Jamie, sort of unworried. But lately, you've been – different. Not all the time, just now and again, you know, as though you've something on your mind.'

'Well, that's it, isn't it? I do have something on my mind. Haven't you?'

'Yes, but it doesn't stop me being happy to be with you.' Roz turned away. 'I do get a bit depressed sometimes, about the difficulties, but when I'm with you I feel better.'

'I'm the same.' He caught her hand and squeezed it. 'If I seem a bit depressed, it's over the difficulties, just like you.' He gave her one of his old smiles. 'We'll just have to sort them out, Roz. Of course, at the moment, you're sad about your sister – I wish there was something I could do to help.'

'There's nothing—' she was beginning when the door opened and Mr Wray looked round it.

'Busy?' he asked. 'Or can you spare a moment?'

'Just finishing coffee,' Jamie told him. 'Come on in.'

Thirty-Three

'Can I get you a coffee, Mr Wray?' Roz asked, but he shook his head.

'No, thanks, Miss Rainey. I've had my elevenses.'

Advancing into the room, the painfully thin Mr Wray took a seat in one of the chairs for clients, adjusted his glasses and gave an uncertain smile. When Roz made a move to excuse herself to return to her own office, he held up a bony hand.

'No, Miss Rainey, please stay. I really want to talk to both of you.'

As Roz instantly looked towards Jamie, she was wondering if he was feeling the same sort of sudden, ominous sensation inside that was gripping her, but as his eyes left hers and met Mr Wray's, he appeared totally calm.

'So, what can we do for you?' he asked pleasantly, at which Mr Wray fingered the frames of his glasses again.

'It's a bit awkward, really. I feel I may sound as though I'm intruding where I have no right . . . It's just that I know I should speak to you – to both of you – and I hope you'll take what I say as concern for your own well-being at Tarrel and Thom's.'

This is it, thought Roz, this is the blow falling. Somehow, she'd always known it would, but now that it had she felt curiously resigned. It had never been possible for her and Jamie to meet, to feel as they did without someone discovering their relationship, and if Norma didn't count because she wouldn't tell, Mr Wray would be very different.

Not daring now to look at Jamie, Roz sat very still, keeping her eyes on Mr Wray, who was himself in fact having difficulty knowing where to look.

'The thing is, Mr Shield, Miss Rainey,' he began, 'I happened to see you both the other evening when you didn't see me. You were, I think I may say, rather preoccupied with each other.'

'Mind if I ask where this was, Mr Wray?' asked Jamie levelly.

'That little restaurant, the Rowan, on the Peebles road. I'd gone there with my wife and a cousin we were entertaining. I saw you as soon as we arrived and meant to come over, but then I realized that you hadn't seen me and maybe didn't want to, and I said nothing.'

Mr Wray waited a moment, perhaps expecting a comment, but when none came he cleared his throat and went on.

'Now, I do realize that every member of staff here is entitled to a private life. Tarrel's doesn't own people body and soul. Nevertheless, Mr Banks has to consider the efficiency of the firm and there's no doubt that when personal friendships develop, efficiency can be affected. That's why such friendships – or relationships, if you like – are not encouraged, particularly when people work together, or, rather, wouldn't be encouraged if there'd been any.' Mr Wray halted. 'Yours is the first.'

'On the strength of seeing us together in a restaurant, you believe we have a friendship that might damage efficiency?' Jamie asked, still keeping his tone level.

Mr Wray now fixed him with his gaze. 'Mr Shield, are you denying there's something special between you and Miss Rainey? I did see you together, I may remind you.'

Jamie was silent. Finally, not looking at either Mr Wray or Roz, he sighed deeply. 'No,' he said at last. 'I'm not denying it. We've become . . . attached to each other.'

'We never meant it to happen,' Roz said bravely. 'It just did.'

'That's true,' Jamie murmured. 'But I take the blame. I knew it wouldn't be accepted here but, as Miss Rainey says, it happened and you can't put feelings back.'

He looked away, his face as serious as Roz had ever seen it. 'I do blame myself,' he said, his voice low. 'I'll always do that.'

Mr Wray looked down at his hands, then slowly raised his eyes. 'The point is, Mr Shield, what can be done?'

'That depends on what you do, Mr Wray. I suppose you'll be informing Mr Banks?'

'No, I don't think so.'

'No?' As he glanced quickly across to Roz, Jamie's eyes were widening. 'You're not going to tell him?'

'I've no wish to bring him in at this stage. All I want to do today is to warn you about the situation here and to tell you to take care.

For a start, be very sure that your work is in no way affected. Can you promise me that?'

'Yes!' Roz cried promptly. 'Work has to come first, we both know that, Mr Wray. But we've discussed something else, Jamie and I, that might be best for us.'

'Oh, no,' Jamie murmured. 'No, Roz, I didn't say it would be best. Don't suggest it.'

'I have to,' she declared, and turned to Mr Wray. 'What we thought – well, I thought – is that I should leave. Mr Shield is the professional, he hasn't been here long and it would be a shame if he had to go. But I'm sure I could find another job and then there'd be no problem.' She sat back in her chair, breathing hard. 'That's the way I see it.'

Mr Wray studied her for a long moment. 'It would also be a shame if you had to leave, Miss Rainey, because I know you're happy here and you're very efficient. We'd be sorry to lose you, but you're right, it would be the best solution to your problems.'

He rose to his feet and moved towards the door.

'I must say, I feel somewhat happier now about this matter. I wasn't looking forward to having to speak to you.'

'Mr Wray, thank you,' Roz said earnestly. 'Thank you for your understanding.'

'We're very grateful to you,' Jamie said. 'Very.'

'That's quite all right.' The lawyer smiled briefly. 'You may not believe it, but I was young myself once. These things happen – they're not difficult to understand.'

'Well, what do you make of that?' Jamie asked when they were alone. 'John Wray is human, after all.'

'I can't believe he's not going to tell Mr Banks,' Roz whispered. 'He's been really nice, eh? And we've been lucky.'

'Lucky, when you're leaving me?'

She hesitated, her eyes searching his face, which had still not really lightened. 'I think it's the only thing to do, Jamie. If we want to keep on.'

'Keep on?'

'Keep on loving each other.'

'I'll always love you,' he said quietly. 'Always.'

'But for now, maybe we shouldn't go out so much? And definitely stick to what we said, about being above reproach at work.'

'I agree. But we can meet sometimes? I mean, what else will we have?'

'Maybe at weekends? Just till I find a job?'

'What a future!'

'When we're not both working at Tarrel's we can go out whenever we like – remember that.'

It was all that made the future bearable, Roz reflected, returning to her office, for it was only the thought that she would be able to meet Jamie freely after she'd left Tarrel's that made it possible for her to imagine going.

Thirty-Four

It seemed right, somehow, that when the lovely summer faded into autumn, the weather should match the mood of Roz and Jamie, Chrissie and Flo. There were golden days, it was true, but still the feeling of melancholy in the air, with the festival over, the exotic visitors departed, the Tattoo stands taken down from the castle to be put away for another year. What would come next? Falling leaves, days shortening, the first fires to be lit – all anyone could do was accept the new season and try to look on the bright side. After all, they did it every year.

At least there was comfort for Roz in knowing that her mother had not gone into a state of depression again, though she couldn't of course be anything but sad over Chrissie's continuing misery. True to her word, Chrissie had not returned to the Café Sunshine, and had instead found herself a job as waitress in a George Street restaurant, much to Flo's disappointment.

'It's not the same at the café without her,' she complained to Roz. 'And she'd have been welcomed back. She needn't have left.'

'Richard used to go there, Ma, that's what she minds. You have to let her do what she thinks is best.'

'Aye, well it would be best if she could stop thinking about that Richard at all. Dougal was all for giving him a punch or two, you know, if he hadn't already gone to Newcastle.'

'As though that would have done any good!'

'Would have done Dougal good, he says.' Flo sighed. 'Och, what a worry it is, having a family! Why, even you are looking for another job, Roz, and I thought you were settled.'

'I explained how things are, Ma. It'll be better for me and Jamie if we don't work together. Though I haven't found anything suitable yet.'

'How about finding wedding bells suitable?' asked Flo, narrowing her eyes as she looked at Roz, who merely shrugged and laughed.

'No wedding bells at the moment, Ma. All I'm looking for is the right sort of post. Might take some time.'

And so it did, for October was well advanced before a likely job for Roz turned up in a New Town law firm requiring a typist and assistant for their property department. Exactly what she was looking for, she told Jamie, as he prepared to leave for a valuation in Murrayfield – she would get her application in that very day.

'I suppose I should be pleased,' he said gloomily.

'You know what it will mean if I get it,' she told him. 'Freedom!'

'True,' he admitted, brightening, and would have kissed her, except that they no longer kissed at work. 'Can't come too soon, then. Better type out your application now.'

'By the time you come back it will be in the post.'

She was not to know, as she settled down at her typewriter, that by the time Jamie came back to go to lunch, her life – and his – would be changed for ever.

It was some time after eleven, as Roz was sealing up her application for the post, when Norma came into her office, her expression rather wary.

'Roz, there's a young lady at reception who wants to see Mr Shield.'

'A young lady?' Roz looked puzzled. 'He's not expecting anyone. Did she say what she wants?'

'No, but her name is Miss Drever. Ella Drever. Mean anything?'

Roz shook her head. 'Better tell her to make an appointment.'

'I wondered if you might see her. Tell her when Mr Shield'll be back.'

And find out who she is, was Norma's unspoken message; clearly, Roz was intrigued.

'All right, Norma. Show her in.'

Moving into the main room, Roz positioned herself near Jamie's desk and waited.

'Miss Drever,' announced Norma, before reluctantly withdrawing as a dark-haired young woman in a tweed suit and brown felt hat advanced to shake hands with Roz.

Tall and well-built, she was probably in her late twenties, strong-looking with large, gloveless hands and a look of competence. Not pretty, but attractive, with wide brown eyes and a friendly smile.

'Ella Drever,' she said in a pleasant voice with a Scottish accent Roz could not for the moment place, until she realized it was like Jamie's. A Borders accent.

'Good morning, Miss Drever,' Roz said politely, offering her one of the customers' chairs. 'I'm Roz Rainey, Mr Shield's assistant – how can I help?'

'Well, I just wanted to see Jamie – surprise him, you know. I came up from Kelder yesterday, but he doesn't know I'm in Edinburgh. I only got a place at the conference at the last moment.'

'Conference?' Taking Jamie's seat at his desk, Roz was becoming aware of something vague beginning to trouble her at the back of her mind, but she kept her smile welcoming.

'A nursing conference on special care right here in this very street, just along from Jamie's office!' Miss Drever's eyes were shining. 'Just right for me! I'm a staff nurse, you see. Special care is what I do and I applied straight away, but I only got in with a cancellation – no time to let Jamie know I was coming. So I thought I'd surprise him anyway. Call in this morning and get him to take me to lunch before the afternoon seminar.'

'I'm afraid he's out on a valuation at the moment, but he'll be back by lunchtime. If you like, you could wait in our clients' waiting room.'

'Oh, that'd be very kind.' Ella Drever jumped to her feet. 'I'd appreciate that.'

'I'll take you along, then.'

'And you'll tell him I'm here?'

'Of course. It will be a nice surprise for him, if you're friends, to see you in Edinburgh.'

'Oh, I think you could say we were friends,' Ella replied, laughing. 'We're probably going to get married one of these days!'

Married. The word reverberated between them as though someone somewhere had struck a great brass gong. Married. Had she said that? Roz put out a hand and clutched the edge of Jamie's desk, which strangely seemed to be rearing up to meet her as blood drained from her face. Was she in a dream? A play? Something where she was acting a part and Ella Drever was the star? 'Going to get married one of these days' she had said, but of course it wasn't true. Couldn't be. Couldn't be . . .

'Miss Rainey, are you all right?' she could hear Ella calling though the mists that were closing round, and then heard nothing at all.

When she opened her eyes, it was to see her own feet in her own black shoes with little black bows, for her head was down between her knees and she was being supported by the strong hands of Ella Drever.

'It's all right,' she heard her say a long way off. 'You felt a bit faint, eh? But you'll be fine. Think you can raise your head?'

'I – don't know . . .'

Slowly, Roz looked up to meet Ella's concerned brown eyes and, after a moment or two, as the strong hands continued to support her, began to struggle to her feet. Oh, see, the floor was rising, she was going to fall again – but Ella was guiding her into a leather chair. As she sank into it, she felt her head begin to clear.

'Thank you,' she whispered, determined not to let Ella see more weakness. 'I'm all right now. I don't know what . . . came over me.'

Didn't she? Didn't she know that her whole world had fallen into shifting sands because of those few light words from Ella Drever?

'I think you need a cup of tea,' Ella was saying firmly. 'Hot, sweet tea – is there anyone who could make it for you? That girl in Reception?'

'Norma, yes, she'd make it – and coffee for you . . .'

'Heavens, don't worry about me! Look, you just wait here and rest and I'll see if I can find her.'

But Ella didn't find Norma, for as she hurried to the door, Jamie came through it. When he stopped short at the sight of her, she threw her arms around him.

'Surprise, surprise! Oh, Jamie, lovely to see you!'

Thirty-Five

'Ella!'

As he freed himself from her hold and looked from her to Roz, he appeared so utterly stricken, as conscious of a world collapsing as Roz herself, that she might have taken pleasure in the revenge of seeing him so – except that she was too wounded to feel anything but pain.

'Ella, what are you doing here?' Jamie asked hoarsely. 'You didn't tell me you were coming.'

'No, as I said, it was a surprise. I'm at a nursing conference here, in this very street – got a place right out of the blue! There was no time to let you know.'

Scarcely seeming to listen, Jamie was already moving to where Roz was motionless in her leather chair. He looked down at her, his eyes fearfully searching her face.

'Roz,' he murmured, 'you've met Ella, then?' He managed a smile. 'A friend from Kelder.'

'Oh, yes, I've met Ella.' Roz's voice low. 'We had a talk.'

'A talk?'

As he grew pale, Ella moved to stand beside him.

'Miss Rainey's not well, Jamie. She feels a bit faint. I was just going to get her some tea.'

'Faint?' Jamie put his hand to his brow. 'You felt faint, Roz?'

'Yes, but I'm all right now.' Her eyes resolutely not meeting his, Roz turned to Ella. 'Miss Drever's been so kind, helping me.'

'Goodness, I didn't do anything!' Ella cried. 'But you're looking better now, Miss Rainey, got a wee bit of colour back. Still could do with that tea, though. You stay there and I'll go find some.'

'Don't worry about it. I can have it when you go to lunch.' Roz, dry-lipped, added, 'With Jamie.'

'How can we leave you?' he asked, desperately. 'You don't look well. I think I should take you home.'

Her eyes, like stones, finally met his. 'I don't want you to,' was all she said, but the words and the way she said them were enough to bring a mottled flush to his pale cheeks, and he turned away.

'You should go home and rest,' Ella told Roz, her gaze now thoughtful as it moved between Roz and Jamie. 'You've maybe had a shock.'

A shock? She'd used that word? Yes, which meant – must mean – she knew or suspected all that Jamie had tried to hide from her. To many women, it would have been obvious from the start, but Roz guessed that Ella was not like many women. She would not see her sweetheart's assistant as any sort of threat until it was made plain, and what could be plainer than the assistant collapsing as soon as she heard the word 'marriage'? It had to happen, Roz argued to herself. Just like Roz, Ella must suffer, because of Jamie. I shall never forgive him, thought Roz. But would Ella?

'I'll take a taxi home,' she announced, rising slowly to her feet. 'Thank you, Miss Drever, for all your kindness.'

'No need to thank me – but do call me Ella.'

'Ella, then. I'm sorry if I've delayed your lunch.'

Steadfastly not looking at Jamie, Roz moved towards her office. 'Goodbye, then.'

'Roz!' cried Jamie, stretching out his hand to her, but without looking at either him or his hand she went into her office and closed the door.

'Jamie, are we going to lunch, then?' Ella asked after a moment of him staring at Roz's door.

'Yes, I think we should,' he answered at last. 'There are – things to say.'

Her eyes wide with apprehension, she put her large, capable hand on his arm and waited, but he said no more and together they left Tarrel and Thom's for a lunch neither of them could eat.

A short time later, Roz called for a taxi on the property department phone and, having left a scribbled note at Reception where neither Norma nor Miss Calder seemed to be around, departed for home. She had said that she felt better but, sitting in the taxi, making sure she had enough in her purse for the driver's tip, she in fact felt much worse. As though without the effort of keeping face before Ella and Jamie she had somehow come apart, as though her strength had left her and she could scarcely face the pain that had been hers since she'd recovered from her faint.

It wasn't just that Jamie had betrayed her, it was that he'd destroyed himself in doing so, had taken away from her all that he'd seemed to her. Where was the sweet, cheerful personality she'd loved so much? The smile, the open face, the genuine kindness in the soft brown eyes? Destroyed by the one word of his other victim: 'Married'. Ella had thought they were to be married 'one of these days', when all the time . . . all the time . . .

In spite of herself, Roz couldn't stem the tears gathering in her eyes, and when the taxi stopped at 35, Deller Street, she kept her head down as she paid the driver and hoped he wouldn't notice. He did, though.

'Got a nasty cold, eh?' he asked jauntily. 'A wee dram's the only thing for that, believe you me!'

'I'm sure,' she muttered, hurrying to the front door with her key, rather wishing she might have drowned her sorrows with a far from wee dram – as though anybody could get whisky these days.

Oh, but how thankful she was to be home, especially as there was no one there, Chrissie and Ma both being at work. As she changed from her office clothes into a jumper and tweed skirt and boiled the kettle for tea, she didn't feel better, only relieved that she could let go and give up all pretence of coping, even lie on her bed and maybe sleep.

When she'd drunk her tea and stretched out on her bed, she did in fact try to sleep, but it was no use. Her thoughts were on a treadmill, going round and round, and the pain that was heartache was just as sharp. Would be for some time to come, she told herself drearily, but then was jolted upright by the ringing of the front door bell.

Would it be Jamie, come to explain himself? No, he wouldn't dare. Her face flushed at the thought. But supposing it was a message about Ma, or something? Slowly, she stood up and, with her hand to her throbbing head, went down to the main door to find Mrs Atkinson already there, shouting, 'Yes? What is it?' at the man on the doorstep. Who was, in fact, Jamie Shield.

Thirty-Six

Of course, she had to let him in. There was no way she could stand arguing with him in front of the interested eyes of Mrs Atkinson, who would already be wondering why Roz was at home during the day and who the young man she seemed about to entertain might be? And why were they not exchanging words, as Roz let him in and closed the door after him?

'All right, Roz?' Mrs Atkinson eagerly asked.

'Fine, thanks, Mrs Atkinson. Mr Shield's just called round with something about work,' Roz answered, keeping her face averted, though she had no hope that her ravaged face would have gone unnoticed. 'This way, Mr Shield.'

With a polite nod to Mrs Atkinson, Jamie followed Roz up the stairs to the first-floor flat, where she showed him into the living room.

'Thank you for seeing me,' he said, standing very still, his face, like hers, showing the effects of the ordeal of the day.

'I had to,' she said coldly, 'but I don't want to talk to you. We've nothing to say to each other now.'

'That's not true, Roz! I have to talk to you – you have to listen to me. Please, let me tell you how it was, how it's all happened. Please, Roz. I'm not the monster you think I am!'

'I don't think you're a monster, just a cheat and a sham. Someone I trusted and who let me down. And Ella, too. I wonder how she's feeling now, at her seminar? I suppose she does know . . . about me?'

He lowered his eyes. 'She knows. Knows I love you.'

'Oh, don't!' Roz cried. 'Don't talk like that any more!'

'You have to listen to me,' he said doggedly. 'At least, give me that.'

They were both silent for some moments, then Roz sighed.

'You'd better sit down,' she told him.

Looking away from each other as they sat apart, they were silent again, until Jamie began to speak.

'The thing is, Roz, Ella and I have known each other all our lives. We went to the same school, our mothers are friends, and I played rugby with Ella's brother. We were all sort of intertwined. Somehow, as we grew up, it just became accepted that we were a couple. There was no more to it than that. And when the war came and I was called up, Ella started nursing. We wrote letters and all that, but I used to wonder sometimes how things would be for us when the war was over. Turned out, they were just the same.'

He paused and shrugged a little.

'I didn't mind. I suppose it was what I expected, but I think now I should have asked myself, why didn't we get married? There always seemed to be something in the way – my studies, Ella's nursing exams – it was always going to be someday. Then I got the job at Tarrel's and couldn't see her so much – she lives in at the hospital and couldn't come up to Edinburgh.'

Turning his head, Jamie fastened his eyes on Roz's face.

'And, of course, at Tarrel's, I met you. That changed everything.'

'Are you trying to tell me that you and Ella were never really in love?' Roz asked curtly. 'You forget – I've met her. She didn't give me the impression that she doesn't care for you.'

'I'm not saying she doesn't care for me, but what you and I have, Roz, is quite different from what Ella and I had. Honestly, it is.'

'Oh, of course, you're in love with me, aren't you?' Roz's tone was icy. 'Well, I don't want to hear about it because none of it was real. If it had been real you'd have told me about Ella, and you'd have told her about me. But you didn't.'

'I couldn't!' he cried. 'I couldn't tell you about Ella because I thought I'd lose you, and I couldn't tell Ella about you because . . . I couldn't hurt her.'

'So you thought she cared enough for you that it would hurt her to know you'd met someone else?'

'Yes,' he said after a silence, as he ran his hand over his face. 'That's true. You've seen those eyes of hers – those brown eyes. So trusting. That first weekend when I went back to Kelder I thought I'd tell her, but I couldn't do it, and then for some reason I didn't feel so bad about it. But the next weekend, when I was with her, I felt so guilty, I knew I had to make the break. But I still never did. The whole thing was like a nightmare, Roz, just a nightmare.' He raised appealing eyes. 'That's why I was what you called "down". You kept asking me what was wrong, but what could I say?'

'You could have told me the truth,' she said quietly. 'Maybe we might have had a chance, then. But it's too late now.'

'No, Roz, don't say that, please. I've explained how it was.'

'All I know is I don't trust you, Jamie. I can't.'

'You can, Roz, you can! Something like this will never happen again, I promise you, because I've learned a bitter lesson.' He grasped her hand. 'So, you see, it's not too late for us. We love each other, don't we? In spite of everything, that's still true.'

'You must face facts, Jamie. We have no future, you and I. All I want now is to say goodbye.'

'How can you want that, if you still love me? Look, I know I've behaved stupidly – badly – but nobody regrets that more than me. Please, Roz, don't throw away what we have. There'll be nothing underhand any more, we can make things work—'

'Goodbye, Jamie.' Roz moved to the flat door and opened it. 'We won't be working together much longer – I'm going to send off my application for that job I saw, and if I don't get it I'll get something else.'

'You needn't do that,' Jamie said quietly. 'I'm the one who'll be leaving.'

'You?'

'Yes. If everything's over between us, I don't want to work at Tarrel's any more. There was some talk when I was down last time of my old firm opening a new office – it would be a chance for me.'

'I see.' Roz held the door open. 'Good luck, then.'

His face struggling to contain his emotions, he gazed at her for a long moment, then turned away and went down the stairs while she listened to every step. When the outer door had banged behind him, she stood like a statue, feeling as cold, until at last she moved to her bed, where she flung herself down and let the tears flow.

'Oh, Jamie,' she sobbed, 'Jamie.'

And it was there Flo and Chrissie found her when they returned from work, and the three of them clung together, trying to bring comfort, but they all knew in their hearts that there would be no comfort for some time to come.

Thirty-Seven

It was a warm May evening in 1951 and Mrs Burr's art class was hard at work, painting the portrait of the Art School caretaker. He was not young, which made it easier, for an earlier subject had been a seventeen-year-old student they'd managed to make appear at least thirty-five every time they added a little shadow to her lovely, unlined face.

'So frustrating, do you remember?' Roz whispered to Norma, who'd joined the class with her in the previous September, glad to see her interested in something new after her unhappy love affair. 'This chap's much easier, eh?'

'Aye, he's got so many wrinkles, it doesn't matter what we add in,' Norma agreed. 'But I don't mind having a go at any subject, do you? The main thing is to get painting, to have an interest outside work.'

'Very true,' Roz agreed, smiling to herself, for though Norma had enjoyed painting Mrs Burr's earlier cones and spheres, still-lifes and bunches of leaves, her real interest now was something quite different. Oh, yes, a certain young man named Tim Clunie, who sat behind them in the class, painting in a great, bold, dashing style and frequently calling out remarks to Roz and Norma, but mainly Norma. In fact, he had already taken her for a drink after class several times. Roz had always excused herself, not wanting to play gooseberry and hoping that this could be the real thing for Norma, who so desperately wanted a 'young man' in her life. It would be wonderful to see her happy.

As for herself – well, she wasn't unhappy any more. She did have serious anxieties concerning Dougal, who, after all he'd said about never fighting battles, had been posted to the war in Korea, and also for her mother, who was only just coming to terms with that, but the searing pain of her split with Jamie was over. Now she could get on with her life, which, if it was not very exciting, at least did not hurt.

It was true, there'd been disappointment, when she'd crazily thought Mr Banks might just possibly have considered her for Jamie's job after he'd left for the Borders, but she'd never really had hopes of it. When, therefore, he'd appointed the plump candidate at the original interview to run the department, she'd accepted it with good grace. She and Mr Appin got on together from the start, for he proved as easy-going as Mr MacKenna, and the calmness of the new arrangement after the roller-coaster of the time with Jamie quite suited her, she being something of a convalescent.

But then she'd begun to look around for new interests, this evening art class being one, though she was also considering trying a second class in social studies in the autumn. All in all, life was becoming bright again for her and for Chrissie, who now had a new man in her life, if Bob MacGarry from up the stairs at Deller Street could be called new. But Chrissie seemed very happy again, except, like Roz, she worried about Dougal. And, of course, Flo.

Time was passing and Mrs Burr, a sweet-faced woman in her fifties, was making her rounds, putting a touch here, a touch there on everyone's canvases, always being very diplomatic in making suggestions and never upsetting people so that they didn't want to return.

'Oh, very bold!' Roz and Norma heard her commenting on Tim's work. 'I'm not sure if the Cubist style quite suits our Mr Muir, but it's certainly very interesting. Well done! And Norma, my dear, how did you get on? Why, I think you've caught Mr Muir nicely, though you've perhaps made him a little too serious, don't you think? If we were to curl his mouth up a little, maybe? Just a flick of the brush – there!

'And Roz, you've got his eyes just right, haven't you? Deep set, quite dark in colour. But does it seem to you that you've given him a beard, instead of just a little shadow? You can leave adjusting it for now, though. We're running out of time.'

Moving to the front of the class, Mrs Burr clapped her hands for attention. 'Now, listen everyone, we only have one more class before we end the course and then have our outing. This year, it's to be to Kirkcudbright – the artists' town, as it's called. Please give me your names next week so that I can book numbers for the coach. Wash all your brushes and leave your canvases on their easels as usual, but first join with me in giving Mr Muir a big hand for being such a wonderful subject!'

There was loud applause for the caretaker, who came down from the dais rubbing his stiff legs and giving an embarrassed smile, after which Tim, curly black hair on end and paint down one cheek, came over to Norma and Roz.

'You going to Kirkcudbright?' he asked, looking at Norma.

'Oh, yes,' she answered quickly. 'How about you?'

'You bet! Fancy a drink again tonight?' He turned to Roz. 'How about you, Roz?'

'Thanks, but I've got to get home,' Roz replied kindly as she gathered up her brushes, but Norma, blushing, said she'd love to go for a drink.

'Right, let's get tidied up, then. Usual place, eh?'

'Usual place,' Norma echoed, with a beaming smile.

Departing for her tram, Roz was also smiling.

Fingers crossed all goes well there, she thought. And fingers crossed, too, that she would find her mother in a good mood after she'd attended a therapy session at the hospital that day. Following Dougal's posting to Korea she'd been so down that her doctor had recommended a new idea for treatment, which was meeting and talking with other sufferers. After initial hostility, Flo seemed mainly to enjoy it, though as usual with her, you could never tell how things would go. Sometimes she was in a good mood when she returned, sometimes she wasn't. Roz would just have to wait and see how she was that evening.

Thirty-Eight

As soon as she went into the flat, she could tell that this was not going to be one of the good times. Her mother's face was blank of all expression, but her blue eyes on Roz were cold.

'Had a good time?' she asked. 'Enjoyed your painting? You're usually full of it.'

'Yes, I did enjoy it,' Roz replied, taking off her jacket. 'We were painting a portrait of the caretaker this evening.'

'The caretaker?' Flo laughed. 'Not a very expensive model, then.'

'He was a very good model, as a matter of fact. Held his pose well.' Roz washed her hands and filled the kettle. 'And Mrs Burr's fixed on a place for our outing – it's Kirkcudbright, the artists' town, as folk call it.'

'If that's tea you're making, I don't want any. I had enough at the hospital, with all those folk nattering on. Some of them just like the sound of their own voice, I sometimes think.'

'Well, I want some tea,' Roz said, preparing it. 'And why are you complaining about the other people at the session? You usually like talking to them.'

'Oh, I don't know, tonight I just couldn't be bothered.' Flo moved her head restlessly. 'I keep wondering how Dougal is managing out there in that foreign land. I mean, why do our Scottish soldiers have to go and fight somewhere like that? It's nothing to do with us if those Koreans want to fight amongst themselves, eh?'

'I think the United Nations stepped in when the North Koreans invaded the South, and the Americans and other countries sent in troops to help the South. It's not just our soldiers who are out there, Ma.'

'Seems to me it's a shame anybody is, then. And we just go on with our lives while Dougal's out there, putting up with I don't know what. Look at you, for instance, all excited about going to Kirkcudbright, and Chrissie out enjoying herself with Bob MacGarry!'

'Doesn't mean we're not thinking of Dougal as well,' Roz said, drinking her tea and keeping calm with difficulty. 'And talking of Chrissie, I think I hear her now.'

How pretty she is these days, Roz thought as her sister came in, smiling, her bright hair springing from her brow, her blue eyes shining. So different from the way she'd looked after Richard had left her, when she'd appeared so weary, so woebegone – almost plain. Seemed Bob MacGarry had worked some sort of magic on her since he'd persuaded her to go out with him, even when at first she'd said she wasn't interested. He was interested, though, and maybe that had been the balm that was needed to soothe Chrissie's wounded heart. His interest, his admiration, had certainly given her her looks back, and now probably much more. Were they in love? Roz thought they must be, and this time the love was not one-sided. This time, Roz prayed, all would go well for her sister, and in fact wasn't really worried that it would not.

'Hello, you folks!' cried Chrissie, taking off her light coat. 'I'm back!'

'So we see,' said Flo. 'What was on at the pictures, then?'

'A Hitchcock film. *Strangers on a Train*. Really creepy. I was so scared!'

'And enjoyed yourself no end,' laughed Roz. 'Why didn't you bring Bob in for a cup of tea?'

'He said he'd better not. He wants an early start tomorrow.' Chrissie felt the teapot. 'Cold, eh? I'll make some cocoa instead. Ma, how was the therapy?'

Flo shrugged. 'Waste o' time, in my opinion. What's the good o' talking?'

Chrissie and Roz exchanged glances.

'Now, why say that, Ma?' Chrissie asked. 'You've found it useful before and the doctors recommend it.'

'Doctors.' Flo rose. 'I'm beginning to wonder just how much they know. Anyway, I'm off to my bed.'

'Have some cocoa first, eh? Might make you sleep well.'

'No, I want to go now, rest my legs. But you girls might think about getting a letter off to your brother sometime. You know how much letters mean to him.'

'Ma, I've just sent one!' Roz cried. 'And Chrissie added a note. You don't need to remind us.'

'All right, just as long as you don't forget him. Goodnight, then. And put the lights out, eh?'

'Bad day?' asked Chrissie, making the cocoa, when Flo had left them.

'Seems like it,' Roz answered. 'But you know she has good days and bad days. We've just got to weather 'em.'

'Shame, when she was doing so well before Dougal had to go to Korea. I thought she was better.'

'She'll get better again. It's like being on a see-saw, up and down, up and down.'

'And at the minute, down. Hey, I never asked you about your painting, Roz. How did it go?'

'Fine. We did the caretaker's portrait tonight.'

'The caretaker? Bet that was a first for him.'

'He's very good. And we've got our outing organized. It's to Kirkcudbright.'

'Kircoobray.' Chrissie mimicked Roz's correct pronunciation of the name. 'That'll be nice for you, eh?'

'Very. I'm looking forward to it,' Roz smiled.

Thirty-Nine

'Kirkcudbright?'

When Roz told him where she was going the following day, a Saturday, Angus Appin looked up from his desk with interest. Only thirty-three, his double chin and stout figure added to his years, but on the credit side, perhaps because he was plump, he also appeared pleasant and affable, which went down well with the clients.

'Now, that's a nice place!' he commented. 'Pattie and I had a weekend there once and really enjoyed it. Don't they call it the artists' town?'

'Yes, seemingly a whole bunch of artists came over from Glasgow to paint there because of the light and everything being so picturesque. Our evening class teacher thought it'd be ideal for our outing.'

'Of course, you're an artist too, Miss Rainey. You'll be sure to enjoy it, then.'

'I don't know about being an artist,' she said with a laugh, 'but I am looking forward to seeing what the artists saw that made them want to paint Kirkcudbright. And, of course, where they lived, if possible.'

'Because you like houses. I remember you saying that when I

came to the interview – the one I failed.' Mr Appin locked his desk
and stood up, frowning slightly. 'Often wonder what went wrong
here for Wonder Boy Shield. No one ever says.'

'Nothing went wrong,' Roz said quickly. 'It was just matters at
home, I think. He wanted to go back.'

'Got a job in the Borders now, hasn't he?'

'I'm afraid I don't know.' Roz put on her jacket. 'Time to go.
Have a nice weekend, Mr Appin. Isn't it nice we get the whole of
Saturday off now?'

'Haven't I heard mutterings that it was about time?' Mr Appin
grinned. 'Enjoy Kirkcudbright, Miss Rainey!'

'I will, Mr Appin.'

Seeing Norma at Reception, Roz stopped. 'All set for tomorrow,
Norma? We've got an early start.'

'Suits me. I'm just keen to get going.'

Norma, like Chrissie, was looking very pretty, possibly for the
same reason – a young man had singled her out to be with and
found her attractive. Now why is it always that way round? Roz
mused, after she'd said she'd see Norma on the coach early the next
morning. Why did you never hear of a young man suddenly looking
handsome because some girl had asked him out? Maybe, one day,
women wouldn't be so dependent on men's interest as they were at
the present time, but Roz had the feeling that day was some way
off still.

Not to worry, she wasn't dependent on any man now. She was
living her life and looking to her own future, and that was the way
she wanted it. On the tram home she was feeling quite cheerful,
until she remembered Mr Appin's words on Jamie. Over him as she
was, she still didn't like talking about him, still didn't want to know
just where he was and what he was doing. She'd made a clean break,
and that, too, was the way she wanted it.

'All set for tomorrow?' Flo asked that evening when she returned
from work. 'You've a long drive, eh?'

'Part of the outing, seeing the scenery.'

Flo hesitated a little, her pale eyes moving everywhere except to
Roz. 'Look, I'm not going to make a thing of it, but I'm sorry I've
not been so easy these past few weeks. It's just that things come
over me and I feel – well, you know how I feel.'

'Ma, it's all right, I understand. We all understand.'

'Aye, but it's funny, eh? All the worry's still there for Dougal, but today I feel better, as though I can manage, yet nothing's changed. There's no rhyme or reason in it.'

'If you're feeling better, that's what matters,' Roz said earnestly. 'You just have to take each day as it comes, eh? And if today's a good day, that's grand.'

'Have a good day yourself then, tomorrow. I've never been to Kirkcudbright, but I've heard it's very pretty, with a harbour and sweet little houses. Don't you go fancying living there, though.'

'Now why would I do that?'

'Well, if you're thinking of being an artist, you might.'

'Honestly, Ma, I'm what they call a Sunday painter!' Roz gave a cheerful laugh. 'I could never be a professional. All I want is to work with property.'

'Still dreaming of lovely houses?'

'Not for myself. I've given up on that.'

'Just as well. Dream of something possible, is my advice.'

'At the minute, I'm not dreaming at all,' said Roz.

Forty

As soon as their coach arrived in Kirkcudbright on a perfect May morning, Mrs Burr's students scattered. As she had explained, there was to be no formal organization of the day. They were all free to see what they wanted, but perhaps they would like to take note of the quality of the light in this town, which was that of a place by the sea, for Kirkcudbright was not only by a river but had a harbour overlooking the Irish Sea. The artists, many from Glasgow, who had formed their own colony in the town, had been drawn by that light and the beauty of the area, and all the students, therefore, should try to get a feel of what had attracted the artists of long ago and still attracted the artists of today.

'What to do first, then?' Roz asked Norma and Tim as they stood together in the centre of the town, guidebooks at the ready. 'I'd like to see where Jessie M. King lived. You know she did those beautiful illustrations for children's books? The guide book says she had a house in one of the closes off the High Street.'

'I'd like to see her house, too,' said Norma, looking at Tim, who shrugged.

'Not really my style. I'd rather see that old ruin over there – MacLellan's Castle.'

As they turned to study the roofless tower house near at hand, Tim consulted his guidebook. 'Says this MacLellan man was once very powerful, and built his castle in 1582. Might get some ideas for pictures there. Or maybe from the Tollbooth – it used to be a prison. Good and dark, eh? Just right for me.'

'Could just be offices now,' said Norma doubtfully. 'I think I'd rather see the pretty houses in the High Street.'

'Why don't we split up, then, and meet for lunch?' asked Roz. 'There's a nice-looking café over there.'

It was agreed that they should do that, and while Tim went looking for ideas for his own paintings, Roz and Norma enjoyed themselves walking in the wide High Street, soaking up the atmosphere, admiring the houses and closes, particularly Greengate, where the exquisite book illustrator, Jessie M. King, had lived with her husband until her recent death.

Jessie came from Glasgow, Roz had read, and had arrived in Kirkcudbright around the same time as the so-called Glasgow Boys, one of whom was the well-known E.A. Hornel, whose home and beautiful garden – Broughton House – was open to visitors. After lunch, Roz told Norma she would like to look round it and also see one of the museums, but again, Tim had other ideas.

'I'd rather go to the harbour, if you don't mind. They say it's one of the best around here, and I might sketch a few boats. But you go ahead with what you want, girls. Don't mind me.'

'Maybe I'll go with Tim,' Norma said apologetically. 'I'd really like to see the sea.'

'Fine,' Roz agreed, happy to let them do what they wanted. 'I'll see you back at the coach, then.'

She would be better off on her own, anyway, she decided: able to choose just what she wanted to see without worrying about Norma. So it proved, and having done the tour of Broughton House, which she found fascinating, she spent some time looking round the little art shops and galleries where she bought small gifts for Flo and Chrissie, before heading towards one of the museums.

Inside, there were so many paintings to see, so many collections to study, that by late afternoon she was so exhausted all she wanted to do was find somewhere to sit down and have a cup of tea. Is there a café? she asked an assistant and, having been told there was, heaved a sigh of relief and made for it, only to find it crowded, every table taken.

Oh no, she groaned and was standing hovering in the doorway when a waitress beckoned her to a table where one young man was sitting alone.

'Mind if this young lady sits here, sir?' the girl asked brightly, at which the solitary male rose to his feet.

'Not at all.' A pair of blue eyes went at once to Roz, who was feeling at something of a disadvantage, sure that her face was flushed and shiny and her hair untidy, but she managed a grateful smile as she moved to the table.

'Please, do sit down,' said the young man, now coming round to set a chair for her. 'May I help you with your packages?'

Heavens, how polite!

Covertly, she studied him as he helped to place her paper bags of presents, guidebook and spare cardigan on a vacant chair, noting that he was handsome in a low-key sort of way. Short fair hair, face rather long, nose very straight, all sort of a match to his accent, which was English – the sort you heard in British films, though there was nothing of the actor about this particular chap. Very genuine, she judged him to be, in his shabby tweeds and striped tie; probably better off than he appeared. He wasn't worrying about how he looked, anyway.

'Thank you,' she murmured, pushing back her hair and taking her seat opposite him, 'this is very kind.'

'Only too happy to help, but here's the waitress to take your order.'

'Tea and a buttered scone, please,' Roz told her.

'And cakes? We have a nice selection of fancies – or there's Madeira. No Dundee at the moment, I'm afraid.'

'Er – fancies, then.' How silly the name sounded, thought Roz, aware now that her flush was deepening under the young man's blue gaze, and wishing he would look away.

'And another pot of tea, please,' he told the waitress as she cleared away his cup and plate. When they were alone, he gave Roz a charming smile. 'A warm day, isn't it? Makes one thirsty. Thank God for the Scottish tea room, I always say.'

'Oh, so do I,' Roz agreed and, under the influence of the smile, gradually began to relax, and feel ready to talk.

Forty-One

'Tiring work, going round museums,' the fair-haired young man remarked. 'I suppose you've just been round this one?'

'Yes. I enjoyed it, but we're over from Edinburgh. It's been a long day, really. So much to see.'

'I'm from Edinburgh, too, or at least only a few miles away. Did you drive over?'

'No, I'm with an art class – we came by coach. Our teacher wanted us to see what the artists found to make them come here to paint.'

'And did you?'

'I think so. Partly the light – seems so different from a city – and then it's all so open and airy, being on the sea and with the lovely hills around.'

'I agree. This is one of my favourite places. I've got a few paintings by the Glasgow Boys myself. Give me a lot of pleasure, though I've just sold one, as a matter of fact.'

'Sold one?' Roz's eyes were wide, then she looked down, embarrassed that she'd seemed to query his decision. Nothing to do with her, was it? It was a relief to see the waitress back at their table with her loaded tray.

'Now, a scone for you, miss, wasn't it? I've brought you butter and jam, and tea, with a separate pot for the gentleman. Oh, and I'll leave the fancies for you to choose one when you're ready.'

'Thank you very much,' Roz said, finally having to look up, but still not meeting the young man's eyes as he murmured his thanks to the waitress and poured his tea.

'Yes, it's a wrench,' he said, appearing not to notice her confusion. 'But I thought it should be here, as it was painted here, and the museum was very happy to have it. Also, it means more people will see it.'

'Oh, yes, that's true,' Roz agreed eagerly. 'I'm all for lovely things being seen by as many as possible.'

'True, but don't you think there's a case for certain works of art being seen in private houses, too? I mean, if they're right for the setting.'

'Then they wouldn't be seen by as many people, would they?'

'Unless the public were to visit?'

'You mean as in stately homes? I haven't much experience of them, though I do work with houses.'

'You work with houses?' His interest was clear as he drank his tea.

'I'm an assistant in a lawyers' property department in Edinburgh.'

'Sounds fascinating.' He laughed a little. 'Selling dreams, then.'

'That's one way of putting it.'

'Well, isn't it everyone's dream to own the perfect property?'

'If they can afford one at all. There are plenty who can't.'

'I know,' he said quietly, and for a little while they were silent, Roz finishing her scone and he his tea.

'Mind if I ask which lawyers?' he said eventually. 'Might be mine.'

'Tarrel and Thom's in Queen Street.'

'Good Lord!' His eyes were bright. 'They are! What a coincidence. This calls for a celebration – have one of your fancies!'

'How about you?'

'I haven't a sweet tooth, but if you press me – why not?'

It was a strangely happy shared moment between them as they took their little cakes and laughed as they ate. How quickly her unease had faded, Roz was thinking as her eyes met his. How soon he'd appeared no longer a stranger, yet she didn't know him from Adam and after this meeting over tea would probably never see him again.

'I've never seen you at Tarrel's,' she remarked. 'Which partner do you see?'

'Oh, Mr Banks, the odd time I venture in, but I haven't been to see him for some time.'

The young man leaned forward, his eyes very direct on Roz. 'Look here, this is absurd – we've been talking all this time and we don't know each other's names. I'm Laurence Carmichael.' He held his hand across the table and Roz, after a moment, shook it.

'I'm Roz Rainey.'

For a second or two longer than was necessary he held her hand, then let it go.

'Miss Rainey, I'm very glad we've met.'

'Me, too.'

Carmichael, Roz was thinking – there was something familiar about the name. Had she heard it at Tarrel's? She couldn't be sure. Suddenly, she looked at her wrist watch and gave a little cry.

'Help! I think I've got to go. We have to meet in the car park in half an hour. Where's the waitress? I'd better get my bill.'

'I'll get the bill.' Laurence Carmichael stood up, his eyes searching the café for their girl. 'But couldn't I drive you back to Edinburgh? I have my car.'

'Oh, thank you, that's very kind, but I think I'd better go back with the others. Our teacher will be checking us all into the coach.'

'It would have been no trouble, but I understand.'

Roz hesitated. 'And it's really nice of you to offer to pay for my tea, but there's no need. I mean, why should you?'

'Why shouldn't I? I feel we're already friends.'

As their waitress came hurrying up with her notebook, Laurence looked down at Roz, his gaze serious.

'I'd like to, anyway.'

'Oh, well, thank you,' she murmured, gathering up her packages. 'Now, I'd better go. It was very nice, talking to you.'

'Hang on, I'll just pay this and then I'll walk with you to the car park. I have to collect my car.'

Saying that would be fine, Roz was already wondering what Norma would say when she saw Roz arriving with this tall stranger in tweeds. 'Where'd he come from?' she was bound to ask, and if Roz had to tell her they'd met over tea in a café, she'd put on one of her funny looks and think Roz had been some sort of pick-up.

Perhaps that was true, but when she glanced up at the man walking by her side, pulling on a tweed cap and smiling down at her, she knew it wasn't. To use her mother's phrase about Richard Vincent, Laurence was what Richard was not, a 'perfect gentleman'. Even on their short acquaintance, Roz knew she could trust him, and that was the difference between him and another man, wasn't it? But Roz would not think of *that* one.

'There's the coach in the car park now,' she said quickly. 'Thank you for coming with me.'

He smiled and put out his hand. 'Well, it's been good to meet you, Miss Rainey. Perhaps we'll meet again. If I come into Tarrel's, I'll be sure to look out for you.'

'Please do,' she said politely, shaking his hand. As she began to walk away, she looked back and waved. 'Thanks again for the tea.'

'My pleasure, Miss Rainey.'

She did not look back again.

Mrs Burr and a number of her students were already milling round the coach as Roz arrived, and amongst these were Norma and Tim.

'Who was that fellow you were with just now?' Norma asked at once, as Roz had known she would.

'Just one of our clients. We met in the museum café.'

'I don't remember him. Who does he see?'

'Mr Banks, but he doesn't come in much.'

'What's his name, then?'

'Mr Carmichael.'

Norma wrinkled her brow. 'Seems familiar.'

'Look, can we get on the coach now?' Tim asked impatiently. 'What does this client matter, anyway?'

Nothing at all, thought Roz, as she followed Norma and Tim on to the coach once Mrs Burr had ticked off their names on her list. Except that she had enjoyed meeting Mr Carmichael and did wonder if she might see him again. It was possible, wasn't it? Better not count on it, though. As though she would! Why, she wasn't looking for any kind of new relationship. She'd burnt her fingers once and that was enough. All the same, it had been very pleasant talking to him. Even if she never saw him again, she would remember that.

Forty-Two

In the days that followed her meeting with Laurence Carmichael, Roz continued to wonder who he was and why his name seemed familiar, but she knew she couldn't ask Mr Banks, who would not take kindly to enquiries about his client. Why the interest? she asked herself, and wasn't sure. Just curiosity, perhaps, or more that he'd been very nice to talk to and she might like to meet him again? Pointless, anyway, thinking about him, because he hadn't come into Tarrel's and it seemed it was unlikely there'd be any more meetings. Probably he was the sort of client who never needed to visit his lawyer more than once in a blue moon, and as June succeeded May and the summer weather sparked off interest in property buying and selling, Roz became too busy to think of anything but work.

'Just the way I like it,' Mr Appin commented on their increased business. 'Our figures are going to break records at this rate.'

'I like to be busy too,' said Roz. 'But you mustn't forget your summer leave, Mr Appin.'

'September will do for Pattie and me. No kiddies with school holidays to worry about, you see.' He gave a self-conscious smile. 'Though, of course, we hope that won't always be the case.'

'Oh? Does that mean . . .?' Roz was looking interested.

'Nothing on the horizon at the moment,' he said hastily. 'As I say, we're just hoping. But what about a holiday for you, Miss Rainey? You know what they say about all work and no play?'

She laughed. 'Oh, I don't forget to play sometimes, Mr Appin. As we're so busy, I'll be happy with a break in the autumn when you come back.'

He looked at her thoughtfully and she knew just what was in his mind. Attractive girl, only seems to think about work in spite of saying she likes to let her hair down – why hasn't she got a young man? At least no one had told him about her affair with his predecessor, though they could only have had their suspicions, apart from Norma and Mr Wray, and they wouldn't say anything. It was all in the past now, and if she did seem to prefer work to having a young man, that was her business. Mr Appin was far too tactful ever to question her private life, anyway, and for that she was truly grateful.

'Coffee time!' she announced now. 'I think we could do with it – we've a lot on this morning.'

But before she could depart to make it, the door opened and Mr Banks himself came in, causing Roz and Mr Appin to exchange glances, each thinking, what could he want? Must be something important.

'Had a good holiday, Mr Banks?' asked Mr Appin, for the senior partner had recently taken a few days in Bamburgh. 'You're looking well.'

'Excellent holiday, thanks.' Mr Banks, who was indeed looking unusually tanned, gave a beaming smile. 'And I found some interesting news waiting for me on my return.'

'Oh?' Mr Appin pushed forward one of the leather chairs. 'Won't you take a seat?'

'No, no, I shan't stay long – I've a mountain of work to get through. I just wanted to advise you both that a significant property will be coming on to the market shortly and is to be sold through Tarrel and Thom's.'

'Sounds good. Which one is it?'

'A house called Bellfields. A Georgian place a few miles from Edinburgh, off the Galashiels road. You may not know it, Mr Appin, but Miss Rainey will, I'm sure?'

'Oh, yes, Mr Banks. At least, I've heard about it but I've never seen it.'

'It's only open a couple of times in the summer – not one of your tea room and gift shop sort of places. But now it's coming on the market and we're the sole agents.' Mr Banks's smile was now showing his satisfaction even more. 'Of course, it's only to be expected – the Carmichaels have been clients of ours for generations. I remember Laurence Carmichael's father consulting my father – keeping up the tradition, you understand, but I'm glad there's been no question of calling in one of these smart London agents. It's a Scottish house and should be sold by Scottish lawyers.'

'Did you say Carmichael?' Roz asked, her thoughts in turmoil. 'It's Mr Laurence Carmichael who owns Bellfields?'

'Yes, yes, exactly so,' snapped Mr Banks, annoyed at being interrupted. 'I thought I'd made that clear!'

'I know, sir, I'm sorry. It's just that I met Mr Carmichael not long ago and he never mentioned Bellfields.'

'You met him? Where?'

'It was in Kirkcudbright. I'd gone there with my art class and he had been to the same museum I'd been visiting.' Roz was now blushing hard. 'I think he'd just sold a painting to the musuem.'

'I see.' Mr Banks and Mr Appin were both staring at Roz as though amazed at this insight into her life outside Tarrel's, and perhaps also at her little piece of information about Mr Carmichael – something she was already regretting having mentioned.

'Poor fellow,' Mr Banks said, 'he's had to part with quite a number of assets lately to try to avoid selling the house, but it looks as though he's lost the battle.'

'I should have thought he'd have rents and so on from his land,' Mr Appin remarked. 'He must have tenants, surely?'

'Very few now. I'm afraid we sold a good deal of the land for his father years ago, and that wasn't the first time land had been sold.' Mr Banks sighed, then brightened. 'Well, if it has to go, it's good that Bellfields will be sold by us. And that's why I wanted to speak to you, Mr Appin. We must make the best showing we can for this sale. There's to be no auction, but plenty of advertising, the price to be made on application only. I want special brochures printed and interior photographs taken by the usual professional fellow we employ – what's his name, again?'

'Reginald MacEwan,' said Roz. 'He does the exterior shots of houses while we usually do the interiors.'

'As I say, no disrespect to you or Mr Appin, but I'd like him to be booked to do all the photography for Bellfields. Mr Carmichael is relying on us to do a good job for him – we must not let him down.'

'Certainly not, Mr Banks, we'll do our very best,' Mr Appin said at once. 'You can be sure of that.'

'I'm sure I can. Well, I'd better get back to my desk.' Mr Banks moved to the door. 'As soon as I get the official instruction to sell from Mr Carmichael, you must arrange a visit with Mr MacEwan to take particulars. Then you and I can discuss the brochure.'

'And the valuation, Mr Banks?'

'Don't worry about that. I'll arrange the asking price with Mr Carmichael myself. All right, Mr Appin?'

'Fine, Mr Banks.'

'As I say, I've every confidence in you – and Miss Rainey.'

With a slight inclination of his head, Mr Banks left them and again Mr Appin and Roz looked at each other.

'Thank God he's doing the valuation,' Mr Appin said, sitting down at his desk with a sigh of relief. 'At least I needn't worry about that, but the rest of this sale looks like being one big headache. Obviously, the house needs a fortune spent on it. Nobody will want to shell out for it, and if we don't do well for this Carmichael guy, we'll get the blame. Or I will.'

'Don't say that, Mr Appin. He's very nice, Mr Carmichael. You'll like him, and you'll do a good job, so stop worrying.'

'How about that coffee, then?' Mr Appin, unusually, lit a cigarette. 'I rather wish your old boss was still here to hold my hand.'

'My old boss?'

'Mr MacKenna. Calm as a cucumber, wasn't he?'

'Why, so are you, usually!'

He smiled wryly. 'Think so?'

'Well, aren't you?'

'I put on a good act. It helps being somewhat fat.'

'You're not fat, Mr Appin!'

'Plump, then. People expect me to be unflappable. Goes with the double chins. In fact – oh, look, forget I said anything! I'm calm as a cucumber, apart from melting like a jelly. We'll get through this sale, of course we will.'

'Honestly, you've no need to worry,' Roz told him firmly, concealing her surprise at his concern. 'You'll do a lovely brochure, there'll be lots of offers, and there you are – job done!'

He looked up at her and nodded. 'Thanks, Miss Rainey. Think I don't need Mr MacKenna, after all. You're just as good.'

She laughed, but as she went away to make the coffee, the laughter died. If she'd discovered a side to Mr Appin she didn't know existed, she'd also found out all she needed to know about Laurence Carmichael, and what it added up to was that if she saw him again it would be purely on a business footing and that was the way it would stay. Why hadn't he told her he owned a place like Bellfields? Because he knew she wasn't the sort of person who knew people like him. Just for a little while that afternoon in the museum café, she'd thought . . . wondered . . . what? Nothing worth thinking about now, that was for sure. Thank heavens she'd found out who he was before she'd indulged in any more thinking and wondering. Thank heavens, as usual, for work.

Forty-Three

The visit to Bellfields was arranged for a day in July. As soon as Roz leaped out of bed in the early morning after a troubled night, she saw that the weather was perfect – calm and still, with not a cloud in the azure sky. What to wear, then? Something cool, in case it became very warm. There might even be thunder.

'Aren't you dressed yet?' cried Chrissie, throwing back her sheet. 'Anybody'd think you were going to Holyrood, the time you're taking.'

'The thing is, I should wear a jacket,' Roz murmured, not admitting that she felt as nervous as if she were in fact going to the royal palace. 'But I don't want to be too hot.'

'Well, you've got that nice green one you bought lately. Won't that do?'

'If I wear it with my sleeveless white blouse and my light skirt it might be OK. Just wish I hadn't to go. It'll be a bit of an ordeal for us all.'

'Fancy! And Ma and me were saying how much we'd like to see Bellfields.'

'But you're not having to sell it,' sighed Roz.

As they had their light breakfast, Flo and Chrissie insisted on talking about the lovely country house Roz was going to see and saying how much they wished they could be going too.

'I've seen pictures in magazines,' Flo remarked. 'And on a calendar we had once. It looks really beautiful. You being so keen on houses, Roz, you'll have a grand time there, eh?'

'She's worried about the sale,' Chrissie told her. 'They'll have to get a good price.'

'No need to remind me,' Roz said bleakly. 'Look, I've got to go. See you tonight, eh?'

'Good luck, pet!' cried Flo. 'You'll feel better when you're away, and you look really lovely.'

'Very smart,' Chrissie agreed. 'Just right for Bellfields.'

They were due at the house at ten o'clock and left in good time, Mr Appin driving the firm's Vauxhall that had succeeded the old Hillman with Roz next to him and Reggie MacEwan, the photographer, following in his own ancient sports car. Roz, full of nerves herself, though controlling them well, was relieved to see that Mr Appin seemed to have recovered his confidence and was looking his usual calm self. He'd asked if she would like to drive, for, after some hard saving up, she'd finally taken lessons and passed her test a year ago, but though she frequently drove on their usual visits, she knew she'd be happier as a passenger on this one.

Why make such a thing of this? she asked herself. Seeing Mr Carmichael again, but in his grand home – what did it matter? She had no answers, only concentrated on looking out at the scenery, which was pleasant, and checking the road map for their turning off the A7.

'The instructions we were sent said Bellfields would be signposted,' Mr Appin reminded her. 'It should be coming up now – hey, there it is, and that daredevil Reggie's gone ahead!'

With a wave of his hand, the photographer was already turning off for the minor road and roaring away from the Vauxhall, which only made Roz and her boss laugh. Reggie MacEwan, in his late twenties, straw-haired and craggy-faced, was known as a law unto himself, very good at his job but also very unpredictable. As Mr Appin said to Roz, still laughing, 'Now you know why I'm glad he doesn't usually have to do the interiors with us. I only hope he doesn't break any treasures at your friend's house.'

'My friend?' Roz stopped laughing. 'I've met him once.'

'Well, I've never met him at all. Suppose I'll have to mind my p's and q's, eh?'

'I told you – he's very nice. But, look, there are the gates – we're here!'

'Thank God for that. I can't wait to get started. The sooner we begin, the sooner it's over.'

The wrought-iron gates to the house were open, but there was no one looking out from the little lodge nearby, and Mr Appin drove straight in and began to negotiate a winding drive. Though there were trees either side, glimpses of parkland could be seen, but there were no deer or anything else to be spotted until the drive left the trees behind and the house itself came into view.

'Oh, yes,' Roz whispered, 'there it is. Bellfields. Just like the pictures – it's beautiful.'

'Very fine,' Mr Appin commented. 'Very fine indeed. Reggie should have a field day, taking photos here.'

For a moment, he stopped the car and they both sat gazing at the elegant, honey-stoned façade of the house they had come to sell.

Not overpoweringly grand or particularly large, it was everyone's idea of a gracious country house; a family house, maybe, but of a special kind. Though it was not actually designed by one of the Adam family, as they'd read, it did have the Adam look, with three lines of long, white-framed windows symmetrically placed at intervals from a central front entrance which was reached by curving stone steps. A stonework balustrade over the top storey added decoration to the roof, where, on such a fine day, smoke wouldn't be seen rising from the forest of chimney stacks.

All the same, as he drove on, Mr Appin murmured to Roz, 'When every one of those chimneys is working, what on earth do you think the fuel bills will be? It's no wonder Mr Carmichael wants to sell.'

'Has to sell, you mean. He doesn't want to.'

'The problem is, will anyone want to buy? Mr Banks is putting it on at offers over fifteen thousand, which is no snip if it needs a lot of work.'

'I see the owner's talking to Reggie,' Roz observed, keeping her voice level. 'There you are, Mr Appin, that's Mr Carmichael.'

Wearing a light summer jacket over a blue shirt and corduroy trousers, he was looking very casual and relaxed, but as soon as he saw Roz stepping out of the Vauxhall, his eyes went to her. With a polite word to Reggie, he moved fast towards her, his hand extended. 'Miss Rainey, we meet again! How are you?'

'Very excited to be here today,' she answered, proud of her own formal manner as she shook his hand. 'May I introduce Mr Appin, head of Tarrel's property department.'

'Mr Appin, it's very good to meet you,' Laurence Carmichael told him as they shook hands. 'I've been so busy trying to get the place looking decent, I'm afraid I haven't managed to see you to discuss the sale personally. I do apologise for that.'

'No need at all, Mr Carmichael, that's quite all right,' Mr Appin told him smoothly. 'The main thing is we're all here now and ready to begin. I see you've already met our photographer, Mr MacEwan?'

'Reggie, please!' cried the photographer. 'I've just been telling Mr Carmichael that this job is not going to be a quick one. Just from looking at the outside, I can tell that we're going to need a lot of time to do Bellfields justice.'

'Please, take as long as necessary,' Laurence said earnestly. 'There's no hurry at all. The longer you take to prepare the sale, the longer I'll be here.'

'Might take some time to make the actual sale, sir,' Mr Appin said after gazing in some surprise at his client. 'One never knows just how things will go.'

'As I say, the longer it takes, the better.' Laurence shrugged. 'I'm in no hurry to leave. I know it has to come, but I needn't wish it to come soon.'

At the expressions on the watching faces, he suddenly smiled.

'But first, before you do anything else, come and have some coffee. My housekeeper has it all prepared for you in the morning room.'

The morning room . . . When they entered the spacious apartment from the long, elegant entrance hall, the same thought occurred to all three visitors: that in most of the houses they usually saw, this would have made a very grand drawing room.

Here, however, it seemed to be their client's living room, for there were books and newspapers scattered on a low table in front of the marble chimneypiece, a jacket on the back of a chair, and on the chintz-covered sofa two spaniels lay before leaping off to make themselves known with tremendous fuss.

'Down, Hector! Down Mascot!' Laurence cried, as the room came alive with noise and bustle and a middle-aged woman in a dark blue dress appeared with a trolley, on which sat a large silver coffee pot, fine china cups and saucers, and a plate of shortbread.

'My housekeeper, Mrs Meldrum,' Laurence announced, before introducing the team from Tarrel's. 'Mr Appin, Miss Rainey and Mr MacEwan will be here for some time, writing, measuring, photographing, and I know you'll do your best to make the house available to them.'

'Oh, certainly, sir,' said Mrs Meldrum calmly. 'Anything the young lady and the gentlemen want, they've only to ask.'

'Thank you very much, Mrs Meldrum,' Mr Appin said quickly. 'We'll try not to get too much in the way of you and your staff.'

She smiled a little. 'The only staff are two girls, a handyman and a part-time gardener from the village, sir. The girls come in most mornings. Ben, the handyman, is here most of the time, doing odd jobs. Now, may I pour everyone some coffee?'

Forty-Four

'So good to see you again, Miss Rainey,' Laurence murmured, coming to join Roz as she sipped her coffee and looked out at the drive from one of the long windows. 'I've been thinking about you.'

'In the middle of all your tidying?' she asked lightly.

'Oh, Lord, yes. Had to have something to take my mind off things.'

'It all looks very nice in here.'

'You think so?' His mouth twisted a little. 'Look a little more closely.'

She turned and looked back at the lovely room and, as she saw Mr Appin and Reggie staring up at the cornice of the finely plastered ceiling, let her eyes follow their gaze. Oh, God, it was out of line, it was slipping! There must be some subsidence to have that effect – the very thing any surveyor would instantly find. Was it just this room, or elsewhere?

'I see you've all found the cornice,' Laurence was saying drily, moving to the centre of the floor. 'Not to mention the ancient window frames, damp on the ceiling, the threadbare curtains and rugs. You'll also be seeing the chimneys that smoke the entire winter, the temperamental boiler, and the roof missing tiles.

'Trying to make the place look decent, did I say? Only works in the main apartments. Some of the top-floor rooms haven't been used for half a century or more, and the kitchens – well, only a saint like Mrs Meldrum would work in them. You didn't bring your own surveyor with you, did you?'

'It's up to prospective buyers to send in surveyors.' Mr Appin's face had taken on a hunted expression. 'But it might be a good idea if you had your own structural survey done, sir. Just to let you know the situation.'

'Far too expensive, Mr Appin.' Laurence's tone was decisive. 'I believe most people interested in Bellfields will expect to find it needs money spent on it. Isn't the phrase in the adverts "some modernization required"?'

'Got it in one,' Reggie cried with a laugh. 'But by the time they've seen my pictures of this stunning place you'll have people queuing up to buy, I promise you. So, let's to work.'

'To work,' Mr Appin agreed. 'May we look around, Mr Carmichael? We usually like to begin at the top.'

'Oh, hell, I told you about the top storey, didn't I? Better watch where you walk. Some of the floorboards are pretty rotten.'

Afterwards, Roz was to conclude that looking round Bellfields might be considered a mixed experience, except that she'd already lost her heart to it. But, there it was . . .

On the one hand, there was the beauty and splendour of the principal rooms – the drawing room, the dining room, the library and the main bedrooms, where, if there were obvious repairs needed and the furnishings were old and shabby, there was still so much to admire.

On the other hand, she had to admit, there was the terrible top floor, where paper was peeling from the walls of the rooms used by servants long ago, the floors were positively dangerous and the ancient windows hadn't been opened for years. Were there mice, too? Awful thought! Roz had been relieved when they'd moved down a floor to view the guestrooms, which at least were still swept and dusted by the 'girls', and where there were a couple of tiled bathrooms, though because of the boiler, Laurence said, the provision of hot water for these would be a very hit and miss affair.

What to make of the prospects for a good sale? Mr Appin had to confess that this was unknown territory for him. Some buyers would be put off by the amount of work needed to be done. Others, if they could afford the outlay, might be desperate to own such a house as Bellfields, or keen to start a school there, or even a hotel.

'We'll just have to see how it goes,' Mr Appin told Roz when Laurence was talking to Reggie about which rooms he wanted to photograph. 'In the meantime, we do our best.'

For the rest of the morning they worked hard, though by lunch-time they felt as though they had still only scratched the surface of what had to be done.

'We haven't even thought about the grounds, or the stable block and offices Mr Carmichael tells me are at the rear,' sighed Mr Appin, who was feeling the heat and mopping his brow. 'As for the property department, that's on hold for today but we can't leave it too long – we're definitely going to have to stagger our visits here to take that into account. Or you might have to hold the fort while I finish up here. You can do that, of course, Miss Rainey?'

'Oh, yes, Mr Appin!' At the thought, Roz's eyes were shining. Hold the fort? Take charge? Wasn't it what she'd always wanted? 'Of course, I'll have to make appointments for the valuations, but I can do everything else.'

'That's settled, then. I know Mr Carmichael seems in no hurry to sell, but I'd like to get on with it. In the meantime, what about lunch?'

The pub in the village was Reggie's suggestion, to which the others agreed, and though Laurence said Mrs Meldrum would have been glad to rustle up a light lunch for them, he understood that they'd like to relax on their own.

'Miss Rainey,' he whispered as she was about to leave. 'May I have a word when you come back?'

'Of course, Mr Carmichael.'

'I wish you'd call me Laurence.'

She met his blue gaze with a direct look of her own. 'I don't think—'

'Oh, come, I told you when we first met that I felt we were friends. I can't be Mr Carmichael to you. And you can't be Miss Rainey. May I call you Roz?'

'They're waiting for me; I'll have to go,' she said hurriedly, running out to join the men, colour rising in her face.

'We're taking our car, Miss Rainey,' Mr Appin told her. 'Reggie wants to be able to drink. I want to keep my head clear.'

'What's all this formality?' asked Reggie. 'I'm Reggie, but you two are Miss Rainey and Mr Appin – how about Roz and Angus? You're not in the office now.'

'Would you mind, Miss Rainey?' Angus Appin asked, as they drove away.

'Not at all,' she answered quickly, and looked back at the fine entrance to the house where Laurence was standing, watching.

Would she be Roz to him, too? She knew she would. It was just a question of facing up to what was happening. He was attracted to her, there was no doubt of it, and she felt drawn to him – at least, she thought she was. Really, she was in such a daze she didn't know what she felt. But, yes, she would call him Laurence, he would call her Roz, and they would see where they went. If anywhere. At which point, she remembered that she would not be seeing him the next day and, in spite of looking forward to being in charge of the property department, felt suddenly rather low.

When they returned from the pub, having enjoyed ham and eggs outside in the sunshine, they found Laurence waiting for them, wondering if they'd like him to show them the stable block and offices. At one point, he explained, there'd been an agent to manage the estate, but he'd been gone for some time and hadn't been replaced.

'I'm sort of a jack of all trades now,' he explained, as they moved to the rear of the house, Reggie with his camera, Roz and Angus looking round with interest at the extensive stabling and other buildings, all so quiet now, though once of course alive with activity. Certainly, there were no horses in the stables any more. The building was now a garage, housing Laurence's old Alvis and a battered Land Rover.

'I gave up riding some time ago,' he remarked cheerfully. 'If there's one thing that literally eats money, it's a horse. But I still use my office next door – even have a typewriter and use all my fingers, would you believe?'

'I think you do very well,' Roz told him quietly as Angus and Reggie moved a little away. 'It must be hard for you, the way things are.'

'No, I'm lucky. Lucky to have known Bellfields all my life.' His handsome face was serious as he looked down at her. 'Roz – will you have dinner with me one evening?'

'Dinner?' She glanced quickly to where Reggie was now preparing for a shot of the stable, while Angus was looking on. 'I—'

'Don't say no straight off. Why should you? We're friends – we've met again, it would be natural to have a meal together. I know a very pleasant little place in Edinburgh. I could meet you whenever you like.' He too glanced over at the others, then touched Roz's arm with some urgency. 'Quick, say yes! We can fix the details tomorrow.'

'I'm in the office tomorrow. I have to look after things while Mr Appin's here.'

'In the office? Oh, hell!' He hesitated. 'No, it's all right. I can ring you. That'd be better, in fact.' His smile on her was radiant. 'Be ready to say yes.'

'I'd better get back to the library,' she muttered, as Angus came to join them, 'and finish my measuring for today.'

Forty-Five

In a way, Laurence's promise to call her rather spoiled Roz's first morning in charge of the property department, for every time the telephone rang she thought it might be him. Each time was a bit of a let-down and shouldn't have been. She must be professional, she told herself – she was here to do a job and was trusted to do it well, not to be thinking about Prince Charming calling to ask her to the ball. Sorry, dinner.

Did she really think of Laurence Carmichael as Prince Charming, though? She must do, for the name had come into her head and there must have been something in her subconscious to make that happen. If he was Prince Charming, was she, then, Cinderella? No! Certainly not! She was herself: intelligent, attractive – so people said – not one to be needing a fairy godmother and a pumpkin. All the same, as she bent over the copy she was preparing for *The Scotsman* property column, she knew it had to be admitted that there was no house like Bellfields, no well-known family, no famous school, no experience of being presented to the king and queen at Holyrood in her background, like the girls Laurence must know.

The more she thought about it, the more foolish she thought it would be for her to have dinner with him. She was as good as anyone, she truly believed it, but others wouldn't, and why should she risk putting herself in that sort of situation? As soon as he rang, she decided she would tell him she didn't want to have dinner with him, and that would be that. No involvement, no pain – that was the golden rule.

Help, there was the phone! Another client wanting a visit, or an appointment, no doubt—

'Tarrel and Thom's, property department,' she intoned in her best telephone manner, 'how may I help you?'

'Hello, Roz, it's Laurence here,' came the voice she'd been waiting for. 'How are you? All alone in the property department?'

'Yes, I'm enjoying it.'

'Good. But you know why I'm calling, don't you? Just wanting to arrange a time for our dinner.'

'Oh, well . . .' She cleared her throat. 'I'm not sure about it, really. I don't think I actually said I'd come, did I?'

'Not in so many words.' He sounded a little stiff, a little taken aback. Perhaps he'd thought she'd jump at the chance to have dinner with him. 'But you didn't say you wouldn't, either.'

'The thing is, I don't think it's a very good idea.'

'Why ever not?'

'I'd rather not go into it all over the phone.'

'Over dinner, then. You can tell me all your objections then.'

She couldn't help laughing. 'When I've come anyway?'

'That's what I'm hoping. Look, why don't we just give it a go? What's one dinner? We could just meet, talk, have a nice meal – what do you say?'

Despite her best efforts she could feel her resolutions fast sweeping away, as the sea bore away the sand from a castle on the beach, and couldn't find the one word 'no' that would stop the flow.

'Why don't we say we'll meet tomorrow night?' he pressed on. 'I'll book us a table at Duthies and call for you about seven. Would that suit?'

Call for her at seven on a light summer evening when all eyes in Deller Street would be riveted on Laurence's Alvis, not to mention Laurence himself? It was the last thing she wanted, but she didn't say, as she'd said to Jamie on their first date, that she would meet him at the restaurant, for she knew it would be best if he did collect her from home, neighbours' eyes or no neighbours' eyes. Deller Street was Deller Street, a perfectly respectable place to live, and if it was different from Bellfields – well, there was her point made.

'That will be fine,' she said clearly. 'I'll give you the address. Have you got a pen?'

It was only when she'd put the phone down that it came to her that though she'd been worrying about the reactions of the neighbours to Laurence Carmichael, she hadn't given a thought to her mother's. Or, Chrissie's. When she told them she was going out with him, they'd think her crazy. Well, she was. She thought so herself.

At least she could say that it would just be a once-only time, this dinner. She wasn't stupid enough to get caught up in a relationship that might cause her more heartbreak. Not that she thought of Laurence in the same way as she'd thought of Jamie. Not yet, but it could happen. For he wasn't just attractive in his own right, he was the owner of Bellfields. For someone who cared for beautiful houses as she did, that was a tremendous pull; she must be on her guard, not to let it sway her from being sensible. Armed with her good intentions, she felt ready to face her family.

It was late evening when they'd both returned from work that she told them, very casually, of course, about the dinner invitation from Mr Carmichael.

'So, I won't be having tea tomorrow, Ma. He'll be collecting me at about seven.'

Flo's pale blue eyes were mystified; Chrissie's interested.

'Mr Carmichael's asked you to dinner?' Flo set down her cup of tea and her cigarette. 'The man who owns Bellfields?'

'Yes, you remember, I first met him on that trip to Kirkcudbright? I told you, didn't I?'

'I don't remember that. Do you, Chrissie?'

Chrissie shook her head. 'I know you went on the trip, but you never mentioned Mr Carmichael.'

'Oh? I thought I had.' Roz poured herself more tea. 'Anyway, when we went to the house, to take particulars, you know, we met again and today he rang me at work and asked if we could meet for dinner. It's just a friendly thing – nothing romantic.'

'A friendly thing, but he wants to take you out for a meal?' Flo and Chrissie exchanged glances. 'That's usually the start o' something, eh?'

'That's the way it goes,' Chrissie agreed. 'He must be attracted to you, Roz, or he wouldn't want to take you out. Fancy, a guy like that!'

'What do you mean, exactly?' Roz asked, knowing full well. 'You think it's surprising? That he'd want to take me to dinner?'

'Aye, it is,' Flo declared. 'When you think of who he is.'

'He's just like anyone else!' Roz cried. 'Only nicer. We got on really well. We enjoyed talking to each other. OK, I know I don't come from his sort of background, but I don't see why that should matter when we're just having a meal somewhere.'

'It's what that might lead to,' Flo said solemnly. 'I'm starting to worry already.'

She picked up her cigarette and smoked it rapidly.

'I don't want you hurt again, Roz, and if you get involved in something with no future, you will get hurt, eh?'

'Ma, it's not going to lead to anything!' Roz said desperately. 'This is just a one-time thing – nothing to get worried about.'

'Roz, you're as good as anybody,' Chrissie declared, 'but folk are always keen to point the finger and make you feel miserable if you don't fit in. That'd be what you'd be up against, if this did lead to anything.'

'I know all that, but it'd only happen if I got involved, and I'm not going to get involved, so just let me have a nice dinner and a chat with Laurence – Mr Carmichael – and leave it at that.'

'As long as we can,' sighed Flo. 'I think I'm away to my bed.'

'Me, too,' said Roz. 'I'll just pop down to the bathroom.'

As she hurried out, anxious to get away from the heavy atmosphere of concern, Chrissie looked at Flo.

'You all right, Ma?'

'Aye, just worried, that's all. I mean, Roz is that sensible, usually – what's got into her?'

'I think it's the house, Ma. You know what she's like about houses and she's never met a man before who owns a house like Bellfields.'

'She's dazzled, you mean?'

'That's the word.'

'So, this dinner's not likely to be a once-only, is it?'

'Roz says it is, but this Mr Carmichael might have other ideas.'

'Aye, ideas that won't end in a wedding ring. He might be attracted to Roz, but when it comes to marriage he'll choose one of his own.'

'We'll just have to keep our fingers crossed, Ma, and hope for the best.'

'Bathroom's free!' cried Roz, putting her head round the door, and with some relief they gave themselves up to the ritual of going to bed and putting aside worries until the morning. Except that sleep came late to Flo and Roz, and only Chrissie was soon away, breathing deeply, dreaming no doubt of her dear Bob. How Roz envied her!

Forty-Six

It was a relief to Roz that her mother and Chrissie were both doing a late shift again the following evening, and were not there to watch her getting ready. Changing her mind about what to wear as usual, she ended up in the same green jacket she'd worn at Bellfields but with a pale green blouse Laurence wouldn't have seen before. Not that he'd have noticed, if he was like most men, but she didn't know him well enough to be sure. What did it matter, anyway?

'Have a good time,' Chrissie had said at breakfast, as Flo had sat, sighing, but Roz had only shaken her head.

Fat chance after all the gloom you two were spreading last night, she'd wanted to say, but had thought better of it. All she wanted now was for the evening to be over, for her confidence had been so dented, her pleasure in the thought of it had quite evaporated. It was only when she saw him again, leaping out of his car to open the passenger door, the sun glinting on his fair hair, that her heart lifted slightly and she found herself smiling as though nothing had ever been said by Chrissie or Flo.

'I see you found Deller Street all right,' she murmured as she settled into the seat next to his, noting that his eyes were on her and not on the buildings, and wondering how many neighbours' eyes were watching him. 'That's our flat there – the middle one – at number thirty-five.'

'Oh yes—' He turned his head to look, but only for a moment. 'Very nice.'

Just what Jamie had said. Now, why remember that?

'Where are we going, then?' she asked quickly as they drove away. 'Where's this nice little place you told me about?'

'Off Forrest Road. I used to go there when I was at the university.'

'Oh, I envy you! What did you study?'

'Architecture. Only did a year, then the war came and I joined the Scots Guards. Never went back.'

'Why, that was a shame! Didn't you want to?'

'Yes, though I don't suppose I'd have been anything wonderful. Thing is, my father had died in nineteen forty-two and I had to take over when I was demobbed. There was only me. My brother had been killed at Dunkirk, and we never knew our mother. She died when we were very young.'

'Laurence, that's so sad!' Roz cried. 'My dad died in the war so I know what it's like to lose someone, but you've lost all your family.'

'Yes, it's sad, but we must talk of other things.' He gave her a quick smile. 'Our first time out together, we mustn't be gloomy.'

First time out together? Only time, it had to be. But she said nothing.

'It'll be your turn to talk at Duthie's,' he warned. 'And it's coming up soon. I hope you'll like it.'

She told him she was sure she would and, it was true, she did. A comfortable Scottish restaurant without too much tartan, it wasn't a place she'd visited with Jamie, which meant she needn't be reminded of him. Needn't, but somehow was, which presented a mystery. She was long over him, so why all these memories? Perhaps because this was her first time out with another man and she was subconsciously comparing them? If that were true, she knew that the man she was with now was very different from Jamie. Thank the Lord for that!

'This is so nice,' she told Laurence as they took their table in the restaurant amongst a number of other diners. 'I like it very much.'

'I'm glad. My choice, so I feel responsible. Now, what shall we have?'

For some moments they studied their menus, Roz trying not to be too worried about the prices; there would be no point in trying to choose the least expensive dishes for everything seemed to be equally dear to her eyes, and she could only hope that Laurence was not so strapped for cash as he'd indicated. Everything was relative, of course. His idea of having no money, for instance, might not be the same as hers.

'How about salmon soufflé for the first course?' he asked, his blue eyes seeking hers over the top of his menu. 'Or, smoked salmon pâté, perhaps?'

'I think I'll pass on the first course. Sometimes seems too much.'

'All right, then. How about going straight to the gigot lamb chops, with the mushroom sauce?'

'That would be lovely.'

Having ordered the lamb and a half bottle of wine for Laurence, with a soft drink for Roz, who said she was no great wine drinker, they gazed at each other across the table, not speaking yet seeming quite at ease.

'Remember, we said it would be your turn to talk when we were here,' Laurence said after a little while. 'But of course you needn't, if you don't want to.'

'Talk about myself, you mean?' Roz shrugged. 'I don't mind.'

'That's good, because I'm interested. I've been interested in you from that first time when we shared a table for tea.'

'Most people would think you were more interesting.' Roz twirled the stem of her glass.

'Most people would be wrong, then. Bellfields is interesting. I'm not.'

'Well, maybe there's more to say about you, anyway. Not much to say about me. My dad worked for the electricity station at Portobello, until he got called up in the war. When he was killed my mother took it very badly. For a long time she was very depressed and we had to look after her – I mean, my brother and I, and my sister.'

'I'm sorry to hear that,' Laurence said quietly. 'It must have been hard.'

'Yes. Well, she's much better now and has a job in a restaurant on the cash desk. My sister's a waitress and my brother's in the army.' A shadow crossed Roz's face. 'He's in Korea now, in fact, fighting in the war.'

'Oh, God, that's a worry!' Laurence stretched his hand across the table and touched Roz's. 'I am sorry, Roz. We thought we'd finished with war, didn't we? And now some of our chaps are back in it. Let's hope they sort that one out soon and send our soldiers home.'

Their lamb arrived and, as they began to eat, Laurence pressed her for more details about herself. 'I haven't heard much about you yet. How did you come to work in Tarrel's property department?'

'I did reasonably well at school, and while it wasn't possible for me to go to university, I did a typing course and found a job. I'd always been interested in houses, so when the Tarrel job eventually came up, I applied and got it.'

'And you've been happy there?'

'Yes, very happy. I'm not a lawyer, though, which means I'm not likely to be able to run the department myself.'

'Though you could,' said Laurence, drinking his wine. 'I bet you could do it standing on your head. Why don't you move into an estate agent's office? Somewhere where you don't have to be a lawyer?'

'In England, you mean? That's been suggested before. Perhaps I should try it.'

'Oh, Roz, please don't! Don't go away over the border! I was a fool to mention it!'

They both laughed then and continued their meal, choosing Drambuie cream as a pudding and finishing with coffee, after which Laurence called for the bill.

'That was truly delicious,' Roz told him when they were out in the warmth of the fine July evening. 'Thank you very much, Laurence.'

'My pleasure, Roz.'

'I just feel . . .' She stopped and he bent to look into her face.

'Feel what? Don't tell me, I can guess. If I've been giving you the impression that I can't afford a decent dinner, that's not true. Refurbishing Bellfields from top to bottom is one thing. Affording a dinner is quite another.' He took her arm and tucked it into his. 'Now, it's a fine night. The car's quite close but I was thinking we could drive to the Meadows and walk a bit, couldn't we? Before I take you home?'

The Meadows. Another reminder of Jamie. His flat had been in that area.

'Good idea,' she said swiftly. 'Let's do that.'

Though the children had left the Meadows, there were still plenty of people about, walking, playing ball games, enjoying the summer evening. Roz and Laurence were enjoying it too.

'The perfect end to a perfect evening,' Laurence remarked. 'Our first time out together has been terrific – don't you think so, Roz?'

'It's been lovely, Laurence . . .' She hesitated.

'Hey!' He stopped and turned her to face him. 'Do I detect a "but" in there somewhere?'

'Well, you said our first time out together was terrific—'

'So? It was, wasn't it?'

'Yes, but I don't really think there should be any more times. Together, I mean.'

'No more times together?' His look was baffled, almost stunned; it was clear he'd never for a moment expected her not to want to see him again. 'Why do you say that, Roz? If you're happy being with me, why not want to see me again?'

'It's not that I don't want to see you, Laurence. It's just that – well, for a start, you're a client. It's not really the thing, is it? For us to go out together?'

'Oh, come on! Are you telling me anyone's going to object? Why should they?'

'Mr Banks can be a stickler for, you know, doing the right thing.'

'Well, we're not doing the wrong thing, in my view. I've a perfect right to ask you to dinner, and you've a perfect right to say yes. If that's all that's worrying you, we can forget it.' He gently held her shoulders, his gaze seeking hers. 'But you said for a start, didn't you? Is there something else troubling you?'

She looked away, desperately watching some young men in the distance packing up their cricket stumps, for the fact was she didn't know what to say. How was she to put into words what the problem was? How to explain what he should be able to see for himself?

'So, there is something else,' he said softly, releasing her. 'Look, there's a vacant bench over there – let's sit down for a minute and knock this thing on the head once and for all.'

Sitting close on the bench, he took her hands in his. 'I think I know what it's about, and it's to do with Bellfields, isn't it?'

'I suppose it is.'

'You won't go out with me because I live in a place like Bellfields, and you don't?'

'That's a funny way of putting it.'

'It's true, though, isn't it? The point is it doesn't matter. It doesn't matter where either of us live, or who we are, or what we do, if we're attracted to each other and want to meet. If we enjoy being together, why shouldn't we be just that?'

'You make it sound so easy, but people don't live in a vacuum, do they?' Roz shook her head. 'Look, I'm going to be very honest, Laurence. Going out with someone can lead to a relationship and I don't want one. I've been hurt once and I don't want to be hurt again.'

'And you think I would hurt you? Roz, that would never happen.

Trust me, it wouldn't.' He made her look at him, meet his eyes that were so sincere. 'Please believe me.'

'I believe you wouldn't want to, but things might be too difficult for you if we went any further.' Roz stood up, glancing at her wrist watch. 'I think we'd better go back now, Laurence. It's getting late.'

After a long pause, he sighed and turned to go. 'As you wish,' he said quietly and, without speaking again, they returned to the car.

Forty-Seven

It was only when they were back in Deller Street again, with welcome dusk enfolding them, that Laurence stopped the car and turned to speak to Roz.

'I've no right to ask, but this chap who hurt you – who was he? What sort of an idiot was he?'

'He wasn't an idiot. He did love me, but I don't want to go into it. He let me down – and someone else too. I couldn't trust him.'

'You can always trust me.'

She smiled sadly. 'I know you'd want to do the right thing.'

'Well, then!' He took her hand. 'But I hate to think of you being hurt. I know what it's like.'

'Laurence!' She sat up straight. 'I never thought – who could have hurt you?'

'Oh, it was some time ago. We were almost engaged, Meriel and I – until she said I cared too much about Bellfields.'

'Cared too much for Bellfields? I can't believe anyone could say that!'

'Well, it didn't interest her, you see. Her family has several properties and to her they're just places to live. They're not important. So, we said goodbye.' Laurence smoothed Roz's fingers. 'No need to worry, I've quite forgotten her now. Have you forgotten your chap?'

'Oh, yes.' It was true, she was well over him.

'But you haven't forgotten the pain. Roz, there won't be any with me, I promise.' He lowered his voice. 'Look, won't you reconsider – about seeing me again? I do want so much to be with you. Ever since we met in that café in Kirkcudbright, I've hardly stopped thinking of you. I kept wondering how I could see you at Tarrel's, and then it came to me – you worked in property, so when I put Bellfields on the market, which I knew I had to do, I guessed you'd come to the house, which, thank God, you did.'

He let go of her hands and drew her towards him, holding her lightly, then releasing her again.

'It seemed like the answer to a prayer. We could meet naturally, I could ask you to see me, it was exactly what I wanted – what we both wanted, I believed. You can't really mean I was wrong, can you? You can't say you don't want to see me again? Not now we've found each other?'

It was beginning to seem to her more and more like one of her dreams, that this man, the owner of a dream house like Bellfields, had somehow become dependent on her – had, you might say, put himself in her power, which was not something she could ever have expected, or even wanted. How had they reached this stage so soon? Was he really in love with her? She couldn't help feeling touched by his words, by the depth of the feeling he'd expressed for her when they'd only just met, when he didn't even really know her.

Perhaps he didn't need to know her? Had she really known Jamie when she'd found herself so drawn to him? Events had proved that she hadn't known him at all, yet the strange thing was that though she didn't really know Laurence, she really felt that she could trust him. He'd said she could, and she believed him. And if, as yet, her own feelings might not match his, they might – probably would, in fact – if she gave into them. And for now? She felt herself weakening, all the resolve she'd thought she had drifting away on a cloud of longing to please him, to make him happy – herself too.

'Don't turn me down,' he was saying, his face close to hers. 'Don't end things for us before they've even begun . . .'

'I don't want to,' she whispered. 'I don't, it's just . . .'

'Just nothing!' he cried, taking her into his arms. 'Roz, be happy! Let's both be happy! Let's take what comes – why not? Is it dark enough for me to kiss you? Are you afraid people might see?'

'No, no!' She was still up on her cloud as their mouths met, and for long moments they clung together before finally drawing apart and facing each other with shining eyes.

'I'll ring you,' Laurence said. 'Soon. Very soon.'

'I'll be waiting.'

'I was thinking we might go to a play. There's a good one at the King's. You'd like that?'

'I would.'

They were silent for some time, until Laurence leaped out and opened the car door for her. As she stepped out, he put his hand on her arm.

'Roz, thank you.'

'Thank you, for a lovely evening.'

'Was it this evening we had dinner? Seems a long time ago.'

They laughed, and finally, reluctantly, parted – Roz to go to her door, Laurence to watch as she stood and waved, before taking his seat in the car again and with a last lift of his hand, drove away.

'You're back, then?' cried Flo, when Roz appeared in the living room. 'I was just going to bed. You're even later than Chrissie.'

'Sorry. We went for a walk in the Meadows after dinner.'

'Nice meal?' asked Chrissie. 'Which restaurant was it?'

'Duthie's, off Forrest Row.'

'Oh, pricey! Top quality Scottish, eh?'

'It was certainly very good.'

'Glad to hear it,' said Flo. 'Seeing as it was a once-only thing.'

There was a silence as Flo's pale eyes went over Roz's face and Chrissie gave a knowing smile.

'Was it?' Chrissie asked.

'No,' Roz answered, looking bravely from her sister to her mother. 'No, it wasn't.'

'I knew it!' cried Flo. 'I knew you'd never say no!'

'I'm keeping my eyes wide open,' said Roz. 'I'll be all right, Ma, I promise. Now don't be down-hearted, I mean it.'

'After all you said! It's just friendly, nothing romantic, it's not going to lead to anything, just this once – why did I listen to you?'

'Ma, just believe me. I trust Laurence, I'm going to be all right.'

'Oh, dear,' sighed Flo. 'Oh, dear, oh dear.'

'Don't be down about it, Ma. Promise me! Think of me being happy, eh?'

'If only I could. Chrissie, give me a hand to bed, will you?'

'Yes, Ma.' Chrissie, catching Roz's eye with a sympathetic glance, went with her mother from the room, leaving Roz to sigh as deeply as Flo before a smile curved her lips and she sat on, lost in remembering. She should have felt bad, giving in as she had, but in fact she felt good. 'Be happy,' Laurence had said. 'Let's take what comes – why not?' Why not, indeed? OK, she'd said she didn't want to risk being hurt again, but she'd changed her mind. Now she was prepared to take any risk there might be, and if the worst happened, it happened. But there'd be no regrets. That was a promise she'd make to herself. No regrets.

Forty-Eight

Everyone agreed that Tarrel's Bellfields brochure, produced by Angus Appin and Reggie MacEwan, was a great success – a triumph, no less, with much interest being shown by prospective buyers who'd received it after following up advertisements. There'd even been enquiries from over the border, and as the requests for viewing came flooding in Mr Banks expressed himself well pleased, which, if it didn't surprise Reggie, smoothed the worried frown from Angus's brow. The only person who didn't seem happy was the owner, whose spirits grew ever lower the more likely it seemed that there might soon be a sale.

'Laurence, I know you don't want to sell,' Roz told him over one of their frequent dinners, 'but if it has to happen, at least you should get a good price. I mean, Angus and Reggie did such a wonderful job – a lot of people have been attracted and that's sure to bring in the offers.'

'Oh, I know,' he said, drinking wine despondently. 'I know I should be grateful to the chaps. Reggie's photographs were amazing – how he managed to make everything look so perfect, I can't think. And Mr Appin's write-up was excellent. Even got in a bit about my family history, did you notice?'

'Certainly did. I was really interested.'

Roz paused to reflect on what she'd learned about those early Carmichaels, wealthy Edinburgh merchants who'd built a fine country house on the site of the present Bellfields, only to see it burn down and require re-building in the eighteenth century – this at the same time as they'd lost most of their money in the South Sea Bubble trading disaster. They hadn't given in, though – they'd held on to the new house and handed it down to their descendants, even if with little capital, who in turn had kept it going until Laurence had made the decision to sell.

'I don't like talking about my family much,' he told Roz. 'It brings it home to me that I'm the one who's let them down. There never was much money around – I think you know that the land had to be sold, which meant that there were no rents coming in, but everyone before me kept Bellfields afloat. Now it's going and I'm responsible. Don't expect me to be happy about it.'

'You have to remember that you had no choice!' cried Roz. 'Things aren't the same for you as for your ancestors. You need staff to maintain Bellfields and in the old days workers were cheap. Now – and I'm glad of it – they expect better, which means it's just too much for you to hang on any longer.'

She covered his hand with hers and held his eyes with her own direct gaze. 'Don't blame yourself, Laurence. You've done all you could. Try to think of that.'

His look still moody, he shook his head. 'I bet if the house had been yours, you'd never have given it up, would you? You're a fighter, aren't you? You'd have kept it even if you were living on beans on toast and doing all the work yourself. Come on, admit it!'

'How can I say what I would have done? Maybe, like you, I'd have had to sell in the end.' Roz lowered her eyes. 'But it would have broken my heart.'

'Now you know how I feel, Roz.'

'Laurence, I've always known how you feel. About Bellfields, anyway.'

The wonderful thing was that they were so happy together. In the long days of August, when possible buyers were still going round Bellfields, they met often, for meals, for theatre visits, shows at the festival, or long walks on Sundays, always ready to kiss and caress when they could, longing sometimes to progress but never quite going so far. Even in the privacy of Bellfields, where Laurence liked Roz to come, they kept on the safe side of passion – especially as Roz was always nervous when visiting the house privately, conscious that the housekeeper, Mrs Meldrum, didn't approve, though showing it, of course, only by her manner and never by words.

Why should I care? Roz asked herself. No reason, of course, but she did care. Not that there was anything she could do about it, any more than she could persuade her mother to meet Laurence, either in her home or anywhere else.

'No, I'll wait till I'm feeling happier,' Flo told Roz. 'Till I believe you're going to be all right with this grand fellow. Time enough to meet him then.'

'Ma, I tell you I am all right!' Roz would cry, but Flo would only set her mouth and look away, and Roz knew it was useless to say any more.

'She's got a lot on her plate,' Chrissie told her. 'Worrying about Dougal, eh? Seems so long since we saw him. He does get leave now and then but only over there.'

'I know, and of course in his letters he makes out he's fine, but who knows?' Roz sighed heavily. 'You're right, I shouldn't try to pressure Ma into anything, just in case.'

'She's been OK lately. Maybe she's getting better?'

'Maybe. And maybe not.'

Meanwhile, it gradually became apparent that the supply of prospective buyers was drying up, and that of all those who had so far been shown round Bellfields by Angus or Roz, not one had even expressed interest to a lawyer, never mind making a genuine offer.

'I don't understand it,' Angus said worriedly to Roz. 'I know some will have been put off by what's to be done, but you'd have thought that out of all the droves we took round Bellfields somebody would have wanted it!'

'It's disappointing,' Roz agreed. 'Though Laurence isn't too worried.'

'You'd know, of course,' Angus said, giving her a shrewd look.

He was one of two people at Tarrel's who'd been told by Roz that she was going out with Laurence, the other being Norma. Best to put them in the picture from the beginning, Roz had decided, for in some ways it would be easier not to hide things from the two who knew her best, and both could be trusted not to say anything to Mr Banks. Really, she would have preferred to have no secrets at all after her early experiences with Jamie, but it might be better if Mr Banks didn't know just yet of her relationship with a client.

Norma, so much wrapped up in her own love life, had opened her eyes wide at Roz's surprising news, but had commented very little, and Angus had simply told her that it was her business and hers alone. He couldn't see any harm, if she was happy about it.

'Of course I'm happy!' Roz had cried, and he'd nodded and said no more.

Now, when she smiled but said nothing about Laurence, Angus

remarked, as he'd done before, that Laurence Carmichael was one of the strangest clients he'd ever known. What seller didn't want any buyers?

'One who wants to keep his house for himself,' Roz told him.

Forty-Nine

At last, on a golden day in September, things began to look a little more hopeful when a Mr and Mrs Elphick, who'd made an appointment for a viewing, arrived at Tarrel's and appeared very excited about Bellfields. They were from Perth, looking for a property near Edinburgh to convert into a hotel, this being their way of investing a recent inheritance, and from the brochure which they'd only just read Bellfields seemed to fit the bill. Now they were to be taken by Roz to see it and couldn't be more keen.

Fingers crossed, her eyes had said to Angus as she escorted the middle-aged, smartly dressed couple to the car, and fingers crossed was his unspoken reply as she drove away. They had a splendid afternoon for viewing, that was true, just as long as the sunshine didn't show up all the defects, of course. But one must look on the bright side, Angus decided – Roz was now so expert at showing buyers round, she knew exactly how to present the house to its best advantage.

'Lovely country,' Mrs Elphick remarked. 'And so close to Edinburgh, it would be a perfect location.'

'I agree,' said her husband. 'Miss Rainey, we have great hopes of this place, I can assure you.'

'You won't be disappointed,' she told them, her heart lifting as it always did as they neared Bellfields and turned into the drive. Would Laurence be waiting for them at the entrance? she wondered, and when he wasn't, rang the doorbell for Mrs Meldrum while the Elphicks looked around with every appearance of pleasure.

When the housekeeper answered the bell, Roz smiled and introduced her prospective buyers, asking if Mr Carmichael was at home.

'He is, Miss Rainey, but he has visitors,' Mrs Meldrum answered coldly. 'Please come in. I'll tell him you're here.'

'Splendid hall,' Mr Elphick was whispering, looking up from his brochure.

'Perfect as a Reception!' his wife murmured.

'Here is Mr Carmichael,' Roz said happily as Laurence appeared, his eyes quickly going to her before he shook hands with the Elphicks and welcomed them to his house, assuring them that Miss Rainey would tell them all they needed to know. Now, if they would excuse him . . .

He turned to Roz. 'Miss Rainey, if I'm needed, I'll be on the terrace with my visitors.'

'Thank you, Mr Carmichael,' she said, wondering who his visitors might be. His accountants, maybe – they did come to see him from time to time.

The day had been going so well, Roz had no great worries about showing the Elphicks the house. After all, they'd liked everything they'd seen so far, and if they liked the main reception rooms and could face any sinking cornices, there'd only be the top floor to navigate and then they'd be home and dry. True, many others had fallen at that hurdle, but Roz remained more confident over this viewing than any other so far, and even if Laurence would be downcast if he really had an offer to accept, he knew it was what he had to do. What choice did he have?

All continued to go well as the Elphicks were shown the magnificent drawing and dining rooms, the morning room, the library and the grand staircase, and expressed themselves delighted with everything. As Mr Elphick explained, they were not interested in superficial decoration, only in the size and proportion of the rooms and how well they would respond to the changes required. And though their eyes went over the cornices in the morning room, they didn't actually mention them. Could it be that in these two Tarrel's had found buyers who wanted a house, come what may? Were they the sort of buyers every estate agent dreamed about?

'I really do like this house,' Mrs Elphick was murmuring. 'I feel it's right for us – such a lovely atmosphere.'

'So glad you think so,' said Roz. 'Should we go upstairs?'

After the Elphicks had admired the principal bedrooms, she told them there were also a number of guest rooms, as they'd have seen from the brochure. Though there was work to be done on these, there was no doubt that the whole place could easily be transformed.

'Lead on, Miss Rainey!' Mr Elphick cried, laughing, his wife joining in, and Roz, after showing them the guest bedrooms, was beginning to think they were, yes, home and dry – until they reached the top floor and no one was laughing any more.

It was unfortunate that the strong afternoon sunshine had reached the stage of shining directly in through the windows, lighting up in cruel detail all its damp misery of unsafe floorboards, peeling wall paper and general neglect, so that it looked worse than Roz had ever seen it.

For heaven's sake, she thought, why hadn't Laurence done something to make this top floor look even a little better when he'd embarked on his tidying up programme? Just because the maids who'd slept there had been long gone and no one else had used it for years, did he have to ignore it? Even the Elphicks must be dismayed, yet if they really liked Bellfields, they'd be able to look ahead and see how this part could be changed, wouldn't they? But they were both suddenly very quiet.

'There's a lot to do,' Roz remarked with an effort at cheerfulness. 'But of course it would be worth it.'

'A lot to do,' Mrs Elphick said, shivering. 'My heart fails me to think of it.'

'And coupled with the work needed on those cornices we saw downstairs, God knows how much it would all cost,' her husband said flatly. 'What on earth would a structural engineer make of this place?'

'But if it ended up as the place you wanted, as I say, it would be worth it, wouldn't it?' asked Roz eagerly, but Mrs Elphick was shaking her head.

'I don't know – there's something upsetting to me, seeing a place like this. Were the maids up here? Was this where they slept? I hate to think of their lives, you know. All those poor girls . . .'

'I do, too, but it wouldn't have looked like this when they were here, Mrs Elphick. It would look completely different with just a coat of paint.'

'Not like those cornices, then,' Mr Elphick declared loudly. 'Shall we go down, Miss Rainey? I think we've seen all we want to see now.'

'These rooms could very easily be transformed,' Roz said quickly. 'Don't let them put you off if the rest of the house is what you want.'

'I'm still thinking of those cornices,' Mr Elphick answered. 'Maybe we should see Mr Carmichael?'

'I'll find him for you,' Roz said quietly. 'Let's go back to the hall.'

Her heart weighing like a stone in her chest, she gave the Elphicks seats and made her way out of the house to the terrace overlooking parkland at the rear. The sun that had done so much damage was still radiant in the sky, and as she approached she could see three figures sitting back enjoying it, one being Laurence, another a dark-haired man, and the third a blonde young woman wearing a white shirt and shorts. She had excellent legs.

'Roz, there you are!' cried Laurence, rising with the dark-haired man. 'Come and meet Paul Ferris, my accountant, and Miss Leys – Meriel.'

Meriel? At the name which she recognized instantly, Roz wondered why she'd thought her heart felt heavy just a few moments ago? It must have been as light as a feather, compared with the way it was feeling now.

Fifty

'Meriel, Paul – may I introduce Miss Rainey from the property department at Tarrel and Thom's?' Laurence was saying easily. 'Tarrel's are handling the sale of the house – and working very hard, I may say.'

The dark-haired man, who was thin and lithe, with a beaky nose and sharp, dark eyes, inclined his head, smiling, while Miss Leys drawled a greeting without rising from her chair.

'Do excuse my dress, Miss Rainey.' She laughed a little. 'I thought I was going to play tennis, but have you seen the tennis court? Laurence really should let his handyman just dig it up and plant vegetables or something.'

Her short blonde hair was well-styled, her eyes blue-green and rather narrow in shape with long, dark lashes, and her teeth so dazzling white they told all Roz needed to know about her background. No one without money and a good diet had teeth like that. She couldn't be blamed for that, of course, but Roz rather guiltily knew that she would never want to be generous towards Miss Meriel Leys.

'My tennis court is the least of my problems,' Laurence said, taking up a pitcher of lemonade. 'Miss Rainey, may I offer you a drink?'

'No, thanks, Mr Carmichael, I just came to tell you that Mr and Mrs Elphick are ready to go. You might like to have a word?'

'Oh, of course.' He set down his pitcher, glancing quickly at Paul Ferris. 'Any luck with them, do you think? Did they like the house?'

Roz hesitated. 'To begin with, they were keen, but I'm afraid they rather think there's too much to do.'

'Blast! What changed their minds, then?'

'Not much doubt of that,' Paul said shortly. 'Laurence, I did advise you to improve the top floor and get a surveyor in to give you the full picture on subsidence.'

'That sort of thing costs money I haven't got. You know I tried a loan and the bank turned me down.'

'Well, something's going to have to be done. You don't need me to tell you that you can't keep going as you are, and that's a fact.'

'I've managed so far.'

'But not for much longer.'

'Look, I'd rather not discuss it now,' Laurence said curtly. 'This isn't the time or the place.'

'I know, I'm sorry. It's just so difficult to pin you down, Laurence. How often have I asked you to come into the office?'

'I'd better see these people,' Laurence muttered. 'Will you excuse me, Meriel?'

'Of course.' She stood up, smiling at Roz. 'Goodbye, Miss Rainey. Nice to have met you.'

'And you.'

As they returned to the hall, Roz shot a questioning look at Laurence. 'How come Miss Leys is here? I thought you and she had parted.'

'Oh, we have. It's just that she saw an advert for Bellfields in one of the glossies and decided to look me up to ask about the sale. For some reason, she thought we could still play tennis.'

'I see.'

'No need to worry about it.'

'Why should I worry?'

'I'm saying you needn't.'

She could say no more as the Elphicks were in sight and Laurence was advancing to shake their hands, courteous as ever, thanking them for coming as though they were his guests.

'We did like your house, Mr Carmichael,' Mrs Elphick said earnestly, 'but I'm afraid it would need too much spent on it for our purpose.'

'Far too much,' put in Mr Elphick. 'It might have been made clearer in the brochure what the position is. No point in trying to cover up what has to be done.'

'I'm sorry you feel we didn't give you a true picture,' Roz said quickly. 'It wasn't our intention to deceive.'

'Oh, yes, you just rely on that old saying, "let buyers beware" and all that, eh?' Mr Elphick gave a snorting laugh. 'We all know what estate agents are like.'

'I really don't think there is any point in insulting Miss Rainey,' Laurence said coldly. 'Good afternoon, Mr Elphick, Mrs Elphick.'

'Kenneth didn't mean to be rude,' Mrs Elphick said hurriedly. 'I'm sure Miss Rainey has been very kind – it's just that we're so disappointed.'

'I'll drive you back.' Roz took out her car keys. 'Goodbye, Mr Carmichael. We'll be in touch.'

'Of course, Miss Rainey.'

His gaze on her was tender but she said no more as she shepherded the Elphicks out to the car, uncaring that the atmosphere on the drive back would be distinctly chilly, glad only that it would also be silent. She wanted to think her own thoughts.

Fifty-One

It was October. No sign of any change in the Korean War, and no hope of seeing Dougal yet. No hope, either, of a buyer for Bellfields, which no longer seemed to cheer Laurence's spirits. Perhaps he had at last realized that to save his house he must in fact let it go but, with no buyer on the horizon, was depressed that even that option might be lost to him.

Certainly, he seemed depressed about something, preoccupied, anyway, though he refused to admit it when Roz tackled him, and sometimes his mood reminded her of Jamie's before the fateful day when Ella Drever had blown away his pretences. She never let herself go too far down that road, but at the back of her mind there was anxiety. Could this change in Laurence be anything to do with Meriel Leys?

She'd never asked him about her after that one meeting she'd had with her, believing it best not to mention her name, which could come between herself and Laurence and maybe even cause trouble. But then, one evening when they were going home after a theatre outing, she found herself suddenly, out of the blue, asking if he'd seen Meriel again. She hadn't meant to do it and once she'd spoken the words, regretted them, especially as Laurence, driving the car, seemed to stiffen.

'Why do you ask?' he demanded.

'I was just wondering, that's all.'

'The answer is no, I haven't seen her.'

That should have been the end of it, but at her little sigh of relief, he cleared his throat and spoke again. 'As a matter of fact, though, she has telephoned me.'

'Telephoned?'

'Once or twice.'

'Why should she do that? If it's all over between you?'

'Oh, she keeps wanting me to do things. Go riding, for instance. She'd supply the horse.'

'You're going to do that?'

'No. I don't want to ride anyone else's horses.'

'So, what else does she want you to do?'

'Buy raffle tickets for some charity or other.' Laurence laughed. 'That's a joke, eh? I could do with somebody running a raffle for me.'

'Oh, Laurence—'

'I said it was a joke, Roz.'

'I just wish you didn't have to worry so much about money.'

'I'm like most of the population there.'

'But not Miss Leys?'

He glanced at her quickly, then turned back to the road. 'You're right, not Meriel. Her father's in shipping.'

Roz stared. 'Oh, no, not Leys and Son, of Glasgow?'

'The same.'

She was silent then, still not speaking, even when Laurence drew up a little way from her home and turned to look at her.

'Now what's going through your beautiful head?' he asked lightly.

'I'm only wondering what it would be like to have that sort of money.'

'Let's not waste time brooding on it. We shall never know.'

You might, she thought, but did not put the thought into words. She could, after all, be wrong even to think it, and as he drew her into his arms and began to kiss her, that was what she hoped.

Nothing more was said of Meriel Leys in the days that followed, and Roz, allowing herself to relax, took pleasure in going to her art class again, where on a November evening she and Norma were copying landscapes, while Tim nearby was absorbed in something of his own creation.

'Nothing like painting to concentrate the mind,' Roz remarked to Norma. 'Makes you forget all your troubles, eh? For a while, anyway.'

'Wouldn't say that!' Tim called across. 'Doesn't make me forget that Churchill won the election, when it should've been Attlee!'

'Oh, don't get on to politics!' cried Norma, carefully outlining a cloud and frowning. 'I'm more interested in why this cloud doesn't look like the one in the picture I'm copying.'

'Because you're not Constable!' Tim said with a laugh.

'If I was Constable, I wouldn't be coming to this class!' Norma answered spiritedly.

'You'd be very welcome all the same,' said Mrs Burr, joining them and smiling. 'Actually, your cloud's not too bad at all, Norma. Just lighten it up a little with your brush – there, that's better! Everything all right with you, Roz?'

'Yes, thanks, Mrs Burr. I was just saying how painting takes your mind off your troubles. Don't you agree?'

'Indeed, I do, except that you often end up with a different sort of trouble.' Mrs Burr laughed. 'How to get your clouds right!'

As she moved on, Norma glanced at Roz 'You haven't any troubles, have you, Roz? I mean, apart from your Dougal being in Korea?'

'No, no, I'm OK,' Roz answered quickly.

'Still seeing Mr Carmichael? What a shame you never sold his house for him, eh?'

'There's still hope of that. Someone'll want it someday. And I'm still seeing him.'

'That's good.' Norma looked at Tim, who was covering his canvas with large black shapes. 'And I'm still seeing Tim,' she added in a whisper before raising her voice to call, 'What's that then, Tim?'

'Can't you tell?' he asked with a grin. '"Election Night"!'

'More like "Black-Out"!' Norma declared, at which Roz laughed and thought again how much she was cheered by her painting class. Whatever happened, she'd still have that. But what should happen, then?

What happened, in fact, was something good, for when she returned home that evening it was to find Chrissie and Bob sitting with her mother round the kitchen table, on top of which was a bottle of wine and five glasses. As soon as she came in, all three leaped to their feet, their eyes shining, and Chrissie cried, 'Oh, Roz, we've been waiting for you! We have some news!'

'Grand news!' added Flo, her voice trembling.

'Wonderful news,' said Bob, already opening the bottle.

'Is it . . .?' Roz began. 'Are you . . .'

'Yes, yes, we are!' Chrissie was running to hug her. 'Roz, we're engaged!'

'Oh, that is such good news!' Roz cried, kissing her sister's cheek. 'Oh, I couldn't be happier. Bob, congratulations!'

'Got that right,' said Bob. 'I'm the one to congratulate. Mind if I join in this kissing?'

After kissing Roz, he embraced the tearful Flo, while Chrissie showed off her pretty diamond ring to Roz's admiration and called out as a knock came on the inner door, 'Come on in, Evan! We're waiting for you!'

'I was wondering who the fifth glass belonged to,' said Roz as Bob's tall older brother joined them, with a hand outstretched to Flo and smiles all round. There had to be more kissing, with Evan making up for lost time and kissing everyone, beginning with Chrissie and ending with Roz, while Bob poured the wine and Chrissie handed out crisps and everyone sat enjoying rare, cloudless happiness.

Not altogether cloudless, perhaps, for after sipping her wine, Flo set down her glass.

'If only Dougal could have been here,' she sighed, and everyone sighed with her, but only for a moment, till Roz said, 'He is here! He's here in spirit. And he couldn't be more pleased!' And the moment passed.

Looking at Chrissie, seeing her happiness and remembering her misery over Richard Vincent, Roz felt she couldn't have been happier herself. Somehow, it seemed a good omen for them all that Chrissie should have come through her bad time to find a love that was true and promised so much hope for the future. Perhaps some of that will rub off on me, thought Roz as the evening finally drew to an end, with the MacGarry boys making their way home up the stairs, leaving the Raineys to go to bed and lie awake, reliving their joy.

But for Roz the joy was to be short-lived, for it was only the following Saturday, when they'd met for the afternoon, that Laurence said he had something to say to her. And she had a terrible feeling she knew what it was.

Fifty-Two

In the car, after he'd collected her from home, he suggested they should go to Bellfields where they could spend time in private, then return to Edinburgh for a meal.

'Private, so that you can talk to me?' asked Roz, studying his profile. She'd thought when they'd met that he was not looking well – rather haggard, in fact, with dark shadows beneath his eyes. Perhaps he had not been sleeping? Clearly he had something on his mind.

He nodded, staring into the mist, the famous Edinburgh haar that had so far refused to lift, making the day chill and damp with drops of moisture hanging on the trees like tears.

'Miserable day,' Roz remarked after a silence.

'Yes.'

'Typical November.'

'It is.'

'Laurence!'

'What?'

'Will you just tell me what this is about?'

'I'm sorry, Roz. It's not that easy. Let's leave it till we get to the house.'

She sighed and said no more, twisting her gloved hands on her lap and gazing out at the familiar road, or what could be seen of it, while Laurence beside her sat hunched over the wheel, his presence, usually so pleasant to her, now a source of deep anxiety.

It was a relief to reach the house, where the spaniels gave their ecstatic welcome with Mrs Meldrum inclining her head, but Laurence said the only place that would be warm was the morning room, where there was a log fire.

'Elsewhere, it's cold, cold, cold.' He smiled briefly, looking no less haggard. 'As you would expect.'

'It's certainly warm enough here,' observed Roz, admiring the fire and taking one of the shabby old chairs close to it. How old were its faded, crumpled loose covers? Twenty years, thirty years? What on earth did it matter? She knew she was trying to fill her mind with something other than the blow that must be coming her way.

'Oh, God, I feel so bad!' Laurence suddenly cried, flinging himself into a chair near hers, while the spaniels looked at him in surprise and came to rest their heads against his knees. 'So bad, Roz. You don't know, you can't know!'

Should she tell him she'd already guessed? No, why should she? Why should she lighten the load for him? Remember what he'd said, 'There won't be any pain with me, I promise . . . You can always trust me . . .' Always trust him? Well, she had trusted him, there was the irony, but he'd turned out like Jamie all the same. Strange, that two men who'd loved her – and she believed they had – should both have let her down. No, he must find the words to tell her himself that he was saying goodbye.

As she looked at his ravaged face, however, her heart softened. He was suffering, there was no doubt of it, for what he wanted to do went against his whole code of behaviour. When he'd told her she could trust him, he'd truly believed it, but now he'd broken that trust. He couldn't face her, tell her what must be told, because he couldn't face himself.

'Laurence,' she said, taking the decision to raise the issue herself, and putting her hand on his. 'This is to do with Meriel Leys, isn't it?'

He raised his head. 'How did you know?'

'I didn't, I guessed. I mean, it was pretty obvious, really.'

'But we'd parted, she didn't want me . . .'

'She changed her mind. Decided she did want you after all, so you changed too.'

'Not about you, Roz, never about you!'

'You still love me?' She sat back in her chair.

'I do, Roz, I do!'

'But you love Bellfields more.'

He looked down, putting his hand to his eyes, while his dogs left him and moved away to lie down, resting their heads on their paws but watching him all the same.

Suddenly, Laurence rose and stood gazing at Roz. 'Look, I've let you down, as I thought I never would, but I don't know what to do, which way to turn. Paul says there's no way out without a sale, and there's no sale on the horizon. The banks won't help and, as you can see, the place is in a bad way. Country houses do get like that if they're not kept up; I know of dozens that have had to be left, or have just mouldered away around the owners' heads.'

He took her hands in his and held them tightly. 'It's true what I said, Roz. I do love you, and I don't want to let you go, but if I don't take Meriel's offer, it will be Bellfields that will go, and I can't let it happen, Roz, I can't!'

'Her offer?'

He hesitated, letting her hands go. 'She says she'll take care of the house. Do what's necessary to make it safe.'

'If you . . .?'

The question hung between them, both already knowing what he must do, until Laurence turned away, shaking his head.

'There's nothing I can say to defend myself, Roz. I can't even say I'm sorry. It's too much, what I've done, isn't it? To say sorry for?'

As Roz was slowly rising to her feet, the door opened and Mrs Meldrum appeared.

'Shall I bring in tea now, sir?'

'Tea?' He stared blankly. 'Oh – Roz, would you like some tea?'

'I don't think so, thanks. Must get back.'

'Right. Thanks, Mrs Meldrum, we won't be wanting tea. We'll be going back to Edinburgh now.'

'Very good, sir.'

After the housekeeper had withdrawn, Roz stood for a moment, looking round at the morning room, then stooped to pat the heads of Hugo and Mascot.

'If there are any more people wanting to view Bellfields, I'll ask Mr Appin to bring them,' she said over her shoulder, then caught her breath. 'Oh, but there won't be any more people, will there? You'll be taking the house off the market.'

'On Monday,' he answered hoarsely. 'I'll – I'll just get your coat.'

The drive back to Edinburgh was silent, each of them sitting like strangers with nothing to say, until they were nearing the city and Laurence asked if he could take Roz to dinner.

'No, thank you. I'd rather go straight home.'

'You must have something.'

'I'm not hungry.'

As he drove on, sighing deeply, Roz said lightly, 'You know, I think I knew as soon as I saw her that Meriel had won. Strange, isn't it? I didn't even know there was a contest.'

'I think actually it was when she saw you that she decided to change her mind about me.'

'When she saw me? But I was just someone from the property department.'

'No, she asked me about you later. I told her.'

Roz gave a brittle little laugh. 'That's the way it goes, eh? But I got it wrong, didn't I? It wasn't Meriel who won, it was Bellfields. I've lost out to a house.'

When Laurence stopped the car outside her home, Roz immediately put out her hand to open her door, but he held her arm.

'Roz, weren't you going to say goodbye?'

'Oh, I think we've said that, haven't we?'

'Listen, I know I can't ask you to forgive me, but try to remember how I feel about you, and why I'm doing what I'm doing, will you? You've taken it so well – I can't believe you've been so good to me. Don't forget me, please.'

'Goodbye, Laurence,' she answered. 'Enjoy Bellfields.'

And then she did open her door and was out, running into her house without looking back, while he sat on in his car until he saw passers-by peering in and finally, slowly, drove away.

Fifty-Three

The days that followed her break with Laurence were dark, not just for Roz, but for the nation, caught up in anxiety for the health of the king, George the Sixth, who had had serious health problems for some time and was looking increasingly frail. After an operation in September, described as a 'lung resection', there were rumours of cancer, and when more and more of his duties were seen to be taken by others, everyone wondered just what the future held.

Flo, though not a great royalist, admired the king for his work for his people during the war, and read with interest all newspaper reports of his health, which rather surprised Roz, who'd expected her to be more concerned with the ending of her own affair with Laurence. Still, it was refreshing not to have her sympathy, for to have everyone feeling sorry for her over the loss of her 'Prince Charming' was proving very irritating. Oh, those sad-eyed looks from Chrissie, Nora, Angus and others were almost more than she could bear. It wasn't the end of the world for her, was it?

She wasn't sure. Though it was true she wasn't suffering the same sort of pain she'd had after her split with Jamie, she did feel a deep regret for the loss of Laurence. And not only Laurence, but Bellfields. For the first time she'd encountered a true dream house that for a little while had become part of her, as Laurence, also something of a dream, had seemed to be a part. He wasn't, of course. Wasn't at all what she'd thought – though he might have meant to be – and it was as though a light in her life had been put out and she must manage for some time in the dark. Even her pleasure in her work seemed to have deserted her, though she flung herself into it, making herself think of something other than Laurence, who had traded her in for a woman he didn't love in exchange for a house.

'Aye, it's a good job you've got your work,' Flo said one evening when Chrissie was out with Bob. They had been listening to dance music on the wireless, but Flo had switched it off – a sure sign she wanted to express her views. 'Takes your mind off things, eh?'

'Usually,' Roz answered, busy knitting a sweater for Dougal which she'd just begun.

'You could've seen this coming, though, if you'd wanted to. I mean, I always knew he would marry one of his own, and you must've known that too.'

'We never discussed marriage.'

'Well, there you are! You both knew it'd never work out, a fellow like him and you. You're a lovely, clever girl, and I'm sure he was very keen on you – though of course I never met him—'

'Your decision, that.'

'Never mind now. The thing is, like I say, he was keen on you, but what about his friends? They'd all be very different, eh? Have

every advantage and expect you to be the same. You'd never have
been happy, Roz.'

'I think I might have got on with his friends, Ma.' Roz laughed
shortly. 'It was his housekeeper who disapproved.'

'Cheek! Now she'd no right to take that line, and you an educated
girl!'

'Ma, it's all over and done with now. I'm just going to get on
with my life and put it all behind me.'

'Very wise. You stick to that, Roz, and you'll come through well.'
Flo opened the evening paper and sighed. 'See this about the king?
They're wondering if he'll be able to do his Christmas broadcast,
the poor man.'

'I haven't begun to think about Christmas yet.'

Roz finished a line and wrapped her knitting up in her work
bag. 'Don't think I'll be feeling much like it, anyway.'

'If only Dougal could come home, eh? Whenever are we going
to see him again, Roz?'

'I shouldn't think it'll be too long now. The papers are saying
that the Korean War's reached a stalemate.'

'That just means it might go on longer,' said Flo glumly.

In the event, Christmas and Hogmanay turned out to be as cheerful
as usual, with even the king managing to make his customary broadcast on Christmas Day. The fact that this was done by recording
small passages at a time was kept quiet, it being considered enough
for the nation to know that he'd made it, and that was certainly
good news.

No good news came out of Korea, though, at least as the stalemate
between the two sides continued. There was no bad news either,
and Dougal's letters home always looked on the bright side. His
Christmas parcels had arrived safely, he told Flo, and he and his
mates sent heartfelt thanks for all the goodies they'd contained. If
and when Roz finished his sweater he'd be truly grateful. 'What
have you been doing, then?' he asked cheekily. 'Going out gallivanting
like Chrissie and Bob?'

'No need to tell him what's happened,' Roz said earnestly.

'Oh, but he must be told,' Flo insisted. 'No need to send bad
news, of course, but he wouldn't think your parting from a fellow
like Mr Carmichael was bad news. He'd be happier to see you with
someone like Bob or Evan.'

'Evan?' echoed Roz. 'I scarcely know him.'

'Didn't take long for Chrissie to get to know Bob, did it? And now they're engaged.'

'Ma, don't start match-making for me, please. I don't want to get involved with anyone else for some time to come.'

'But Evan's attracted to you, Roz. I could tell, that time he came down for Chrissie's little celebration. And he's got a good job, you know.'

'Look, I'm not interested. Just leave it, eh?'

'Aye, sorry, pet. I know you're still upset over Mr Carmichael. You won't mind if you see Evan at Hogmanay, though? Chrissie's invited him to come with Bob to see the New Year in.'

'No, I won't mind,' Roz said with an exasperated sigh. 'Though if I had my way I'd go to bed early and not give a damn about nineteen fifty-two. I don't suppose it'll be any better than nineteen fifty-one.' Seeing the look on her mother's face, she added quickly, 'Unless Dougal comes home, of course.'

Fifty-Four

The day before New Year's Eve, a small staff party was held in Mr Banks's office, this being a custom everyone enjoyed. Wives were invited, as well as anyone who was officially engaged to a member of staff at Tarrel's, and this was where Norma sprang her surprise by appearing at the party accompanied by Tim Clunie and exhibiting a quite large, handsome ring.

'Tim's grandmother's!' she announced, as Miss Calder and Roz bent over it with exclamations of admiration, while Tim stood modestly by and Mr Banks and everyone else clapped their congratulations.

'This calls for an extra celebration!' Mr Banks declared. 'Miss Calder, please bring out the champagne I was keeping for our last drink – I think we ought to have it now.'

Champagne! Who'd have thought old Banks would have splashed out on that? But, as he said, this was a special celebration, for Norma had now worked for some years at Tarrel's and deserved some recognition.

'We couldn't be happier about this,' he told her and Tim when he made the toast, 'though we hope we won't be losing you, Miss Ward?'

'Not yet, Mr Banks,' she answered, blushing, as Roz exchanged glances with Miss Calder. There had been a time when Mr Banks would have wanted no married women whatsoever at Tarrel's, and of course he had not yet appointed a woman lawyer – but things were changing in the modern world and perhaps even Mr Banks was changing with them.

After they'd drunk the toast to Norma and Tim and people circulated, Roz caught Norma by the arm and drew her to one side.

'You slyboots!' she cried. 'Why didn't you tell me about you and Tim?'

'Oh, Roz, you know how it was. I didn't like to, that was all.' Norma was looking embarrassed. 'I mean, after you and Mr Carmichael split up.'

'Oh, heavens, as though I can't be happy for you, just because of that! It doesn't matter about me and Laurence, I'm just glad for you and Tim.'

'But I feel so sorry, Roz. You went through a lot over Mr Shield, as well – it just doesn't seem fair.'

'Haven't exactly got a good record, have I?' asked Roz. 'Och, it's just the way things work out. I'm OK – don't worry about me.'

'There'll be someone else,' Norma said eagerly. 'Someone right for you, you'll see!'

'I'm not looking,' Roz said firmly and moved away to talk to Mrs Appin – Pattie – a fair-haired young woman as slim as Angus was plump, who was very interested in his work, though not a lawyer herself as she freely admitted, being 'just a secretary'. What was interesting her that evening, she told Roz, was the waste of all Angus's work on his beautiful brochure for Bellfields, and wasn't it a shame that Mr Carmichael had now decided not to sell?

'I think it's criminal, I really do!' Pattie cried hotly. 'I know he'll still have to pay the bill for it, but that's not the point. Why can't people make up their minds what they want to do, without causing so much waste? I'm sure Angus regrets all the time he spent on that now!'

'Darling, it's par for the course,' Angus said, joining them in time to hear his wife's views. 'Clients buying and selling houses change their minds all the time, which is why we're lucky that their offers are binding. Now why don't you go and have a chat with Mrs Wray – she's looking your way – and I'll get some more drinks.'

As Pattie hurried off with cries of, 'Vera, how are you?' Angus gave Roz an apologetic glance.

'Sorry about that, Roz. Pattie doesn't know about you and Mr Carmichael, of course – you'll have to forgive her for jumping in with both feet like that.'

'It's quite all right, Angus,' Roz told him, feeling grateful that he did not talk gossip at home. 'Maybe she's got a point, anyway.'

'Not at all. I quite enjoyed working on the brochure and if Mr Carmichael is happy not selling, that's all right by me. We haven't lost out.' He lowered his voice. 'As long as you're all right, Roz?'

'I will be, Angus, I will be.'

When she arrived home after the drinks party, it was to find a surprise waiting for her.

'You'll never guess what's come for you!' cried Flo. 'From one o' the good florist's and all!'

'Flowers?' asked Roz. 'For me?'

'Got your name on 'em,' said Chrissie, watching her closely. 'Look lovely. Ma's got 'em in a bucket of water.'

The great sheaf of white flowers – lilies, small chrysanthemums and gardenias, were wrapped in cellophane with a small attached envelope. As Flo hauled them out of the bucket, Roz took the envelope and, after a moment's hesitation, opened it.

'Are they from him?' asked Chrissie. 'I bet they are!'

'Yes, they're from him,' Roz said quietly, her eyes on the card she'd taken out.

'So, what does he say?' cried Flo.

'What on earth can he say?' Chrissie was sniffing the scent of the flowers. 'I bet you feel like chucking 'em out, eh, Roz?'

'He doesn't say much,' Roz said, taking the flowers from her mother. 'Just best wishes for the New Year.'

'What a nerve!' cried Flo. 'But if you're not throwing 'em out, I'll have to find a vase. Give 'em here, Roz.'

'It would be silly to throw them out,' said Roz, putting the card in the pocket of her cardigan as Flo bore the flowers off to the sink while she found a vase. 'I think it's quite a nice gesture, really, to send me flowers.'

'As though it makes up for anything,' said Chrissie.

'Oh, it doesn't. Just shows how he feels.'

In the bedroom, Roz looked at the little card again, which read not just 'Best wishes for the New Year' as she'd said, but 'To Roz, with best wishes for 1952. May it be a better year for you than I made 1951. Yours, Laurence.'

There was no way of knowing whether 1952 would be better than 1951 or not, but there was no doubt that Laurence's flowers, as well as his message, had made Roz feel better. At least there was no bitterness between them. She felt she would be truly better soon.

Fifty-Five

'I'm afraid I've a confession to make,' Flo announced a short time before Bob and Evan were due to arrive on New Year's Eve. 'Don't be cross, girls, but I've invited the Atkinsons up for tonight – I mean, it's only neighbourly, eh?'

'The Atkinsons?' Chrissie exclaimed. 'Todd and Gerda coming here? Oh, Ma, what a thing to do!'

'Our favourites,' said Roz, smiling. 'Just the ones to make a party go.'

'Well, they're on their own – no family – and I thought it'd be nice to ask 'em. Might make Todd a bit easier to deal with in the future as well.'

'That'll be the day,' said Chrissie. 'But if you've asked 'em we'll just have to put up with 'em. Let's check everything's ready.'

They were all ready themselves, wearing their best woollen dresses, Flo with a Paisley shawl round her shoulders and a little make-up, which made her look attractive and well. It was such a relief that she had been so well lately, her daughters thought as they set out plates of sandwiches, sausage rolls and mince pies, together with glasses for the port wine and bottles of beer. Maybe she was truly recovered from her depression? Even with Dougal still in Korea, and with Roz's problems as well as her anxiety over the poor king, it seemed so. If true, it would be the best present the New Year could bring, but as usual they'd have to wait and see.

'Going to put the wireless on?' asked Roz. 'We must be sure not to miss the countdown to midnight.'

'Plenty of time,' Flo replied. 'But, oh, there's a knock! See who it is!'

'It's Bob and Evan!' cried Chrissie, leading Bob in by the hand, her face alight, while Evan followed carrying a bottle of wine.

'Happy Hogmanay, Mrs Rainey!' the brothers cried. 'Happy Hogmanay, Roz!'

'Don't you ladies look grand?' said Bob. 'And what a spread, eh?'

'And flowers,' observed Evan, taking in Roz's bouquet on the sideboard. 'They're beautiful.'

A short silence fell, as Roz looked at the floor and Flo began fussing with the table, moving plates for no reason and placing a bottle opener at the ready.

'Is that some wine you've got there, Evan?' she asked at last. 'That's so kind. Will you or Bob do the honours, eh? Or shall we wait for the others?'

'Others?' asked Bob, as another knock sounded.

'You're in for a treat,' Chrissie told him. 'Ma's invited the Atkinsons.'

'Todd?' cried Evan.

'And Gerda,' said Roz. 'I'd better let them in.'

Both were large people and, once in, they seemed to fill the room, Todd in a new blue jumper, his heavy face for once all smiles, while Gerda, in a bright red dress with her mouse-brown hair newly permed, rushed up to embrace Flo and hand over two bottles of beer.

'Happy Hogmanay, dear!' she cried. 'Now, isn't this nice of you, to ask us to be here with all the family!'

'Not quite all,' said Flo quietly. 'Dougal's still in Korea.'

'Oh, I know, I'm sorry. But you've got Chrissie's young man, eh? Hello, Bob! Hello, Evan! Happy New Year!'

'But where's Roz's fella?' asked Todd cheerfully. 'The grand one with the snazzy car! We like to watch him in that car, coming calling for you, Roz, don't we, Gerda? I was sure he'd be here tonight – I was looking forward to having a wee chat with him aboot motors, seeing as I ken a fair bit.'

'He won't be coming,' Roz told him with stiff lips. 'But would you like a drink? Mrs Atkinson, what about you? We've got quite a selection.'

'I'll open the bottles,' said Bob grimly.

'Put the wireless on!' cried Chrissie. 'Let's have some music!'

As Scottish dance music echoed around them and the glasses were

filled, the atmosphere lightened a little, but Evan, coming close to
Roz, murmured, 'Sorry about that, Roz. It must have been hard
to take.'

'Oh, I'm OK, Evan. We all know what Todd's like. If he's been
watching out for Laurence's car he'll know he hasn't been lately and
probably guessed we've split up. He just likes giving things a stir.'

'Well, I felt like punching him in the nose, I don't mind telling
you.'

'A lot of good that would do for neighbourly relations! And that's
all Ma was doing, trying to be neighbourly.'

'Are you really OK?' he asked quietly. 'I mean, generally.'

'Getting there, I think.'

'I'm glad.' His dark blue eyes rested on her. 'Wish I'd sent you
flowers.'

'Like a sandwich?' she said quickly. 'Or a sausage roll?'

Time passed. The wireless played on and the food was eaten –
most of it by Todd who, after he'd downed several beers, suggested
a sing-song, which was instantly vetoed by Bob and even Gerda,
who said warningly, 'Now, Todd!'

He replied, 'Aye, OK, then.' And fell asleep on the sofa.

'Thank goodness it's nearly twelve o'clock,' Flo whispered as the
music on the wireless was replaced by an announcer telling a studio
audience and all who were listening to charge their glasses and be
ready to welcome in 1952. 'Who'd like what for the toast? Port or
wine?'

'Whichever it is, I don't want much,' said Roz. 'I'm not one for
drinking.'

'Nor me,' Gerda said eagerly. 'Just a wee dram now and again,
eh? Why don't we have the port, Flo? Then you can keep the wine.'

'Aye, pour the port, then, girls,' Flo ordered. 'Must be ready for
the toast.'

'I'll wake up Todd,' said Gerda, knocking his shoulder. 'He'll no'
want to miss the chimes.'

'Wha's going on?' he asked, struggling up. 'Is it morning?'

'Och, no! It's time for the countdown to midnight – last moments
of the old year!'

'Twelve, eleven, ten, nine,' boomed the voices from the wireless,
'eight, seven—'

'There it goes,' whispered Flo, taking Roz's hand, as Chrissie took
Bob's and Evan stood with his glass in his hand, joining in.

'Six, five, four, three, two, one – midnight!' came the shout, and 'Welcome to nineteen fifty-two!' called the announcer over the sound of the tolling of Big Ben. 'Get ready for Auld Lang Syne!'

'Everybody on their feet!' shouted Bob. 'Come on, Todd, Gerda! Join hands, now, and start singing!'

Standing in a wavering circle, they joined hands and sang Burns's famous words, 'We'll take a cup o' kindness yet for the sake of Auld Lang Syne!', finishing up meeting together and kissing whichever neighbour was nearest. Chrissie and Bob, of course, Flo and Roz, Todd and Gerda, but then, as Flo turned to Chrissie, Evan moved towards Roz and kissed her gently on the cheek.

'My second kiss,' he whispered.

'Second?'

'Don't you remember? I kissed you at the engagement party?'

'Well, stay close – I see Todd coming!'

Too late. His great, rough-chinned face was next to hers and his beery breath wafted over her as he planted a kiss on her brow, while Gerda was kissing Evan and looking round for Bob.

'Aye, now where's wee Chrissie?' Todd was asking as he lumbered away, followed by Gerda, and Evan turned to Roz.

'Survived?' he asked, smiling.

'Only just.'

'Don't look now but I think they're going. Chrissie's with Bob and Gerda's decided to get Todd home.'

'Flo, it's been grand,' Gerda was saying as she hugged her. 'We've really enjoyed it, eh? Todd, come on, now, and thank Flo for a grand Hogmanay do!'

'Nice to have you both,' Flo said politely. 'Take care on the stair, mind.'

'Aye, and you send one o' thae dark-haired laddies down to be our first foot, eh? Don't you lassies come in the front door first, mind, or else we'll have bad luck the whole year.'

'Cheek of it!' cried Chrissie. 'Saying girls bring bad luck.'

'Och, it's just a custom, dear. Take no notice,' said Gerda.

'Where's our piece of coal, then?' asked Bob. 'That's a custom, too.'

'And your piece o' Christmas cake,' said Flo. 'Now I've got some left—'

'Mrs Rainey, I'm only joking! I'll be your first foot – don't need any coal or cake. Chrissie come down with me, eh? But don't step out of the door!'

The little party was breaking up, with thanks and goodnights and waves, as Bob and Chrissie went down the stairs so that Bob could go out of the front door and come in again, while Todd and Gerda tottered home arm in arm, and only Evan was left to go up to the boys' flat.

'Thanks again, Mrs Rainey,' he told Flo. 'We've had a wonderful evening. Roz, so nice to see you.'

'And you, Evan.'

Briefly, their eyes met, until Evan turned away and began to climb his stairs, looking back to wave. 'Happy nineteen fifty-two!' he called.

'And to you!' Roz called back, then she and Flo went into their flat and closed the door.

'Now to clear up,' sighed Flo, surveying the plates and glasses and empty bottles. 'Think it went well?'

'Sure it did. They all had a grand time. Especially Todd.'

'Aye, well, that was a mistake, inviting him. I should never have done it.'

'It was a nice idea.'

Flo flopped down into a chair. 'Why don't we have a cup o' tea, eh? Before we clear up?'

'No need for you to do it, Ma. We'll clear up – you've done enough. I'll just put the kettle on.'

'I think it did go well,' Flo said thoughtfully. 'And it's done me good to have a few folk in for Hogmanay. Had such grand times in the old days, when your dad was alive.'

'I know, Ma.'

'That's what the war took away from us, eh? Just ordinary family do's.' Flo turned her gaze on Roz. 'But that Evan MacGarry, just like I said, he's got an eye for you, Roz. Oh, it was that obvious tonight, seeing the way he was looking at you.'

'Oh, Ma! The things you see!'

'Ah, now, I shouldn't be surprised if he asks you out pretty soon, and you should go. Forget that Mr Carmichael for good.'

'Evan won't ask me out. Even if he wants to, he'll know that I'm not ready for it. I don't want to get involved.'

As a door banged and Chrissie came in, rosy and smiling, Flo shook her head. 'Always so stubborn, Roz. You're your own worst enemy.'

'Are you making tea?' asked Chrissie. 'I could do with it. Alcohol always makes me thirsty.'

She flung herself into a chair. 'Grand little party, Ma. Thanks very much.'

'You enjoyed it, pet?'

'Apart from entertaining Todd.'

'Don't worry. I shan't make that mistake again.' Flo lit a cigarette and gratefully blew smoke. 'Oh, thank the Lord – the kettle's boiling!'

Fifty-Six

Roz was proved right – Evan did not ask her out. In fact, she rarely saw him, only occasionally meeting him on the stairs when they both came back from work, and then he was usually with Bob. Not that Roz wanted to be asked out. As she'd told her mother, she wasn't ready for another relationship, or even making a close new friend.

'Once bitten, twice shy,' went the old saying, but she, you might say, had been twice bitten, which probably meant that she'd be more than twice shy. Content enough, in that dismal month of January, to go to work and once a week attend the art class where she and Norma would battle on with their landscapes while Tim went his own way, shovelling paint on his canvas with a palette knife.

'We think September would be nice for our wedding,' Norma told Roz one evening. 'Can be lovely weather then, and it'll give us time to save up. My folks are going to pay for it, of course, but Tim and me want to get our own flat. Isn't that right, Tim?'

'Absolutely,' he agreed, screwing up his eyes and standing back to view his work, as Norma added a brush stroke or two to hers.

'I'll do what I can, though I don't earn much,' she went on, 'but Tim's a teacher, as you know, and he's pretty sure we can find something we can afford. Maybe you'll help us to look, Roz, you being the expert?'

'Glad to, though I don't know about being an expert. My sister's keen to get a flat too, but she'll probably have to rent at first.'

'It's exciting, eh, that she'll be planning her wedding, just like me?' Exciting she might have found it, but Norma's eyes were full of sympathy for Roz, poor girl, who had no wedding of her own to look forward to. But had Chrissie fixed a date yet? Norma wondered, and asked Roz.

'Not yet. Might be the end of the year.'

'As long as it doesn't clash with mine, because she's sure to want you as a bridesmaid, and I want you, too. You will say yes, eh?'

'Norma, of course I will!' Roz laid down her paint brush to give Norma a quick hug while the other students looked on, smiling. 'I'll be honoured. Thanks for asking me.'

Chrissie, in fact, was only just beginning on her wedding plans, but it went without saying that Roz would be her bridesmaid and Evan Bob's best man.

'And maybe by the time you fix a date, Dougal will be back,' said Flo. 'He'd like to see you wed, Chrissie.'

'I know, Ma, but we're a long way off it yet. I'm sure he'll be back.'

Of course she wasn't sure. How could she be sure? She'd only said it to cheer Flo up, but there was no hope of Flo's staying cheered up when, only a few days later, on February the sixth, the news broke that the king had died in his sleep. Ill though he'd looked at the airport when he'd seen his daughter, Princess Elizabeth, depart with Prince Philip for a visit to Africa that should have been his, his death was still a tremendous shock to the nation, which immediately went into mourning.

People could talk of nothing else, for so much seemed to have been affected, and while deep sympathy was extended to the king's mother, Queen Mary, and his widow, Queen Elizabeth, everyone wanted to see the new queen arrive back from Africa. She was such a forlorn, sad young figure descending from the aeroplane all dressed in black, and formally greeting her ministers lined up in the cold to meet her.

What would happen now? What would it be like to have a woman for a monarch? One so young, too – only twenty-five – and completely untried. It would be like Queen Victoria's coming to the throne all over again, but look how long she had reigned! Folk could hardly get used to singing 'God Save the King' when she'd died, but now, in 1952, the nation would have to get used to singing 'God Save the Queen'.

Flo took the king's death very badly, seeing it as the triumph of the dark and melancholy over the light and hope of life. Just as it had been for her Arthur, so it was for the grandest in the land, and the poor Queen Mother, as the king's widow had become, must suffer as she, Flo, had done, her whole life changed.

Roz thought her mother was wrong to take such a pessimistic view of death, for if it came as the end and could cause great change to the living, it still didn't mean that life itself must be meaningless and without hope. It was all folk had, after all, and one day she knew she would be taking all she could from it again.

Her own sympathies after the death of the king went of course to his widow and mother, but she also felt for the daughters he'd left, for she'd lost a father, too, and knew what they must be going through. Both would be feeling bereft, though after the funeral the older sister would have to concentrate on her new role, which some parts of the press were already seeing as the beginning of a second Elizabethan age. Not, of course, in the eyes of Scots, who'd never had a first!

As Gerda put it to Flo on the stairs, 'Aye, just as long as nobody tries to call the young lassie Queen Elizabeth the Second when she's in Scotland, seeing as we've never had a Queen Elizabeth the First, you ken!'

'We'll just make her welcome, anyway,' Flo answered with a sigh. 'She's got a lot on her plate, eh?'

'Aye. First, there'll be the funeral to face. They say the Duke of Windsor might be there, the one that gave us all the push, and poor Queen Mary. Who'd have thought his mother would outlive the king then?'

Flo only said she must get on, that she didn't feel too well, but Gerda grasped her arm and asked her to come with her to the cinema when they were showing a newsreel of the funeral.

'You'll no' want to miss it, Flo, and neither do I, but Todd's no' one for funerals – or royalty, come to that – so he won't come. We can go together, eh?'

'Oh, I don't know,' said Flo, but in the end agreed to accompany Gerda, along with Roz and Chrissie. All were much impressed by the solemnity of it all – the silent crowds, the funeral music, the late king's marching brothers, including the Duke of Windsor, who'd been king himself until his abdication, as well as the three royal ladies in their mourning clothes and veils. Such pomp and ceremony, yet underneath the real grief and sense of loss they'd never seen anything quite like it.

'But all so sad,' sighed Chrissie as they came out of the cinema and into the February darkness. 'Whenever will things get cheerful again?'

'Why, dear, you've got your wedding to look forward to!' cried Gerda. 'Should think that'd be cheerful enough!'

'And one o' these days, we'll see Dougal again,' Flo remarked. 'I mean, I hope we will.'

''Course you'll see him, Ma,' said Roz. 'That war can't last for ever.'

They were not to know that Dougal was arriving back in Scotland as they spoke, never to see Korea again.

Fifty-Seven

As soon as she picked up the letter lying on the mat at the main front door some days later, Roz knew there was something wrong. It was addressed to her mother and from Dougal – she recognized his handwriting – but it wasn't in a Forces envelope, as was usual with his letters. It hadn't come from Korea. No, this letter was in a cheap little white envelope and postmarked Glasgow. Glasgow? How could that be? Dougal in Glasgow? Impossible!

Yet, there it was, his letter postmarked Glasgow in her hand. Somehow, he must have returned. But why? Her heart beating fast, Roz went slowly up the stairs to give the letter to her mother, who would be in a state as soon as she saw it, that was for sure. And they were all due to leave for work any minute, but how could they leave for work if there was bad news in Dougal's letter? For though she had no idea what it could be and why he should be back in Glasgow without them being told, Roz was certain that this little envelope contained nothing good.

Bracing herself, she went into the flat and called her mother, who was adjusting her hat at the kitchen mirror. 'Ma, there's a letter from Dougal!'

'Dougal?' Flo's face lit up. 'Give it here, then. Haven't heard from him for a while, eh?'

'Thing is – don't get upset – it's not from Korea. The postmark's Glasgow.'

'What?' Flo's face immediately became a mask of concern. 'Glasgow? What are you talking about?'

'There must be some mistake,' said Chrissie, who was already in her coat. 'Dougal can't have sent a letter from Glasgow.'

'Want me to open it, Ma?' asked Roz.

'No, no, give it here, I say. I'll open it, of course I will!'

Flo was tearing open the little envelope, snatching out the one sheet of paper it contained and fearfully running her eyes over the contents. Then she looked from Roz to Chrissie and, putting out a hand, steadied herself against the table before sinking into a chair.

'He's in hospital,' she whispered. 'He's been sent home.'

'He's wounded?' cried Chrissie.

'No, he says he isn't. But – oh, God – there's something wrong.' Holding out the letter, Flo put her hand to her eyes. 'Read it, read it! See for yourselves!'

'Dear Ma,' the letter began. 'Don't get upset when you see I'm in hospital. I've not been hurt – I'm fine. It's just that they think I need to come home. I can't fight any more. Please ring here and ask when you can come over. They'll tell you all about it. I'm looking forward to seeing you, and the girls. Try not to worry. With love, Dougal.'

Roz and Chrissie raised their eyes from their brother's letter and looked at their mother.

'What does he mean?' Chrissie whispered. 'He can't fight any more, but he's not been hurt? What's wrong?'

'I think – I think it must be to do with the mind,' Roz said hesitantly. 'Must be, if it's not physical . . .'

'There's nothing wrong with Dougal's mind!' Flo cried. 'There couldn't be! He's the most sane and sensible lad you could possibly find. That's a piece o' nonsense, Roz, to say that about your brother.'

'They wouldn't have sent him home for nothing, Ma,' Chrissie said gently. 'I mean, battle can affect soldiers, isn't that right? Didn't they used to call it shell shock?'

'There's never been a hint of it,' Flo retorted. 'All his letters have been cheerful – I'm his mother, I'd have known if there was anything wrong.'

'He hasn't written lately,' Roz murmured. 'Something must've made him stop. What we've got to do now is ring the hospital and find out when we can go.'

'Oh, Roz, will you do that? I canna face it. Will you ring and fix it up so we can go as soon as possible? You'll come with me, eh? Both o' you?'

'Maybe you and Roz should go for the first time,' said Chrissie. 'The doctors will want to talk to you – they won't want three of us. I'll see him soon as you find out what's going on.'

'As long as I don't have to go on my own,' Flo murmured. 'Oh, I feel so bad – I don't think I can go into work today. Will you ring them and say I won't be in, Roz?'

'Might be better if you did go in, Ma. Might help you to keep going till we find out what's wrong.'

'No, no, I'll stay here. I'll have a cup o' tea and a cigarette and wait for you to come back from the phone. That's all I can do.'

'I thought I'd ring up from work – they'll let me use the phone there – and it'll be easier than from the phone box. I'll come back in my lunch hour and tell you what's happening.'

'Can we see him this afternoon, do you think? I'll not sleep a wink if I don't see him.'

'I think we'll have to try for tomorrow, Ma. There won't be time to go today. Now, I'd better go.'

'Me, too,' said Chrissie. 'Oh, Ma, will you be all right?'

'Try for this afternoon, Roz,' was all Flo would say, and with sinking hearts at the dark look on her face, the sisters left her.

'This doesn't look good,' Roz said before they parted for their different trams. 'Sounds to me as though Dougal has got some mental problems, whatever Ma says, and how's she going to be if he has?'

'She might be better once she knows what the problem is,' Chrissie replied. 'It's always worse not knowing what you've got to face.'

'True. Let's hope we find out soon, then. See you tonight, eh?'

'You don't think you'll be going to Glasgow today?'

Roz shook her head. 'More likely tomorrow, when they can give us an appointment with the doctors.'

'And then you'll see Dougal?' Chrissie's lip suddenly trembled. 'Oh, Roz, how d'you think he'll be?'

As Roz shook her head, Chrissie flung her arms around her and for some moments they stood, holding each other, before they separated, tears not far away as they ran for their trams.

When Roz came home in her lunch break, it was to tell her mother that she'd got through to the hospital and been given an appointment with a doctor at two o'clock the following day. Afterwards, they would be able to visit Dougal. That was good news, wasn't it?

'Don't know about that,' Flo answered. 'I was hoping to see him today.'

'He's having tests today – we wouldn't have been able to see him anyway.'

'Tests?' Flo sighed. 'Oh, well, thanks for phoning, anyway. Now, sit down and have some soup – it's only tinned, but it'll do you good.'

Eyeing her mother cautiously, Roz sat down at the table. 'You're not feeling too bad, Ma, are you?'

'I've decided to try not to worry too much, because I don't think you're right about Dougal, Roz. He's got a problem, or they wouldn't have sent him home, but it's not what you say. Not nerves or anything. You'll see when we get to the hospital.'

'Ma, I have to tell you . . .' Roz was looking down at her bowl of soup. 'The hospital outside Glasgow is a military one.'

'So? It would be, eh?' Flo served herself soup and offered Roz some bread. 'Dougal's a soldier, that's where he'd be.'

'But it has a specialist ward for nervous cases, Ma. And that's where Dougal is. They told me on the phone.'

Flo laid down her spoon, her face losing colour. 'They told you?'

'They just said which ward he was in, after they'd given me instructions to find the hospital.'

'That was all?'

'They wouldn't tell me any more over the phone, would they? It'll be the doctor who'll give us information.'

'That's set me back, that has,' Flo murmured, lowering her eyes. 'I don't feel like eating now.'

'Oh, Ma, that's ridiculous!' cried Roz. 'What good is it going to do Dougal if you don't eat?'

'I'll have it later. But you finish yours, and then we can have some tea.'

'Promise me you'll try to be positive about this, Ma. Look on the bright side. Dougal's home and whatever's wrong, he'll be in good hands. Try to think of that.'

'I am thinking of it and I'm thanking God he's home, but I canna stop worrying.'

As Flo took out her cigarettes with shaking fingers, her tragic eyes fastened on Roz's face. 'I canna stop thinking that he's going to be like me, go through what I've been through, and it's what I've always dreaded, Roz, that one o' you would end up like me.'

Her voice dropped to a whisper. 'And seemingly, he's the one, eh? My Dougal – so strong . . . who'd have thought it? But he'll be in the black night, Roz, just like me, and there's nothing we can do!'

'Ma, you're better now,' Roz said uneasily. 'Dougal will get better, too.'

'Will he? We don't know what'll happen to him. Who says I'm better, anyway?' Flo sat back as though suddenly exhausted. 'That night is always there, Roz, somewhere. I never know if it'll find me again.'

Roz, used as she was to comforting her mother, cheering her, encouraging her, was now at a loss to find anything to say. Reaching out, she pressed Flo's hand. 'Let's see how Dougal is tomorrow,' she whispered. 'Maybe he'll be better than we think.'

Fifty-Eight

The following morning, they had finished breakfast, which for Flo consisted of a cup of tea and a cigarette, and Chrissie had just left for work, when a knock sounded at the door and Roz went over. It was Evan.

He was wearing a raincoat over his suit, a trilby hat covered his black hair, and he was carrying a briefcase – clearly on his way to work.

'Roz, I came to ask after Dougal.' He swept off his hat, his look anxious. 'Chrissie told Bob about him last night and we were so sorry to hear he was in hospital. Is there anything we can do?'

'Come in a minute, Evan, Ma will be pleased to see you. No, there's nothing you can do, thanks all the same.'

Flo, tidying away the dishes, gave a surprised smile at the sight of Evan.

'Oh, Evan, have you come to ask after Dougal? We're going to see him this afternoon – he's in hospital near Glasgow.'

'We've to see the doctor first,' Roz put in. 'Won't know what the situation is till then.'

'But he hasn't been wounded? That's something, anyway.'

Flo set her lips. 'Aye, it's something.'

'I just wish there was something I could do,' Evan said earnestly. 'Do you think Bob and I could visit him some time? Which hospital is he in?'

'Rookwood Military,' Roz told him. 'Why, I'm sure you could visit him, but we'll ask today about the times.'

'And if he wants any magazines, or anything, could you let us know? And tell him we're thinking of him?' Evan paused for a moment. 'Such a grand lad – we hope everything will be OK.'

Thanking him again, Roz went with him to the door, where he put on his hat and looked down at her, his eyes so sympathetic, she had to look away.

'We'll be in touch, Roz. I'm glad you're able to go with your mother today. She's not looking well – not surprising, of course.'

'I'll look after her.'

He hesitated, touching his hat. 'Goodbye, then, and good luck with the visit. Let us know how things go.'

'I will. Goodbye, Evan. Thanks for calling.'

She watched him hurry away down the stairs before returning to the flat, where her mother gave her a weary smile.

'Very thoughtful, Evan. Nice of him and Bob to want to see Dougal.'

'Just hope they can. But now, though, we'd better get to the station. If we make an early start we can have something to eat at the railway buffet in Glasgow before we find the bus to Rookwood.'

'I've got some cakes for Dougal, but I don't care about eating.'

Roz sighed. 'See how you feel when we get there. Come on, I want us to give ourselves plenty of time.'

In the event, Flo did manage a cheese roll and tea at the Central Station buffet, while Roz had scrambled egg on toast and coffee, after which they felt fortified enough to find the bus to the hospital, following the instructions given on the telephone.

'Somewhere out beyond Bearsden,' Roz remarked. 'Seemingly, the bus passes the hospital gates, so it couldn't be more convenient.'

To this, Flo made no comment. Nor did she take any interest in the route the bus followed, though when they reached the outskirts of the city, the scenery became pleasant, with golf courses, open spaces and an air of well-being.

'Rather different from some of the rest of Glasgow,' Roz

commented, hoping to get a word out of her mother, but it was only when the conductor called out 'Rookwood Hospital!' that Flo seemed to come alive and scramble hastily out of the bus, while Roz hurried to catch her.

'Name and business?' asked the soldier who'd appeared from the guardhouse near a pair of locked gates.

'Mrs Rainey and Miss Rainey to see Colonel Marsh,' said Roz.

He checked his list and nodded. 'Colonel Marsh, that's correct. Go through the gates, up the drive to the hospital and speak to Reception, OK?'

'Fine, thanks.' Roz took her mother's arm as the gates were opened and they made their way up a short drive to a large, stone building, which might once have been a private house but now seemed very much an institution.

'Here we are,' said Roz when they'd entered the massive front door and found themselves in a long hall smelling of floor polish, carbolic and the pungent smell of rather old chrysanthemums on the receptionist's desk. 'I'll speak to the lady at Reception, Ma. You wait here.'

'I'll speak to her,' said Flo.

As they were a little early, the receptionist, a kindly-faced woman of thirty-five or so, gave them instructions for finding Colonel Marsh's waiting room, which was on the third floor; they could take the lift or the stairs.

'The lift,' chose Flo, and when they were travelling together up to the third floor, Roz pressed her mother's arm.

'Not long to go now, Ma.'

'Aye, if he's on time. These doctors are never on time.'

But Colonel Marsh, a tall, angular man in his forties, wearing a white coat over his khaki uniform, was surprisingly on time, and courteously showed them to chairs in his consulting room before taking his own seat at his desk. His light hair was cropped short, his narrow blue eyes keen, and it seemed to Roz that here was a man they could trust to be frank. Whatever had to be told of Dougal, he would tell it.

'Mrs Rainey,' he began, 'I'm glad to meet you.' He looked at Roz. 'And this is . . .?'

'I'm Dougal Rainey's sister,' Roz said quickly. 'Is it all right if I'm with my mother?'

'Certainly. I want to meet Private Rainey's family.' He gave a brief smile that included them both. 'Now, you'll be anxious to hear how he is and why he's been brought from Korea to this hospital. Feel free to ask me any questions later, but first I'll put you in the picture about what's been happening to him, and will explain something of how we intend to help him.'

'Thank you,' said Roz, as Flo, her eyes riveted on the doctor, made no reply, and after a moment or two, the colonel began.

Fifty-Nine

'Before I say anything else,' he said quietly, 'I must tell you that until his illness, Dougal had always been considered an excellent soldier. He was, in fact, due to be promoted, and his commanding officer in his report to me speaks very highly of him.'

The colonel took up an envelope which he passed to Flo. 'This is a letter he's written to you, Mrs Rainey, so that you can read for yourself how well your son was doing.'

'Thank you,' Flo whispered. 'That's good to know.'

'You'll be wondering what went wrong,' the colonel continued. 'Well, it happens to many good soldiers through no fault of their own, but after a long period of warfare sometimes they are overcome by what we once called shell shock, but now tend to call stress, or battle fatigue. From what he's told me, I believe that Dougal's problem has its seeds in early battles, when he saw comrades cut down or captured. It's clear he couldn't forget what he saw and that he began to feel guilty he'd survived. That's a quite common reaction.'

Colonel Marsh, twirling a pencil, paused a moment, then went on: 'Seems that he managed to keep going, but it began to be noticed that a change had come over him. He didn't refuse to work or fight, but everything he did was done, as you might say, in slow motion. It was as though he was clogged down with heavy weights, and could only move at a certain pace – which of course no sergeant was going to accept. He was disciplined, his chance of promotion was lost, and no one knew what to make of it. Finally, he was sent to the medical officer, who diagnosed battle fatigue.

'This can take several forms – sometimes loss of memory, or

physical troubles with eyesight or hearing. Or, as in Dougal's case, depression.'

'Depression?' cried Flo. 'Oh, no, not Dougal! No, no, it canna be!'

Looking at her in some surprise, the colonel said gently, 'It's all right, Mrs Rainey, we're going to treat it. We'll do all we can, I promise you.'

'Oh, no, no,' Flo only wailed. 'Oh, I was so dreading – I was so hoping—'

'Colonel, my mother's better now, but she has suffered from depression herself,' Roz said, leaning forward. 'That's why she's so upset about Dougal.'

'I had no knowledge of your illness, Mrs Rainey,' the colonel said gravely. 'I'm very sorry to hear of it, and I do appreciate that it must be very difficult for you to accept your son has it too, but I've every hope that he will be completely restored to health. Please believe that.'

'I don't see what you can do,' Flo muttered. 'I had treatment, but if I'm better, I got better myself. How do we know that'll happen to Dougal?'

'Much depends on the patient, you're right about that, but all approaches are different. My own for Dougal is psychotherapy.'

'Psychotherapy?' Roz repeated. 'Can you tell us what that is, exactly?'

'Certainly. It involves dialogue with the patient, talking with him and encouraging him to talk himself, to explore his own fears, to look into his own mind. This takes time, which means that the patient might need a fairly long stay in hospital before he can become an outpatient, depending on his response.'

The colonel gave an encouraging smile. 'As I say, I've every confidence that Dougal, who is usually from all accounts a well-balanced, practical young man, will respond very well. Please have every hope that he will soon be well again.'

'Thank you,' Roz said quickly. 'You've been very helpful.'

She glanced at Flo, who nodded. 'Aye, very helpful,' she said after a pause. 'But when can we see Dougal?'

The colonel rose. 'You're very welcome to see him now.'

Escorting them to the door, he shook their hands and smiled again. 'I know it's useless to tell you not to worry, but please try to be positive, think of how Dougal was and how he will be again. Now, I'll just ring for one of the nursing assistants to take you to his ward.'

Thanking the colonel again, they turned to follow the young woman who had arrived to take them to Dougal and, as they were taken up in the lift to a corridor of several doors, all they could think of was how he would be. How would they find him? Their Dougal?

'Here he is!' cried their guide, opening a door. 'He's in a two-bedded ward, but his roommate's with one of the doctors, so you'll be able to have a nice wee chat. Dougal, you've got visitors!'

Eagerly, fearfully, they entered the ward.

Sixty

At first sight, as he rose from a chair by his bed, he didn't look any different. Still the same Dougal, even in hospital-blue clothes, his short fair hair neatly parted, his face tanned and healthy-looking. But it only took a moment for Roz to recognize, with a sinking heart, that the face he turned to them might seem tanned and healthy but was in fact like her mother's when she was ill. Shuttered, expressionless, the eyes without light. Oh, God, how much would Flo see? What would she do?

But Flo was already embracing the tall, silent figure, hugging Dougal tightly and smiling radiantly, not seeing what Roz had seen.

'Dougal, son, how are you?' she was crying. 'Oh, it's so grand to see you, it's the day we've been waiting for! I've brought you some shortbread and the ginger cakes you like – they had 'em in the baker's today. I ran out and got 'em first thing—'

'Very kind,' he said quietly. 'Very thoughtful.'

She held him at arm's length, studying his face.

'Are you glad to see us, Dougal? Look, here's Roz – and Chrissie will be coming tomorrow. We're that happy to see you after so long. Such a long, long time. You feel the same, eh, seeing us?'

'Yes, of course I do. I've been looking forward to it.'

Flo glanced at Roz, her eyes shining, as though to say, you see, he's not depressed, whatever the doctor thinks! But Roz was pulling forward two chairs she'd found and not answering the look. Soon enough, her mother would realize that the Dougal she was so glad to see again was not the Dougal who had left them to go to Korea. Soon enough she would realize what they were up against.

'How are you feeling, now you're back?' she asked Dougal herself.
'A big relief, eh?'

'I don't feel much at all,' he said after a pause.

'But you must be glad to be here. I mean, they're going to get
you better.'

'Roz!' cried Flo. 'Don't talk in that way!'

'We've had a talk with Colonel Marsh,' Roz said evenly. 'He told
us you were very well thought of as a soldier, Dougal, but things
got difficult for you, didn't they?'

He turned his expressionless gaze on her. 'They said I was too
slow. Everything was slow. It was like – being weighted down.'

'Oh, Dougal!' sighed Flo. 'Why should that have happened? You
were always so quick!'

'I didn't want it to happen.'

'Of course you didn't!'

'But then I got to thinking, maybe it's a punishment, eh?'

'A punishment?' cried Roz. 'Why ever should you be punished,
Dougal?'

'For being alive,' he said simply. 'They went, you see. My pals. I
saw 'em go. I couldn't save 'em. Well, one was saved, but not by
me. He got taken away – we never saw him again. But Roddie and
Tiger – we used to call him Tiger, he was that fierce, always the
daredevil, risking his neck – well, they died. Not the only ones,
either.' Dougal heaved a deep sigh. 'I don't know why I was left.'

'There'd be others left,' Roz told him, holding his hand. 'You
wouldn't be the only one, eh? You were in a battle, it was only to
be expected some wouldn't survive.'

'Like your dad,' said Flo. 'But you were all right, Dougal. You
were saved. It was a miracle.'

'Ma, there are no miracles!' he suddenly shouted, his face turning
red. 'No miracles, I say! Look, I don't want to talk any more. Just
don't talk any more.'

He left his chair and flung himself on to his bed, turning his face
away, leaving Flo to look into Roz's eyes and let her see at last that
she understood. Oh, yes, too well, so that her lip trembled and the
tears gathered, though she did not let them fall. Not in front of
Dougal, even if his face was turned away.

Into the silence, they heard clicking footsteps and then the door
opened and a voice called brightly, 'Mrs Rainey? You've found him,
then?'

And a military nurse, rather plain of face, but very friendly in manner, came hurrying in, hand outstretched in greeting.

'Hello, there! I'm Joan MacEwan, the QA who's looking after Dougal. Looks like he's feeling tired again – comes over him, you know. But someone's bringing him tea and that'll wake him up. Maybe you'd like to go for a cuppa yourselves? We have a very good canteen.'

'Thanks, I think we would,' said Roz, introducing herself. 'I think Dougal has talked enough for today.'

'I want to say goodbye,' said Flo, dabbing her eyes. 'He'll want me to say goodbye.'

When she bent to kiss his cheek he sat up, resting against his pillow, and gazed at her without smiling.

'Goodbye, Ma, goodbye, Roz. Thank you for coming.'

'We'll come again soon,' promised Flo. 'And Chrissie will be coming tomorrow.'

'And the MacGarry boys are keen to see you, too,' added Roz, but Dougal showed no interest in the MacGarry boys and, after a long moment, Roz and Flo quietly left him, the Queen Alexandra's nurse following.

'I'm sorry if you found Dougal not much like himself,' she said seriously, her dark brown eyes very sympathetic. 'But it's early days, you understand. He will improve, now he's home. We all feel that.'

'Thank you,' said Roz. 'You're very kind.'

'Very kind,' Flo agreed.

'Not at all,' said Joan. 'Dougal is a fine young man. We all want to see him better. Now, shall I tell you how to find the canteen?'

In the canteen, which was full of smoke, it being the only place in the hospital where smoking was permitted, Flo and Roz chose tea and rock buns.

'Safer than the scones,' Roz murmured. 'At least, they're meant to be like rocks.'

Flo lit a cigarette without speaking, but Roz, knowing her so well, was relieved that, though her mother was certainly unhappy, she did not appear to be actually depressed. Perhaps seeing Dougal had given her a strange strength to try to keep well for his sake, to do what she could to help.

'It's worrying, Ma,' Roz said as they drank their tea. 'I mean, seeing Dougal as he is, but I'm sure he'll come through. It'll take time, but the colonel's good. I think we can trust him to get Dougal better.'

'Can only hope.' Flo sighed. 'But it's terrible, eh, to think of what he's seen, poor lad. Makes me wonder what sights your dad had to face before he died.'

'That's war, Ma. Dougal's done well to keep going as long as he did.'

'That reminds me . . .' Flo opened her bag and took out the letter the colonel had given her. 'Let's see what the officer had to say about our Dougal.'

As Roz crumbled her rock bun and waited, Flo's eyes rapidly scanned the letter, then laid it down, her face brightening.

'Roz, read it! It's so nice – says what a grand soldier Dougal was, how proud they were of him, and that what's happened to him could happen to anyone. Wasn't it kind of the officer to write to me like that? To make me feel better?'

'You're right, it's a grand letter,' Roz said softly, replacing it in its envelope. 'I never thought commanding officers could be so understanding.'

'Just shows, eh? You can never tell how folk'll be?' Flo ground out her cigarette and stood up.

'Aren't you going to finish your rock bun?' asked Roz.

'No, let's go for the bus, eh? I'd like to get home.'

Better though they both felt after the commanding officer's letter, as they made their way to the bus stop they found their hearts were heavy again. It was the thought of having to leave Dougal back in the hospital in the way they'd seen him, looking into the abyss, unable to take comfort as yet from them or anyone. How long would it be before he was better?

When the bus finally came and they were on their way back from Glasgow, neither could find any more to say.

Sixty-One

How long would it be before Dougal was better? As the year moved slowly on, from February to March and then to April, nothing in the situation seemed to change, though Colonel Marsh seemed hopeful that the breakthrough would soon come.

Meanwhile, everyone visited him – his family, his friends – mainly at the weekends, which the hospital preferred. Everyone tried to talk to him, make him return to their world, but he seemed to want to stay outside it, and even though he was encouraged to take exercise to keep himself fit and so always looked well, he was still far away from the Dougal they'd known.

At times, the load he put upon those who cared for him seemed too much, though they did not complain. Chrissie, for instance, had declared that she and Bob would not marry until Dougal was well enough to attend the wedding, and as the weeks went by, there seemed little hope of arranging a date when he had made so little progress.

'I don't mind, I understand,' Chrissie told Roz. 'But it's hard, eh? I mean, for all of us.'

'I suppose we could still make our dresses,' said Roz. 'I'm booked to be bridesmaid for Norma in September and I was thinking I could use the same outfit. If you don't mind?'

'Mind? I don't care what anyone wears, just as long as there's a wedding sometime!'

'It'll come, Chrissie, try not to worry. People do recover from this battle fatigue and the colonel is sure Dougal will.' Roz paused. 'Don't like to say, but we've been lucky so far that Ma's been all right. Things could have been a lot worse.'

'Oh, you're right!' Chrissie agreed. 'We'll just keep going, then, and hope for the best.'

'That's the spirit!' said Roz, putting on a cheerfulness she didn't feel, for she could see no light appearing yet at the end of the tunnel. Even work, which had always been her saviour in the past, seemed no longer to help. She got on well with Angus, and worked as hard as she'd ever done, yet she knew her heart wasn't in what she was doing as it had once been, and that this was perhaps due to the parting from Lawrence Carmichael. It was not Lawrence himself she was missing, but the pleasure she had taken in his house, a house that had brought her closer than any other to the realization of her dreams. Try as she might, she could not bring back her own enthusiasm for houses, and one day was taken aback to find that Angus had noticed it.

'Roz, mind if I have a word?' he asked one day in late April when they were having their morning coffee.

'Please, do.' She looked at his pleasant, plump face that always filled clients with such confidence. 'Haven't blotted my copy book, have I?'

'No, no, quite the reverse. It's just that . . . well, I don't know if it's because you're worrying over your poor brother – God knows you've every right to – or whether things have just gone a bit stale for you. I mean, with the job.'

'Stale?' She set down her cup. 'You mean, I don't care about my work?'

'Oh, I wouldn't go so far as to say that. I'm sure you care. But it seems not to make you happy any more – am I right?'

She was silent, thinking over his words. 'Maybe,' she said at last. 'The point is, I just don't know what to do about it.'

'I hate to suggest this, because it's the last thing I'd want, but would a new job be the answer?'

She gave a hopeless little shrug. 'Such as what? I can't think of anything.'

Angus sipped his coffee and helped himself to another digestive biscuit. 'Naughty, naughty,' he said to himself, smiling. 'Roz, you ought to slap my hand when you see it hovering over the biscuit tin.'

'Oh, Angus, stop worrying about your weight! You're just right the way you are.'

'So you slim folk say.' He shook his head. 'But we haven't come up with anything to cheer you yet, have we? I have the feeling it may just be that you have a lot on your mind at present, and when your brother gets better, so will you. I mean, you'll get your old feelings back for the property market.'

'I hope you're right. It's all I know.'

'Well, here's an idea – how would you like to try your hand now and again at what I do? I'm talking about writing property descriptions.'

Her eyes widened. 'Write the descriptions? You mean it, Angus? Why, I'd certainly love to have a go. If you're sure? Mr Banks might not approve.'

'He needn't know. And say what you like, Roz, you are a natural as an estate agent. If you were working in England you'd be doing my job already, no question.'

'Well, it's very kind of you to think of me, Angus. I do appreciate it.'

'Say no more. Just put the lid on the biscuit tin, eh?'

★   ★   ★

Walking fast home from the tram that evening, Roz was feeling decidedly better. Whether trying her hand at Angus's work would give her back her enthusiasm for houses she still couldn't be sure, but it was something different and she was indeed grateful to him for thinking of her. People were kind, and there were good things in life, in spite of what poor Dougal thought. If only she could get that through to him . . .

But just the last time she'd visited, when they'd walked in the hospital grounds and looked at the fresh green of the trees and the new buds on the shrubs, he'd taken no pleasure in the renewal of nature, declaring it was all a waste of time, that life bloomed only to end in death, and what was the point of anything? She had talked and talked, but had seen by the closed look on his face that he wasn't listening, and had finally said no more. All that could be done was to wait till he was better. Surely that must come soon?

'Hello, there!' a voice called to her as she reached the door of the flats, and the next moment Evan was at her side.

'Heavens above, do you have to walk so fast?' he asked, smiling and gasping. 'I was on the top deck of the tram when I saw you get off ahead of me and, look, I've only just caught you!'

'Don't tell me you need to get fit, Evan!'

'Think I'd better book in at a gym? No, it's you who's just too speedy.'

Taking out his key, he opened the door, motioning her in before him, his eyes studying her at the foot of the stairs.

'You're looking well, Roz. Has there been good news about Dougal?'

'Not so far, I'm afraid. He's no different from when you saw him – at the weekend, wasn't it?'

'There'll be a change soon – bound to be. I can feel it.'

As she began to climb the stairs, he put a hand for a moment on her arm.

'Roz, I was wondering . . .' He was hesitant, his voice low. 'Would you care to come to the pictures with me one evening? Just as company for an old friend?'

His quiet gaze on her did not seem to be asking more, and put her at ease. But could he truly be called an old friend? She hesitated, but only for a moment. Why not? she asked herself. Why not have a night out for a change? Was she never to take a fellow at his word again? It would be unfair to cast doubt on Evan because of Jamie and Laurence.

'Anything good on?' she asked lightly.

'*High Noon* with Gary Cooper and Grace Kelly. That's on at the Princes.'

'Grace Kelly's lovely.'

'Yes, and everybody likes Gary Cooper. Fancy coming, then?'

'When?'

'Why not tonight?' His eyes had taken on a sparkle.

'All right, I'll have something to eat first. What time shall we leave?'

'Say, seven?'

'Fine. Call for me then.'

Roz ran ahead up the stairs and at her door looked back at Evan hurrying after her. 'See you at seven.'

'Seven.'

Their eyes met. ''Bye till then, old friend,' said Roz.

As she smiled he laughed, a shade self-consciously, and watched her walk into her flat before leaping up the stairs home.

Sixty-Two

Sitting next to Evan in the cinema, as Gary Cooper fought off the bad men in his western town and Grace Kelly watched and waited, Roz found herself wondering why she was there. Had she really only wanted a night out as a change from the usual? Or had she had some more deeply buried reason for spending an evening with Evan? Time had passed. Though she grieved for the loss of Laurence Carmichael's house and did not grieve for him, there was no other man in her life at present, and perhaps subconsciously she would like someone? Was she in fact ready to think of someone else?

No. To think of someone else meant to care, and to care meant you were vulnerable. She'd been hurt twice – she'd been betrayed by men she'd believed in who had turned out to be quite different from what she'd thought. If she were ready to think of seeing someone else, what were the chances that she would be hurt for a third time?

Glancing at Evan in the darkened cinema, it seemed to her that he was very relaxed sitting there, his eyes on Gary drawing his gun, so much at ease she couldn't help but think she would be safe with someone like him. But how could you ever know a person until a crisis came? How could you know what was underneath those layers of calmness that Evan presented to the world?

Another thought came to her – supposing she'd got it all wrong and he wasn't interested in her, anyway? It was her mother who'd put the idea into her head, and of course the invitation to go to the cinema had reinforced it, but the fact was he hadn't even taken her hand that evening. So what was she worrying about, then?

Laughing at herself inwardly, she fixed her attention on the film, taking pleasure in seeing Gary triumphantly defeat the wrongdoers and face a wonderful future with his young and beautiful wife, until the credits rolled and the audience, feeling good, sat blinking as the lights came up.

'Good, eh?' Evan said, turning to her. 'You enjoy it?'

'Oh, yes, it was just what I needed.' She smiled. 'A bit of suspense – worry about Gary – and then the happy ending. Perfect.'

'Want to see the B picture? That'll be next.'

'I suppose we might as well.'

'Let's have an ice cream, anyway, and think about it.'

While they were eating their ice cream with wooden spoons from cardboard tubs, Roz discovered she was feeling surprisingly relaxed herself. There was something to be said for going out with someone who hadn't declared himself, and might not even want to, as long as he was like Evan MacGarry.

'Have you noticed how cinema ice cream tastes different from all other ice creams?' she asked him. 'They must make it differently.'

'I think you're right, but I'm just glad it's around again. Remember during the war? Think the last ice cream I had in the war was in nineteen forty-three, just before my call up.'

'What were you in? One of the Scottish regiments?'

'No, Royal Engineers – the Sappers, as they call 'em. I didn't want to be in the infantry – constructing things was more my style.'

'And now you're a draughtsman. What does that mean exactly?'

'Well, basically, a technical designer. There are quite a few types you can be. Bob's on the electrical side, and I'm what's called a civil draughtsman. I work for a firm of civil engineers, preparing material for construction – could be roads, bridges, that sort of thing.'

'Strikes me you're a talented sort of guy.'

'Wouldn't say that.' He laughed, a little pleased. 'Might say it of you, though. Expert on houses, eh?'

She scraped out the last of her ice cream and shook her head. 'I don't think of myself as an expert. And I'm not sure I feel the same about houses as I did. Going through a bad patch, maybe.'

His eyes had their sympathetic look. 'You've a lot to worry about just now.'

'Yes.' In the midst of the talk and movement around them, they were silent until Roz said, rising, that she'd put their tubs into a rubbish bin.

'You really want to see the other picture?' Evan asked, rising with her. 'Or shall we just get some fresh air? It's a nice evening out there.'

'Let's go, then. After *High Noon* whatever they've got will be a bit of an anti-climax.'

'My thoughts exactly.'

Coming out into the east end of Princes Street from the Princes cinema, the evening air was warm, the light still good, and they decided to stroll a little before going home. Tourists were everywhere, taking advantage of the good weather, milling round the Scott monument, window shopping in Logie's and Jenner's and walking in the gardens, where Roz and Evan joined them.

'Have to take advantage of a nice evening,' Evan remarked. 'With our weather, you never know what you'll get tomorrow.'

'A good motto for life,' Roz remarked. 'Never know what's round the corner.'

'True.' Evan studied her for a moment as they slowly made their way through the gardens. 'But there are times when it's something good.'

'You're an optimist. Hasn't been my experience.'

'Shall we sit down a bit? There's an empty seat over there.'

'Shows it's getting late.' Roz laughed as they took their seats. 'You have to be lucky to get one of these in the daytime.'

'Not too late, is it? I'm enjoying myself.'

'Me, too, but time's going by. These spring evenings never seem to get dark.'

'We'll just sit here a minute. There's something I'd like to say, Roz, before we go back.'

'Oh?'

'I daresay you can guess what it is.'

'I'll wait till you tell me.'

'Well . . .' He ran a hand over his face. 'All I want to say is that I'd like it very much if we could go out now and again. I'll have to be honest, I don't mean just as friends.' He smiled quickly. 'That's the bit I thought you might have guessed.'

'I wasn't sure what you felt, Evan.'

'But you knew I was attracted to you?'

'I thought you might be. But then, you might not.'

'I thought women knew these things!'

'They can't be sure.'

He reached for her hands. 'You can be sure, Roz. But the thing is, I know the situation. I know you've been hurt and might not want to be involved with anyone else, and I can understand that. If you really don't want to see me, well, so be it. But if you do, maybe we could just take things slowly – go out from time to time, don't rush – see how things go.' He released her hands. 'Then you could see if you were interested in me, the way I am in you.'

'Evan, I like you very much,' she said slowly. 'But you're right – I am wary about seeing someone else.'

'I see.'

'Don't look like that!' She put two hands to his face and turned up the corners of his mouth. 'I didn't say I wouldn't go out with you. If it could be like you said – no rush, just seeing how things go, that would be fine.' Sitting back on the bench, she smiled at him. 'That all right?'

'Oh, Roz, too right it is!' Evan pulled her to her feet. 'So, now we can go home. You don't know what it means to me, to have said what I wanted to say to you just then. I've been lying awake, thinking about it.'

'Have you, Evan?'

They linked arms as they left the gardens to walk back towards the Bridges where they could catch a tram, Evan no longer his calm self but showing signs of walking on air, while Roz was feeling surprisingly happy, not at the thought of taking a risk with him, but over causing him to look as he did. Was it possible she looked the same? She thought she might.

When they'd parted at the stairs, without a kiss but a press of hands and a long look, Roz knew she'd have to tell her mother and Chrissie where she'd been and what it meant. They'd both been at work when she'd left and she'd scribbled a note that had told them very little. Now she'd have to face their reaction.

'Out with Evan?' cried Flo, her eyes alight. 'To the pictures? How did that happen? Why didn't we know?'

'Aye, why didn't we?' asked Chrissie, her blue eyes round with surprise. 'My, Roz, you're a dark horse, eh? Going out with Evan and never a word to anybody!'

'He only suggested going to the pictures when we met after work. You weren't here, I couldn't tell you.'

'You could've put it in your note,' Chrissie persisted.

'Oh, what's it matter?' asked Flo, beaming. 'I'm just so pleased, Roz, so pleased for you and Evan, because I knew he was keen and he'd be so right, eh? Chrissie, aren't you glad?'

'I am – I'm delighted.' Chrissie gave Roz a fierce hug. 'He'd be just want I wanted for you, Roz, and the grand thing is, he's Bob's brother!'

'Hang on, hang on, I'm not engaged, you know,' said Roz, laughing. 'We've only been to the pictures!'

'But you wanted to go,' said Flo. 'That's the thing, eh? You know where it might lead. Ah, I'm that happy – if only Dougal could get better, I'd have nothing else to wish for!'

'If only,' echoed Chrissie.

'There must be a breakthrough soon,' said Roz, her laughter gone, her eyes bleak. 'There must.'

Sixty-Three

And the breakthrough came. Not a complete one, but more as Colonel Marsh described it – a sign that there would be one, a hope that the end might be in sight.

What had happened, he told the family, was that Dougal, though still depressed, was now free of the nightmares that had also plagued him since his return from Korea, bringing disturbed sleep and subsequent daytime lethargy. Without the terrible reliving of his experiences at night he had been able to sleep naturally – a sign, the colonel believed, that his subconscious was beginning to free him from his fears. And there at last was the real hope that he would be better able to face the day. Perhaps very soon he would be allowed home from time to time, for such outings from hospital could be very beneficial.

'Oh, to have him home again, that would be so wonderful!' Flo had cried. 'When do you think it might happen, Colonel?'

'If all goes well, I'd say middle of June.' he told her. 'And after that, we may actually see a true breakthrough.'

'Middle of June . . .' the Raineys echoed and, for the first time, saw a little light shining at the end of the tunnel.

But before it burned brighter, before Dougal was allowed visits home, Roz and Evan embarked on their 'no rush' plan to spend time together, designed to calm any fears Roz might have about going out with another man. In fact, it very soon became clear to her that Evan was not 'another man' to be approached warily, but just Evan, someone to trust. And that was how it had to be. There was no point in being with a person if all the time you were fearing the worst. Where would the pleasure be in that?

But there was pleasure in going out with Evan, and though they'd said they would take it slowly, just see how things went, as the days of May moved by they met more and more often, happy to be together.

Sometimes they'd go to the pictures, sometimes to a play at the King's, or the Lyceum, but what they liked best was to take a bus into the country, to walk in the woods around Swanston, or at the weekend in the Pentland hills. Here they would pause, to kiss and embrace, to delight in physical contact as lovers do, and it seemed to Roz that Evan would be a very good lover, though he would never demand more than would be allowed at the time when all girls had to be 'careful'. It was easy to see how talk of marriage came up so soon between men and women, to provide the fulfilment lovers soon desired, but of course it was very early days for Evan and Roz. So far they had not reached any talk of the future, and were just willing to take their happiness in meeting together. In that sense, it was no different from Roz's experiences with Jamie and Laurence. But she never thought of them.

Something did remind her of Jamie, however, when towards the end of the month Evan announced that he wanted to buy a car, and she remembered for a moment Jamie's joy in his. Bob, it seemed, was also looking around for one – just something second hand, he and Evan said, which suited Roz and Chrissie. Anything on wheels would do, to allow them to drive out in freedom and privacy – that was all they wanted. So, come on, guys! Hurry up and make a decision!

In the end, Bob went for a Hillman, while Evan found a small Morris, both cars seeming perfect to Chrissie and Roz when they were paraded for their inspection, while Flo was delighted at the promise of lifts to Dougal's hospital.

'Do you mean it, boys? Oh, that'd be grand. Specially if one o' you could collect Dougal when he's allowed home – that'll be middle o' June, just like the colonel said – I've just heard.'

'I'm afraid I can't make that weekend,' Evan said sadly. 'I have to go to Newcastle for a conference to do with new ideas for my work. What a shame – I don't want to go anyway.'

'And I don't want you to go,' sighed Roz. 'But you have to keep up with new ideas, Evan. Maybe Bob can collect Dougal that time?'

'Sure I can!' said Bob. 'It'll be a pleasure, Mrs Rainey. Just tell me when to go and I'll be there.'

'I'll come with you,' Chrissie told him. 'It's my Saturday off. Oh, fancy seeing Dougal at home again! I wonder what he'll do once he's back?'

It was a surprise to everyone that what Dougal wanted to do that first Saturday home was go to see an Abbot and Costello film at a cinema in the Haymarket.

Abbot and Costello? Everyone stared. He wanted to see that double act? Those film comedians getting in and out of scrapes? It was the last thing the family had expected.

'Go to see Abbot and Costello on your first night home?' cried Flo, putting their thoughts into words. 'Why, that's not like you, Dougal!'

His face that was still without expression did not change, but he did make an effort to explain. 'It's grand to be back, Ma. I can't tell you how glad I am to be home again, but I saw in the local paper that the Abbot and Costello picture was on and I just felt a sort of craving to see it. Something funny – crazy – you know what I mean? Something right outside my life. Maybe one of you could take me?'

'Are you allowed, though, to go to the pictures?' Flo asked, looking dubious. 'Maybe the hospital wouldn't want that.'

'They needn't know,' he replied calmly, and gazed around at his gathered family. 'Well, who's taking me?'

'I will,' Roz said promptly. 'And Ma will come too.'

'I certainly will!' cried Flo. 'Chrissie, what about you and Bob?'

'Well, I think we'll wait for you here,' answered Chrissie. 'If you go to the early evening showing we'll get a fish supper for when you get back.'

'A fish supper?' For the first time, a gleam shone from Dougal's blank eyes. 'I haven't had one o' those since I don't know when!'

Why, there he is, thought Roz, exchanging looks with her mother, her heart lifting. There's the old Dougal back, just for a minute, not completely, not yet, but he will be, he will be – that was a sign!

'You have a rest,' she told him, 'and then we'll go to this film. What's it called?'

'*Lost in Alaska*. Just the usual thing, you know. Slapstick and comic routines.'

'We can all have a good laugh, then. I'm sure we could do with it.'

'But who says I need a rest?' he asked truculently. 'I've had enough rest to last me a lifetime. I'll go out for a bit of a walk around before we have to get the tram.'

'Are you sure you'll be all right on the tram?' asked Flo anxiously. 'The hospital may not like it.'

'Ma, I'm not an invalid.' Dougal raised his eyes to the ceiling. 'Of course I can go on the tram! Think I'm going to catch some terrible germ, or what?'

'Don't speak to Ma like that!' Roz said sharply. 'She's only thinking of your health.'

'Sorry, Ma.' A dark red colour rose to his brow and he lowered his eyes. 'I didn't mean to snap.' He tried to smile. 'Don't want to spoil my homecoming.'

'Ah, don't apologise!' Flo threw her arms round him. 'We know what it's like for you. Let's go for that wee walk and then go to the film – that'll cheer us up.'

Sixty-Four

The cinema was quite small and rather old, the seats distinctly shabby, the curtains over the screen not exactly threadbare but thin and faded. Never mind, the place was full, with everyone talking and laughing as though in anticipation of the show that was to come, and the atmosphere was so different from the one at the hospital that Dougal actually seemed relaxed – more so than they'd ever seen him since the start of his illness, thought Roz and Flo, and again they took heart for his recovery, marvelling that he had somehow divined for himself what was best to cheer him.

'Remind me who these two comics are,' Roz murmured to him. 'I don't think I ever saw any of their films.'

'Well, the stout one is Lou and the thin one is Bud, and Lou always gets things wrong and Bud tells him what to do – in a funny way, if you see what I mean. There are plenty of wisecracks and gags and all that sort of thing – you'll see when it starts. In fact, I think it's starting now.'

As the lights went down and the curtains parted, Roz glanced at her brother to see how he was looking, and though it wasn't possible to be sure, it did seem to her that he was still relaxed and even smiling as he waited for the credits to pass and the film to begin. Oh, please let this be the real breakthrough, she prayed, closing her eyes and only opening them as the soundtrack alerted her that *Lost in Alaska* was really on its way.

As complicated as any opera plot, the story here had the comic duo cast as San Francisco firemen who rescue a would-be suicide, only to find that the reward he gives makes the police suspect them of trying to kill him, which means that somehow they all end up on the run to Alaska. At which point, Roz rather got lost, but it didn't in the least matter, for there were plenty of opportunities for the humorous situations that the audience had come to see and which did make Dougal laugh out loud, while Roz and Flo could laugh too with the sheer relief of hearing him. When had they last heard Dougal laugh? It seemed so long ago they couldn't help their laughter being mixed with tears, which they did their best not to let Dougal see.

When the film ended at last and the lights went up, both turned to look at him, and weren't really surprised to see that his face seemed to have somehow unfrozen. The closed look, the lack of expression had given way to a softness around the mouth and a light in the eyes that made both Roz and Flo long to speak, to comment, maybe even give him a hug, but they dared do nothing. Supposing it didn't last? Was it only the result of the film? Best to keep still and hope.

'Who'd like an ice cream?' cried Flo, and Roz was instantly reminded of Evan and that first time they'd gone to the cinema and had ice cream in the intermission. How she missed him! If only he could have been with them to see the first signs of recovery in Dougal, to believe with her that that was what was happening! And how strange it was that this new love had come to her in a way she'd never expected, and that she, like Chrissie, had fallen for a 'boy next door'. Wasn't it said you could travel the whole world and not find love, only to find it on your doorstep?

'Come on, then,' said Flo, 'do you want an ice cream or not?'

''Course we want one,' Dougal replied. 'We always have one at the pictures, eh? I'll get 'em.'

'No, I will,' said Roz, jumping up and smiling at Dougal's wish to have everything as it had been before his illness. 'And then it'll be time for the B picture.'

'Only cartoons, I think,' Dougal told her. 'But hurry up anyway, time's getting on.'

Apart from Chrissie not being with them, it was just like the old days; the family at the pictures, sitting together, eating ice cream, and it was what Dougal wanted. Or even needed. There was no doubt now in the minds of Flo and Roz that the light at the end of the tunnel was beginning to shine even more brightly: Dougal was going to get better.

They had finished their ice cream and in the darkened auditorium were waiting for the Disney cartoon film to begin, when – out of the blue – everything changed. One moment they were relaxed, content, and the next, along with everyone around them, spun into fear, rising, trembling in their seats, as the call went up: 'Fire! Fire! Get out while you can!'

And wisps of smoke drifted across the screen.

★　　★　　★

'Go on, move!' cried a large woman next to Roz, pushing her towards Dougal, who standing next to Flo, protectively holding her arm. 'What in hell are you waiting for?'

'Move, Ma!' Roz shouted, as Flo appeared dazed. 'Dougal, get Ma to move!'

'I am, I am!' he called back as they almost fell into the crowd of people in the aisle pushing towards a far exit where a crush was already building. 'Roz, follow me, follow me!'

She could feel the hands of the large woman on her back, forcing her into the aisle after Dougal, but then pushing her roughly to one side and elbowing her onwards into the crowd. 'Dougal!' she screamed. 'Wait for me, wait for me!'

But already she couldn't see either him or Flo – was only aware of strangers around her, pushing against her, and herself falling; falling amongst legs and feet and knowing something was wrong with her arm, something painful, but nothing like the pain in the back of her head that was so sharp, she cried aloud. 'Help me, help me!'

But no one helped. Only the black cloud that descended over her gave her such wonderful relief. She let it take her she didn't know where, and closed her eyes against the world.

Sixty-Five

There was still darkness around her when she opened her eyes, but there were no people and no noise, only a far-away pool of light. Everything was hazy, though, and she couldn't seem to work out where she was; also, she felt rather sick and full of pain from her arm and her head, and heard herself murmuring unintelligible sounds.

'It's all right,' she heard a voice say, and a face swam into view, one that seemed to be shaking to and fro above her but was calm and pleasant. 'It's all right, Miss Rainey, you're safe. You're in the Royal Infirmary.'

'What . . . happened?'

'You've concussion and a broken arm, but we'll talk in the morning. Now you must try to sleep again. Do you need anything? Feel sick at all?'

'A bit, but it's going off.' Suddenly, things seemed to be coming back to her and she tried to struggle up, her eyes full of terror. 'The fire!' she cried. 'There was a fire! Where's my mother? Where's Dougal?'

'They're both safe,' the nurse said soothingly. 'There's nothing to worry about, there was no fire, but you must sleep now and talk in the morning.'

With firm hands she helped Roz to lie back against her pillows, smoothed the sheet and tiptoed away.

No fire – how could that be? Roz, trying to see her surroundings and making out shadowy beds all with sleeping mounds, was mystified. There'd been no fire, Ma and Dougal were safe, but she had concussion and a broken arm? It was too much to take in, too much . . . She closed her eyes, and even without the black cloud to cover her, fell into deep sleep.

It was morning when she woke again, daylight streaming into the long ward lined with beds filled with women patients, while nurses were busy with their duties. By her own bed, however, was a red-haired young man in a white coat who gave her a quick smile and introduced himself as Dr Kerr.

'How are you feeling this morning, Miss Rainey?'

'I – well, I'm not so sick, but I'm a bit muzzy and I've got a terrible headache.'

'The muzziness will soon pass, so too will the headache, probably, but you took quite a blow to the back of your head which has left you with concussion.'

'A blow to my head?'

'Yes, I'm afraid it looks as though someone's boot hit you when you were lying down. I'll be looking at the mark this morning and give you some painkillers for the headache. We'll also have to put your arm in plaster.' He grinned. 'We set it for you last night.'

'How long will I have to stay in?'

'That depends on how you progress – maybe no more than a couple of days. Feel like any breakfast?'

When she shook her head, he told her she'd feel like eating later, but in the meantime she must keep up her fluid intake and rest as much as possible. First, though, she'd have to go down to have her arm put in plaster.

Dr Kerr stood up, calling to a nurse to organize a wheelchair, and Roz, summoning her strength, asked when she could see any visitors. Already she was thinking not only of her family, but Evan. Would he even know yet what had happened to her? And who would explain to her just what had caused the fire that was not, it seemed, a fire at all?

'Visitors this afternoon for a very short time,' Dr Kerr said kindly. 'But remember, it's rest you need to get better.'

It was three o'clock before anyone was allowed in to see her, and then it was Flo and Dougal, Flo carrying a bag of fruit, both looking large-eyed and pale, and sighing with relief when they saw her.

'Oh, pet, we've been that worried!' cried Flo, leaning to kiss her. 'I canna tell you what it was like when we couldn't find you last night – I was nearly up the wall – and then when we did find you, you looked so bad, so white, and unconscious! Wasn't it terrible, Dougal?'

'Terrible,' he said, his voice shaking, but as she looked into his earnest face close to hers, a great joy filled her heart for, worried or not, it was Dougal's old face she saw. Just as at the cinema, there were no more shutters, no longer any darkness in his eyes, only real feeling there for anyone to see, and she could have burst into tears over it.

'We canna stay long,' Flo whispered. 'You've got to rest, they say, but I'll be back tomorrow, eh? With Chrissie and all, but Dougal's got to go back to the hospital tonight. He wants to have a wee word first. Take care, pet, take care!'

There were quick kisses and then Flo left, leaving Dougal, who quickly pressed his sister's hand.

'That fire – it was just a hoax. A damned silly guy getting his kicks from setting off a smoke bomb and frightening everybody. He's already been in trouble for arson, but now they've got him again – he'll be in for it.'

'I should think so!' Roz cried. 'I can't believe anyone could be so wicked!'

'Never mind him. I just want to say, Roz, that I – I think I'm OK.' Dougal bit his lip. 'It's lifted, what was pressing me down, and I think that was beginning to happen before I came home. But it was seeing you, Roz, lying there looking so bad, that made me think – oh, God, I thought you were dead. And when you weren't, I was so glad I knew I didn't believe that life isn't worth living any more – I knew it was all that matters, and if we survive we've got to be grateful for it. And I am grateful, Roz, that I survived – and so did you.'

'Oh, Dougal!'

They clung together for a moment, then Dougal drew away,

smiling. 'I've got to go now, Roz. I'll see you as soon as you can make it to Rookwood, but there's someone else waiting to see you now, and you'll know who it is.'

'Evan?' she whispered.

'Aye, Evan.'

He came hurrying down the ward, his face drawn, his dark blue eyes searching each bed until he found Roz, then almost ran to her side and pressed his lips to hers – much to the interest of nearby patients and their visitors.

'Roz,' he murmured. 'Oh, Roz, what a nightmare! I've been to hell and back since Bob phoned me at the hotel at midnight!'

'It's all right, Evan, I'm all right. I've just got a broken arm—'

'And concussion. My God, if I could find the fellow who kicked you, I'd kill him. To trample on a person, to trample on you . . .' Evan sat back, putting his hand to his face. 'Why are there such people in the world?'

'It's a natural thing to want to save yourself, Evan. He might not even have known he'd done it. Never mind about him, sit down and talk to me.'

'They've only given me ten minutes. It seems that rest is the thing for concussion.' Evan breathed deeply. 'But I'll do anything they say, as long as they get you better.'

'Poor Evan,' she whispered. 'Have you been driving all night?'

'As soon as Bob rang me, I packed my bag, got in the car and drove like the clappers till – you'll never believe this – the car broke down somewhere near Berwick. I had to walk miles to a phone, then when I got on to a garage I had to have a tow that they couldn't do till morning, then I'd to wait for them to fix it so I had to sleep in the car.' Evan, laughing, wiped his brow. 'Got here just before your ma and Dougal went in to see you – didn't even have time to get you flowers – but here I am, at last, thank God.'

'I think I'll be out soon, Evan. I'm feeling much better and they said they'll probably let me go home the day after tomorrow. I can rest there.'

'I'll take you, then, but I'll be in tomorrow afternoon anyway. Oh, look, may I kiss you again?'

'Sorry, sir,' a nurse interrupted, 'but I think Miss Rainey should rest now. I'll have to ask you to leave.'

'Till tomorrow, then,' he whispered, but she smiled.

'Sign my plaster, Evan?'

As admiring eyes followed him, he slowly left the ward after signing his name on her cast, finally turning at the door to wave and, to sighs of approval, she waved back.

'That your young man, dear?' someone called. 'What a dream boat, eh?'

But a nurse was already shaking her head and Roz, feeling amazingly weary, closed her eyes and slept, though her lips were smiling still.

Sixty-Six

It was seven o'clock the following day. Time for the ward's evening visitors, but Roz, lying on her bed in her dressing gown, wasn't expecting any, as she'd seen hers already. So lovely to see dear Evan and everyone, even though she did now feel very tired, but tomorrow – oh, joy – she'd be going home! Evan was to collect her after the doctors' rounds, when she should be judged well enough to continue her convalescence at home.

Her eyes moved to a large get-well card on her locker which bore all the signatures from those at Tarrel's, with a special message from Angus saying she must come back soon, that he couldn't manage without her, and another from Norma, who said she'd visit Roz at home.

How kind everyone had been! How pleasant it was to know that they were thinking of her and that she was missed! Closing her eyes for a moment, Roz tried to ignore the itching beneath her arm's plaster, and wondered when she would be well enough to return to work. Soon, she hoped, for she'd never been one for resting. Strange, though, that she still felt so weary!

In came the visitors, tramping down the ward, but Roz, only listening, not watching, felt she would soon fall asleep. Except that some sixth sense was warning her that someone was near and, opening her eyes, she saw Laurence Carmichael.

'Laurence?' She was trying to make sense of it – Laurence, really here? In the hospital ward? 'What are you doing here?'

'I saw the piece in the paper about you, Roz. It said you were recovering here.' He laid some flowers on her bed and put a hand on the chair by her bed. 'May I sit down?'

When she nodded he sat down, keeping his eyes on her face.

'Such a terrible thing to happen to you. I had to come to see how you were.'

'Did you? Well, thank you. As you can see, I'm not too bad. A broken arm, a bit of concussion, but I'm OK.'

'Thank God for that.'

They were still warily studying each other, Roz thinking he was looking rather strained, even a little older, and he thinking – well, she didn't know what. If she was looking strained, too, he would know it was because of what had happened to her, but her guess was that she was looking happy. She should be, anyway, because she was.

'Everything all right with you?' she asked after a pause.

'Fine.' He cleared his throat. 'Did you see that we're engaged? Meriel and I?'

'I'm afraid not, but congratulations.'

He lowered his eyes and sat for a while without speaking, seeming oblivious to the chattering and laughing of the visitors in the ward, while Roz simply waited. At last, he looked up. 'Made a mistake, didn't I?'

'No, Laurence, you did not. You chose the house – and that was right for you.'

'Houses shouldn't come before people. And I was never fair to you, was I? I let you down.'

'You did what you thought you had to do. Let's not talk about it.'

'I can't stop thinking about it.'

She sighed. 'If you'd been what you call fair to me, it would never have worked out. We'd probably have lost the house and been left with each other – and that wouldn't have been enough.'

'Wouldn't it?'

She shook her head. 'No.'

'You didn't love me?'

'I did, but you were always part of the house, you see. I think now, maybe what I felt . . . wasn't real. So, you needn't blame yourself, Laurence. I was to blame, too.'

'No, no, I won't accept that.'

'Well, it's all over now. You have someone else – and so have I.'

'Someone else?'

'That's right.' She put out her 'good' hand. 'We parted friends before; let's do that now.'

He shook her hand and rose. 'I'll wish you all the best, then. Every happiness.'

'And I wish that for you. It was very good of you to come to see me – I appreciate that. Oh, and thank you for the flowers! I'll get someone to put them in water.'

'Goodbye, then. Get well soon.'

'Goodbye, Laurence.'

He walked away, past the eyes of those patients who took an interest in Roz's visitors, and she guessed they'd be wondering who he was and where he fitted in. What a Prince Charming he was, then – she knew she could still feel that, and was filled with a great sadness for him and the hope that he would be happy. Of course, he would be, she told herself. Meriel would see to it, and he would have his house. It had been his choice, after all.

But why had she not asked him to sign her cast? Because he was part of the past? It was hard to say. But she knew she would not see him again.

Sixty-Seven

The following Saturday afternoon, when Roz had been back at home for several days and was feeling almost her old self – apart from her arm – Flo, who had the day off, said she'd just be nipping out for her messages.

'You'll be all right, pet?' she asked, putting on a cardigan and taking up her shopping bags. 'Anything you'd like, if I can find it? What a disgrace it is we've still got our ration books, then!'

'How about salad?' said Roz, looking up from her book. 'It's so warm, eh?'

'Aye, I'll get some cold stuff and boil some eggs. That'll be fine for when Chrissie comes in, too.' Flo, looking back from the door, said softly, 'Oh, but it's so grand to see you looking well again, Roz! You and Dougal both. I couldn't be happier.'

'Wait till he comes home, we'll be putting the flags out then,' said Roz, laughing. 'Wonder what he's going to do.'

'Shouldn't be surprised if it doesn't involve nurse Joan MacEwan,' Flo said, nodding her head. 'He's really sweet on her, you ken. Not that he's said, but I can tell.'

'Why, I'm sure QA nurses aren't allowed to go out with patients!' Roz cried, looking interested.

'Ah, but Dougal won't be a patient for much longer, the colonel says. Never mind, I must away. See what Dougal says when you see him.'

'I'm looking forward to that. Before you go, Ma, have you seen my knitting needle? I've got to scratch down this plaster again or I'll go mad.'

All was quiet in the living room when Flo had gone. Roz yawned, drank some lemonade, opened the windows wider and had returned to her book when the downstairs bell rang.

Now, who's that? she thought, rising. Norma, maybe?

Down the stairs she ran, rather looking forward to a chat with Norma, hearing all the firm's gossip and more plans for the wedding. But the person standing on the doorstep was not Norma. It was Jamie Shield.

Another ghost from the past.

Yet, in an open-necked shirt and flannels and carrying a bunch of pink roses, he looked very much the same. And when she looked more closely, as she tried to seem completely at ease, she thought she could detect a look in his eye she'd seen once before – apprehension.

'Jamie?' she heard herself say. 'What brings you here?'

'The hospital told me you'd been discharged and I thought – I hoped – you wouldn't mind if I came to see you.'

'Why would you want to?'

'Well, because of the terrible thing that happened at the cinema. I can't tell you how I felt when I read the piece in the paper.'

'You didn't come to see me in the hospital.'

'Roz, I've only just found the courage to come here.'

Slowly, she opened the door wider. 'You'd better come in.'

In the flat, she told him to sit down and put his roses into water.

'I can't think why you've come, Jamie. We can't have anything to say to each other.'

He looked away. 'I came to see how you were. It's natural to want to know that, isn't it? About someone you care for?'

Care for? Roz looked desperately around the living room. Had he said that?

'I'm fine,' she told him. 'I have this broken arm, as you can see, and I had some concussion, but I'm pretty well recovered.' She hesitated. 'But I don't understand what you said just then. Surely, you're not saying you still care for me? After all this time?'

'It's all right – I know you don't feel the same. I'm not asking you to take me back. I wish you could forgive me, though.' He waited a moment. 'Ella has, you know. But she's married, anyway, and expecting a baby. She's well and truly over me.'

'I'm glad to hear it.' Roz moved to fill the kettle, at which he leaped up.

'Roz, let me do that.'

'It's all right, I can manage. I'm good at working with one hand now.' She gave him a steady stare as he sat down again. 'Jamie, it was partly because of Ella that I couldn't forgive you. I couldn't forget that day she came to see you when she'd been so happy, thinking you were hers, and all the time . . .' Roz shook her head. 'I felt as bad for her as I did for myself, even though I understood why you'd done what you did.'

'You did understand?' he asked eagerly.

'Yes, but it didn't mean I could forgive you. Not for a long time.'

'And now, Roz? How do you feel towards me now?'

'I'm like Ella. I've forgiven you, but that's as far as it goes.' She watched the kettle as it sang and finally boiled, then made tea.

'As far as it goes? You don't feel the same as you did?'

'No. That died some time ago.'

His eyes flickered. 'And now . . . is there someone else?'

'Yes, there's someone else.'

She poured the tea and they both drank a little.

'I'm sure you'll find someone else, too,' she added.

'Not yet.' He drank more tea, put his hand to his brow and tried to smile. 'That was a blow, Roz.'

'You said just now that you knew I didn't feel the same. That you weren't expecting me to take you back.'

'All right, I was hoping I was wrong. That's the truth of it. But to hear you speak, so bluntly – that hurt.'

'I'm sorry, I couldn't do anything else.'

'No.' For some time, Jamie sat in silence, finally raising his eyes to Roz as she sat watching him. 'Well, there was something else I wanted to say to you. I know it's not going to happen now, but I suppose you might as well hear it. The thing is, I'm thinking of starting my own estate agency in Berwick and I wanted you to be part of it.'

'Me?'

'Yes. You needn't be a lawyer there. You could work as you want to, become a partner, even. I thought you might consider it. No strings, of course. Coming back to me wouldn't be part of the deal.'

'Jamie, it would once have been all I wanted.' She set down her cup, her eyes suddenly taking on a lost, sad look. 'But you're right – it's not going to happen now.'

'You'd be so good, Roz, working with houses without being held back in any way. It would be the perfect opportunity for you.'

'The fact is, Jamie, I don't care about houses any more.'

His eyes widened. 'Don't care about houses? Roz, what are you saying?'

She smiled a little. 'It's true. Looks like all my life so far, I've been going after the wrong thing. Just came home to me the other day, when someone said that houses shouldn't come before people. I know that's true. There's nothing wrong with working in an estate agency, but now I just want to do something else.'

'What sort of thing?'

'I'm still thinking, but it won't involve selling dreams, I know that.'

Jamie stood up. 'I've certainly given up *my* dreams, Roz.'

She sighed. 'Look, you've made some terrible mistakes and I've had some hard thoughts about you, but maybe it's time now for you to move on. You can forget Ella and me – we're OK. Why don't you try to start again?'

He seemed unable to find anything to say and turned aside, then suddenly swung back and kissed her on the cheek. 'Goodbye, then, and good luck. Don't come down – I'll see myself out.'

But she did come down and opened the door for him, ready to wish him good luck, too, then halted. Just locking his car and turning to greet her was Evan.

Sixty-Eight

There were no smiles. Both men stood staring at each other, their eyes wary, their whole body language showing their deep mistrust. Roz, very pale, took a step towards Evan.

'This is Jamie Shield, Evan. He called to see how I was.' She glanced at Jamie. 'And this is Evan MacGarry, Jamie. He lives up the stair.'

Jamie nodded, and Roz could almost see the thought going through his head, as his eyes went over Evan's handsome face and his black hair from which he'd swept his hat, that this was not just a neighbour. Oh, no, he must have picked up instantly that this was the 'someone else' and wished he were anywhere but on the doorstep.

'How d'you do?' he said politely. 'I was glad to see that Roz had made a good recovery. We worked together at Tarrel's.'

'I know,' Evan said shortly, and that was true – he knew all about Jamie Shield and what had happened when he'd worked with Roz at Tarrel's. But he was taking his cue from Roz, who was evidently on friendly terms with Jamie, which meant that Evan would not be knocking him down, as he might have otherwise done.

'Nice of you to look in. I'm just back early to see how Roz is myself.' His slate-blue eyes moved to Roz. 'Such good weather, I thought we might go for a walk.'

'Oh, yes, I'd like that,' she said at once, but the colour had risen to Jamie's face and he began to move away down the street.

'Good to meet you, Mr MacGarry,' he said in a low voice. 'Roz, take care. I'd better be getting back now.'

'That your car?' asked Evan, looking at a handsome Rover parked a little down the street.

'Yes, I got it last year.'

'This is my Morris just here. Goodbye, Mr Shield.'

The two men, still unsmiling, nodded, then Evan moved to stand closer to Roz while Jamie opened his car door, took his seat, gave a long last look at Roz and drove fast away. In a moment, he was gone.

'My God, the brass neck of that fellow!' Evan cried. 'Coming here, asking how you were – why didn't you just show him the door?'

'Let's go up the stair,' she said urgently, taking his hand. 'I just want to be with you.'

In the flat she leaned against him, taking deep sighs as he carefully avoided her arm in plaster and held her close, looking into her face with wondering eyes.

'What's wrong?' he murmured. 'Has he upset you? I wanted to punch him, but you seemed to want to be friendly.'

'It's best, Evan. Best to have no bitterness. And I'm just so glad to be with you, I don't mind feeling sorry for Jamie.'

'Well, I don't want these fellows coming round you again. You've already had that Carmichael guy turning up at the hospital, and now there's been Jamie Shield. What do they think they can do? Just come back when they feel like it?'

Roz drew him to the sofa where they sat together, she still leaning against him, unable to let him go.

'It did upset me a bit, seeing Jamie,' she admitted. 'He seems so unhappy. People make such a mess of their lives, eh? I can't help feeling bad for him.'

'Just remember he nearly made a mess of your life, never mind his own.'

But as he held her fast, Evan's eyes were tender, as though he'd passed from worrying over Jamie to thinking only about Roz. 'Roz, darling, don't you think it's about time that we . . .'

'What?'

'Well . . . made it official.' He ran his hand down her face. 'We both know what we want, don't we? To be together. And what's the best way of being together?'

'Why don't you tell me?' she asked, breathing hard.

'I'll have to get off this sofa, then. Can't go down on one knee if I'm sitting down.'

'Evan, what are you saying?'

'I'm asking, as a matter of fact.' Gently setting her aside, Evan slid from the sofa on to his knees, and smiled. 'Mind if it's two knees? No? Well, here goes. Roz, will you marry me?'

She threw her arms around him, beaming with happiness. 'Do I need to say? Oh, yes, Evan, of course I will!'

'You won't mind if I keep going to work, at least at first?' she finally asked, when they'd spent some time kissing and gazing into each other's eyes. 'So many women do these days, though some men don't like it.'

'I want you to do just what you want to do. If you're happy with your house-selling, that's OK by me.'

'I'm not really happy with that, Evan. Not now. I'd really like to do something else.'

'Such as?'

'I'm not sure. I want to get my priorities right. Maybe work with people. Women who need help. Or families.'

'You'd be good at that. You have a sympathetic manner.'

'Well, I thought I'd get some advice. See if my qualifications would be OK, and then if there are any courses I could do. Oh, it's all up in the air at the moment.' She kissed him again. 'All I want is to be with you.'

'We have to plan the wedding, you know. How about a double one, with Chrissie and Bob? And Dougal doing double duty as best man.'

'Why, he might be planning to get married himself. Ma says he's keen on his nurse. She's such a lovely person, I hope it's true.'

'If it is she won't want him back in the army. Maybe he doesn't want that himself?'

'We'll have to see.' Roz looked seriously into Evan's eyes. 'Do you think things are working out for us?'

'Sure they are! Why would you think anything else?'

'I don't know.' She laughed a little. 'Suppose I'm not used to too much happiness. But Dougal's better and Chrissie's got Bob . . .'

'And you've got me.'

They kissed long and deeply.

'I've got you,' Roz agreed. 'So there's only Ma to worry about. Never know when the black cloud will land.'

'I'd say she was better now, but if any clouds do come, I'll be here to help, Roz. I always will. I'll be here for you.'

'I know.'

They were silent, and would have gone into each other's arms, but Evan said, 'Hey, isn't that the door?'

'Ma!' cried Roz, leaping to her feet. 'She's been shopping. Oh, wait till she hears our news!'

'Are you there, Roz?' Flo cried, coming in with loaded bags. 'Oh, Evan, how grand to see you! You must stay and have your tea. Everything all right while I was out, Roz?'

'You could say that,' said Roz, then she and Evan laughed and told Flo their news, at which she burst into tears of happiness. And as they hugged and kissed and talked about family, the future for them all, they knew, could hold no fear.